If Only For
ONE NIGHT

Brenda Hampton

Jaylin Rogers

Naughty A

D1253140

Acknowledgements

First, I must thank my Heavenly Father for all that He has done, and will continue to do. To my readers, this one is for you. Over the years, I've appreciated your support and this journey has been more than I could have ever expected.

To the Naughty Angels: Theresa Hodge, Taji Kirby-Hines, Tamika Smith, Kellie Kelly, Tonja Tate, Monique Hampton, Monica Hampton, Mia Geyen, Leslie Gray, Gabrielle Denize Newsam, Nicole Brooks, Joyce Hampton, Debbie DiGerolamo, LaLa Estrada, Krisha Robinson, Patricia L. and Veronica N., who gave so much time and effort to this project, I can't thank you enough. We all got a chance to see how difficult writing a story can be and a special thanks to those who helped me pull it all together.

To Jaylin Jerome Rogers, thanks for all that you give to The Naughty Series. Without you, well, you already know we could have never pulled this off. To your agent, Michelle Tootsie Bell, thank you for being such a big part of this and your creation of The Naughty Angels is what made this all possible.

Finally, a special thanks to Voncile Banner Williams and especially Karla Townson who professed that Jaylin needed a Facebook page to connect with readers. Much love to all, and who would have ever thought it would lead to this...

Book Club Meeting

May 15, 2010

Unlike me at all, I was running late for a book club meeting that I had scheduled with several of my readers from different cities. It was a yearly event that I'd devoted myself to, and there I was, stuck in traffic. I slammed my hand down on my horn at the slow moving car in front of me, wanting to yell out of the window and tell the man to move aside.

Instead, I took a deep breath and slowly made my way to the Renaissance Hotel where the meeting was scheduled. Upon arrival, I let the valet park my car and hurried to grab my carrying bags from the trunk.

"Do you need any help with your bags?" the bellhop asked.

I put one bag on my shoulder and pulled up the handle on my other black case so I could roll it inside. "No, thank you. But could you tell me what time it is?"

The bellhop looked at his watch. "Almost ten minutes after two."

I thanked him again, feeling awful that I was ten minutes late. Some of the ladies had come a long way to see me, and the least I could do was be on time. Hopefully, they would understand that traffic had been unkind to me, but either way, I had some explaining to do. I wanted to be sure that my attire didn't show any wrinkles and that my hair hadn't fallen out of place. Stopping by the bathroom to check myself out would have been a crime, so I settled for the few wrinkles in my navy blue two-piece pants suit and the strands of hair that was probably protruding in different places. I squashed the bathroom altogether and headed to the room that I

1

had reserved for the event. I pulled on the heavy door to open it, and almost immediately, everyone turned their heads. The room was filled to capacity with many women mingling while sitting in rows of chairs. Smiles could be seen everywhere. Thunderous applauses erupted in the room, and late or not, it was obvious that my readers were delighted to see me.

"Thank you," I said with an appreciative smile on my face. I stopped to give hugs to many of the readers that I'd known and even to some of the new ones that I hadn't met before. "I'm so glad to see that everyone could make it and thank you all for coming. I feel so blessed."

I made my way up front, tagging my bags along with me. Some of the ladies were filling their plates with finger foods that were lined up on tables that were decorated with white and blue table cloths. Helium balloons were on the tables, and whenever I hooked up with my readers, it was more like a celebration. I explained to everyone the reason for my tardiness and then fixed a plate as well.

For at least another hour, we all sat eating and talking about my books, particularly the Naughty Series. You couldn't talk about Naughty without bringing up the name of Jaylin Jerome Rogers. I mean, where did he come from? How was I able to create a character that was so addicting? Most importantly, was he real? Now, that was the one question that always made me pause and take a moment to gather my thoughts. I, of all people, knew the story behind this man and I wasn't sure if I was ready to reveal the truth about what so many, especially women, wanted to know.

While in thought, I gazed down at the marble floor, thinking of those memorable times that I shared with Jaylin. How could I forget, as the thoughts of him stayed with me more than I wanted them to, or for that matter, was willing to admit. My thoughts had kept me up in the wee hours of the morning, unable to sleep because I couldn't get him out of my head. At times, it was a scary feeling, and the most troubling thing of all was that I someday had to release him, just as I had done in the past. Looking up at the many readers who sat attentive with their eyes looking straight at me, I let out a sigh and professed with fidgeting hands, "There is a possibility that he is not a fictional character."

As the room fell silent, you could hear a pin drop. No one had moved and many sat with their mouths wide open. One lady in particular stood, placing her hand on her hip.

"If Jaylin Rogers is real, show him to me," she said. "I want to see his butt, as I may have a few things that I want to say to him."

Several ladies nodded, and another stood to voice her opinion. "If he's real, can you please provide me with a phone number so I can call him? That brotha got skills and I want to show him what I'm working with, too."

Laughter followed her comment and high-fives were slapped around the room. It had gotten pretty loud, as well as crazy. Maybe I shouldn't have said anything to that magnitude about Jaylin, after all, this was supposed to be our secret. Then, when one woman stood, claiming that she had personally met Jaylin before, everyone turned around to look at her.

"Ladies, my name is Theresa Hodge," she said with an almost unsure and shy look on her face. "I've met Mr. Rogers and I don't mind telling anyone how well I really know him."

"And just how well is that," one woman snapped.

"Very well," Theresa admitted. "If Ms. Hampton doesn't mind, I'd love to tell my story."

I called Theresa up front, and she took a seat next to me. I had no clue what she was going to say, but the expression on her face said that this would be good. Also, knowing what kind of man Jaylin was, I wasn't sure what to expect. Everyone sat back in their seats, ready for Theresa to tell her story. She crossed her legs and the words that left her mouth were shocking...

One Night's Pleasure

Theresa Hodge

"Theresa, you have got to get out of this funk you've been in for the last two weeks! Jasmine and I are taking you out and saying no isn't an option," Shelia said, over the phone.

"Shelia is right," Jasmine said, adding her two cents on the other end. "So get ready to get your groove on come Friday night girl friend."

"I'm not really into the club scene," I replied. "As my best friends, the both of you know this already."

"Maybe not," Jasmine said. "But you will not waste another minute thinking about *that* bastard. He wasn't good enough for you anyway."

I had the nerve to correct Jasmine, knowing deep down that *he* was a bastard. "That bastard's name is Steven. I know what he did, and I will never forgive him for it. Finding him with my so called stepsister was the ultimate betrayal. I will never forgive that slut, Patriece, or that asshole of an ex-boyfriend. I want nothing whatsoever to do with either one of them."

I knew Shelia would be reluctant to believe me, so she quickly spoke up. "Theresa, you know the best way to get over a man is with another one, right? You can do that by going out with us."

I shrugged my shoulders. "Not always, and going from one man to the next doesn't sound like a good thing. Besides, I've had enough of no good assholes to last me a lifetime."

"Well, at least think about going out with us," Jasmine said. "Shelia and I will call you back tomorrow. If you say yes, we will go shopping, after we get off work and have dinner."

"Okay, but I am not making any promises."

With that, I hung up the phone. I knew my friends were

right about Steven, but I loved him so much. So much that I lost myself in a wasted relationship. I gave that man five years of my life. I'm glad I found out who he was before I married the bastard. I sat on my bed, thinking about the day he'd gotten busted.

If I hadn't forgotten my cell phone the night before at Steven's place that day, I wouldn't have been none the wiser. Using my key and entering his apartment, thinking he had already left for work, I walked in on him and Patriece going at it like rabbits. Literally, Patriece was on all fours and Steven was ramming it in from the back. I was so stunned. All I could do was stand there for a minute, before collecting myself and picking up the nearest vase. I happily smashed it on Steven's head. He must have had a hard head because the vase cracked in a million pieces and all that fool did was scream BLOODY MURDER! His voice went higher than an opera singer at an opera. That slut Patriece scrambled to cover herself, saying over and over that this wasn't what it looked like.

How the hell else was it supposed to look?! My mama and daddy didn't raise no fool, so I collected my phone with as much dignity as I could muster and left. That was two weeks ago, and he'd been blowing up my cell, and banging on my door at all hours of the night ever since. That fool didn't know who he was messing with, but he will if he keeps that shit up. I promised myself this, tomorrow would be a new day. That was the last day I would wallow in misery over that asshole.

Later that day, and after thinking about all that had happened, I decided to take a nice bubble bath. It always relaxed me before bedtime. I went into the bathroom and turned on the faucet, adjusting the temperature of the water. I added my favorite bubble bath, as inhaling the vanilla scent relaxed me every time.

I took off my clothes, while watching the tub fill with water. Looking into the mirror at my 5'2" height, I always wished I was taller and smaller. My friends always complemented me about being so beautiful, thick and voluptuous. Both Shelia and Jasmine were 5'8" and very slim. I was not envious of them, because they had hearts of gold. Sliding into the bubble filled tub, I relaxed my head on my bath pillow and closed my eyes. I must have dozed, because the water had gotten cool. I hurried and bathed, then got out of the tub. After brushing my teeth, I moisturized my entire body with lotion, and slid between the cool sheets. I always did have a habit of sleeping in the nude, ever since I moved into my own apartment seven years ago. I was out like a light, before my head even hit the pillows.

The next day on my lunch break, I called Jasmine and Shelia to let them know Friday night was on. Today, however, we agreed to meet downtown at Dolphins Mall. Christmas decorations were already in all of the stores and it was only the first week of November. We stopped in our favorite store, Macy's. I chose an off one shoulder knee length black dress, not too extravagant but classy all the same. I loved how the dress was cinched in at the waist and the top part helped support my more than generous breasts. This dress would go perfectly with my four inch heels I'd already had in my closet. After picking out a few more accessories, Jasmine, Shelia and I were done. We decided to grab a bite to eat at the food court, so we'd have time to get us a manicure and pedicure as well.

While getting our nails and toes done, we all decided to try this club we had never tried before. It was called Wet Willie's. We were told after hours that they had an open bar and a great view on their second floor patio. Not only that, but a great view of the ocean on Ocean Drive as well. I was glad we would be going somewhere laid back, instead of to a club that was too crowded, with people packed like sardines in a can.

As my friends and I parted, we promised to meet up with each other the next night at Wet Willie's at eleven o' clock. The next morning I awakened early, ready to get my work day started. As I was getting ready, I felt excited about tonight. Being with Steven had really made me dull. He never wanted to take me out or wanted me to go out with my friends. Thinking back, he was definitely more of a hindrance. Good riddance!

The work day went by quickly, and before I knew it, it was five o'clock. I rushed through the Friday evening traffic to get home. I wanted to wash and wrap my hair, intending to keep my hairstyle very simple. My shoulder length wrap really accentuated my round caramel face, so leaving it like that was the plan.

While inserting my key into the lock, I screamed as a pair of arms encircled my waist from behind. "Shhhh" I heard a soft voice say and I knew it was Steven's. He put his hand over my mouth to silence my scream. "You will have the neighbors calling the police."

I pushed his hand away from my mouth, as if his hand was contaminated. Almost instantly, he started to plead with me. "Baby, you know how much I love you. I was drunk and things just got out of hand."

I cut my eyes at him and pursed my lips. "Yeah, like I believe your dick just happened to fall into Patriece's pussy. You know what Steven? I am not even going to go there with you. You are a jerk and I can definitely do better than your sorry ass."

He defensively held out his hands. "Theresa, please let me..."

My hand went up to halt his words, "Whatever else you have to say, tell it to a monkey's ass!" I went inside, slamming the door in his face.

Exhaling, I felt good that I had stood my ground and didn't listen to anymore of Steven's lies. The confrontation did take something out of me, but I had to keep it moving. I set my alarm clock and slept for a couple of hours. Later, I woke up feeling refreshed. I decided to wash my hair while I showered. Freshly showered, I brushed my teeth and flossed. I spent extra time moisturizing my skin and spraying my body with my favorite body spray. Then, I put on my sheer peach half bra with a matching thong. The front of my thong was so sheer, you could see through it. It didn't take long for me to wrap and dry my hair. Spraying on a little hairspray, I brushed out my wrap, allowing my hair to fall on my shoulders, leaving me with a soft bouncy wrap. I was thankful it was still so warm this time of year, and being sleeveless wasn't a problem. I slid my dress over my curvaceous body and zipped it. It looked even better now than it did in the store. I didn't even need stockings, so I slid my feet into my heels. I put on minimum makeup, and added glossy lip gloss to my full lips. I sprayed a little more perfume on my wrist, neck and behind my knees. Ready, I grabbed my purse and phone on the way out the door.

While in the car, I called Shelia and Jasmine to see if they were on their way to Wet Willie's. I was meeting them there since they decided to ride together. We pulled up in the parking lot within minutes of each other. Shelia and Jasmine both wore micro mini dresses. They both looked great as usual. Making small talk as we made our way into the dimly lit bar, we decided to sit toward the back, only because we didn't want to be close to the dance floor. The club was pretty crowded, but not too crowded. The DJ was playing "Nasty Song" by Lil Ru. Shelia and Jasmine were ready to get their groove on and I could tell because they couldn't stop snapping their fingers. I hadn't been out in so long, I sort of felt out of place. The waitress came by to ask if we wanted to order any drinks.

"What is the night's special?" Sheila asked.

The waitress' name was Tina, and she replied, "It's called 'The Call A Cab'. After you have too many of those, you will definitely have to call a cab!"

We all laughed. "Bring it on!" Shelia said.

I was hesitant. "I don't know," I said, skeptical. "Y'all know I'm not a big drinker."

Shelia threw back her hand. "Girl, you need to let your hair down. We got your back, right Jasmine?"

Jasmine had already told the waitress, Tina, to bring her one. "You got that right," Jasmine said. "We definitely have your back."

When the waitress brought our drinks, they were in tall clear glasses. I took a sip of the slushy sweet drink, and it was very smooth going down. It was also much more potent than one may have thought, but I liked it.

The DJ went back a little bit and played "Fire" by Lloyd Banks. By this time, we were feeling the effects of the booze. Two guys came up, asking Shelia and Jasmine to dance. They hesitated, but I urged them to go. As they went to the dance floor, the waitress came by and I ordered another drink. I knew I should be drinking more slowly, because I hadn't eaten much that day. Surprisingly, when I looked up and saw Steven, I lost my appetite. "What the hell," I mumbled out loudly. I had been thinking of the devil and here he walks through the door with Patriece on his arm. She had so much makeup packed on that she looked like a two-bit hooker. I took a big gulp of my drink, hoping I wouldn't be seen.

I wanted to avoid an embarrassing situation at all cost, so I looked for Shelia and Jasmine on the dance floor, hoping we could quietly leave. In a hurry, not looking where I was going, I walked right into a chest that felt like I had hit a brick wall. Looking up, my eyes locked into those of the most gorgeous and tall hunk of a man I had ever had the pleasure of running into. His hair was naturally curly, and it took everything in me not to run my fingers through it. There wasn't too much hair on his smooth light skinned face, only a goatee complimented his strong chin.

"Excuse me," I stuttered in awe. "I...I wasn't looking where I was going." He grabbed my waist to keep me from falling. Surely thought I would slip through his arms like melting butter. My heart rate went up, and I felt as if I had been running for miles. He was impeccably well dressed; black slacks with a button down Italian satin shirt. His sleeves were cuffed up to his elbows. His shoes were leather Italian black squared toed loafers. Dressed in all black, he had "sexy" and "bad" written all over him. His watch was a diamond studded Rolex that glistened on his wrist. Money was written all over him, but that was not what drew me to him. It was his all out blatant sensuous sexuality that his body exuded. Cut to perfection like a Roman god...damn, he had miss kitty purring with just a look.

As I looked into his sexy grey eyes, he smiled, showing perfect white teeth. I almost went down for the count when he licked his lips, leaving them damp and luscious. I wanted to take my tongue and lick what was sure to be the sexiest pair of lips around. I must have been in a trance, because his lips were moving and I didn't hear a thing he'd said.

"I'm sorry. Would you repeat that?" I asked.

"There is no need for any apologies," he replied. "What's your name, beautiful?"

"The...Theresa," I stuttered once again.

This man had my tongue tied up in knots.

"Well, my name is Jaylin. Jaylin Jerome Rogers. Nice to meet you and I'm delighted that we bumped into each other."

As those words left his mouth, the music slowed down. "Trading Places" by Usher started playing.

"Would you like to dance?" Jaylin asked, extending his hand.

I almost threw myself into his arms, but I didn't want to

appear desperate. So I just said, "Yes, that would be nice."

On the dance floor, he held me very close as we moved to the beat of the music. It felt as though I was meant to be in his strong arms. My head only reached his upper chest, and I inhaled his sexy exotic cologne. That smell, in itself, made me think about having hot sweaty sex with such a fine ass man. *What is wrong with me?* I thought. This wasn't like me, wanting to sex someone I'd just met. The song ended much too quickly, and he offered to buy me a drink. I was already feeling the effects of the last two, but what the hell? I had another Call A Cab, and he ordered Remy, no ice. Jaylin asked me about myself, and before I knew it, I was spilling my guts about what had happened between Steven and me. It had to be the alcohol, but he was so easy to talk to.

Out of the corner of my eye, I spotted Steven coming over to our table. Jaylin saw how upset I became and figured out who Steven was.

"Let me handle this," Jaylin said, standing with an intimidating look. "Wrong place, wrong time. The lady doesn't want to be bothered, so I suggest you step back."

Steven couldn't get one word out of his mouth, and I couldn't believe how easily he'd backed away. Then again, all it took was just one look at Jaylin's strong and intimidating stance to make anyone back down.

As Steven walked away, I thanked Jaylin profusely.

"No problem, Theresa. You didn't deserve what that idiot did to you and I wasn't about to let him come over here and ruin your night."

"Thank you again," I said, gulping down my drink much too fast. I would definitely have to ride home with Shelia and Jasmine, unless they were too drunk to drive also. Jaylin noticed the affect the alcohol was having on me, because he smiled and asked if I were okay. I told him that I was, or if not, after tonight, I would be.

Shelia and Jasmine came over to the table with the men they had met earlier. Neither of my friends could keep their eyes off Jaylin, but they didn't want to be disrespectful to the other men.

"We all want to go check out another club," Jasmine said. "Do you want to go?"

I glanced at Jaylin, as he, too, wanted to know my answer. "No, I think I'm going to stay. I'll catch a cab home and pick up my car later."

My friends stood there looking at me with big goofy grins on their faces. I introduced them to Jaylin, and told them to have fun.

After Shelia and Jasmine left, Jaylin offered to take me home. I usually didn't let strange men near my home, but my common sense went out of the window when it came to this sexy man. He even offered to drive my car, so I wouldn't have to come back and get it. Leaving the club, I showed him where I was parked, handing my keys to him. I figured he was use to driving more expensive cars than my Nissan Altima, but he didn't seem to care. It took about thirty minutes to get to my apartment.

I gave him the key to open my door and invited him inside. The least I could do was offer him something to drink, but the only liquor I had was some Hennessy that Steven had brought over a while ago. I told Jaylin to help himself to a glass of it, or even to the assortment of juices I'd had behind a bar. Shortly thereafter, I went into my bedroom and took off my heels, so that I could relax my feet. When I came back into the living room, Jaylin had put on a CD. "Speechless" by Beyonce was playing. The mood was set, so I sat on the sofa to relax. Jaylin followed, sitting closer than I'd expected. His scent had my heart doing all kinds of flips. I looked into his grey eyes as he looked into my brown ones. Before I knew it, our lips were touching. I was taking his tongue and opening my lips so he could intertwine his tongue with mine. He kept nibbling at my lips with his perfect white teeth, almost making me cream in my panties.

Moments later, he directed me on his lap, where I straddled him. I could feel the arousal of his manhood, as my dress bunched up around my knees. He took his hands and palmed my thick ass. I couldn't help myself, as I was grinding into his big, and I do mean, big bulge. I knew Jaylin was blessed by the feel of him. This man knew he could have me cumming with just a kiss. Every time I would grind down, he would rise up, hitting my clit through my thong just right. Easing his hands up my back, he lowered my zipper. He pushed the dress down my shoulders, unsnapping my bra with one hand. My bra was thrown across the room, and then he took my breasts in his hands and squeezed them. Tasting one nipple at a time, he aroused me even more.

The pleasure was building with each swipe of Jaylin's tongue across my nipples. Throwing my head back, I succumbed to my first orgasm, which would only be the first of many to come that night. I took Jaylin by the hand, leading him into my dimly lit bedroom. I turned back the bed, revealing sinfully red satin sheets. Jaylin pushed my dress all the way down, to pool around my feet. Placing my hands on his wonderfully strong shoulders, I finally stepped out of my dress. Don't know how I managed to get Jaylin's shirt unbuttoned, but it wasn't long before that, too, hit the floor.

Finally, free of his shirt, he unzipped his slacks and stepped free of them. God, I will never know how those black briefs managed to hold all of that manhood intact! Slipping off his briefs, I could barely manage to control my drooling. Instead, I licked the wetness from my lips, staring at the biggest dick I had ever seen. It was at least nine or ten inches long, and in addition to being long, it also had width, which was always a plus.

By this time, I was so wet. I could feel moisture saturating my thong. Pushing me back on the bed, Jaylin took total control. He slowly opened my legs, letting his naked body nestle between mine and making me want him with an intensity I had never felt before. Sex had never been this way between Steven and me. Steven had been a very selfish lover. That part of our relationship, I will never miss. In one night, Jaylin had managed to make Steven only a blip on my radar at best.

As Jaylin gave me another soul stirring kiss, he made me moan louder. Kissing all over my face and neck, I felt so cherished. His lips moved down my body, paying special attention to my already aroused nipples. He tackled those for a while, then placed trailing bites and kisses down my stomach while tonguing my navel. Using his teeth, he removed my thong, leaving me bare to his beautiful grey gaze. He licked around his luscious lips, lustfully gazing at me with such hunger. I thought I would burst into flames. My legs were spread further apart and he kissed from my feet, to my inner thighs, leaving wet soft kisses along the way. Finally reaching his destination, I poured both of my legs over his shoulders. That left me open and vulnerable to his questing tongue. Jaylin was eating me out so good, causing me to squeeze his head tight. I laughed, thinking of the possibility of him never coming up for air. He took my clit into his mouth, making me cream as I had never done before. He licked around his creamy, wet lips and moaned with pleasure.

A few minutes later, Jaylin got up from the bed and found his slacks to retrieve a condom. I, of course, could not help but admire his fine ass when he had his back turned. It didn't make sense for a man to have that succulent of an ass, and all I wanted to do was sink my fingers into his muscles. Coming back to the bed, I reached for the condoms and tore off one, placing the rest beneath my pillow for later. I rested Jaylin back on the bed, and put the condom into my mouth. As I went down on his huge dick, I rolled the condom down using my mouth and tongue. Jaylin was so long, I used my hands to finish rolling it on. He then took control, laying his body on top of mine. Once again, he kissed me with those gorgeous lips, tasting my essence on his lips. I kissed him with a hunger I didn't know I was capable of. Throwing my legs around his waist, he entered me inch by glorious inch. I was so tight that I hoped all of his meat would fit. He was all of the way in my tight sheath, finding a rhythm that took me beyond my wildest fantasy. Jaylin was definitely an alpha male who took total control over my mind, body and soul.

By lifting one leg to his shoulder, it took him even further into my tight sheath. Moisture was streaming down my thighs like rain. I couldn't believe I was on the verge of cumming for the third time that night. My toes curled and I was seconds away from screaming in pleasure.

Jaylin lowered his head and his lips touched my ear. "Is this pussy ready to come for me again?"

I couldn't even answer, as his performance was feeling so good. Holding each other's gaze, Jaylin reached between us and flicked my clit with his fingers. I burst into a thousand flames, and he came with such an intensity, I could feel him swell in me even more. Seconds later, we both let out loud roars of pure pleasure.

Exhausted, but well satiated, I lay there in oblivion not knowing that we were far from being finished. Jaylin promptly disposed of the used condom, before he put on another one. Flipping me onto my stomach, he grabbed me around my waist, and eased his fully aroused penis into my still wet canal with ease. Taking me in this position had me fully aroused again within seconds. Jaylin didn't know it, but he had my kitty so tamed, it would never be the same again. I lost count of the many orgasms we had that night, or the many positions we'd tried. One thing I do know is that Jaylin was the best lover I'd ever had, and without a doubt, the most generous.

Falling back onto the bed, with our arms and legs intertwined, we fell into an exhausted slumber. Feeling something brushing my head and lips, I snuggled deeper into sleep. The next morning when I awoke, I was alone in my bed. I would have thought last night was a dream, if it hadn't been for the soreness of my body. Compliments, of course, of the intense love making Jaylin had put on me.

I stretched my arms over my head, immediately noticing a note Jaylin had left on the pillow. Picking up the note, written in Jaylin's bold and sexy scrawl, I read what he had written: *Theresa, what we shared was beautiful and intense. Never let a man define who you are, and never compromise your beliefs for anyone. I hope you will remember this night of passion, as I will never forget you or the night we shared. Never settle for less, because you really do deserve the best. Stay Sweet and All Love,*

Jay Baby

The End

Book Club Meeting...

After Theresa told her story about what had happened between her and Jaylin, there were a lot of whispers going on, as well as laughter. I was pretty shocked, then again, no I wasn't. One lady raised her hand and stood to ask Theresa a question.

"Theresa, I'm not mad at you for doing what you chose to do, and if given the opportunity, I would have probably done the same. My question to you is do you have any regrets?"

Theresa didn't hesitate not one bit. "No. No regrets whatsoever."

Many of the ladies clapped and continued to question Theresa about her amazing night with Jaylin.

"Tell us, was it really as good as Ms. Hampton makes it out to be? And, is he actually that fine?"

Theresa smiled, "Yes, it was really that great. " She turned to me and patted my back. "Ms. Hampton does a great job explaining Jaylin, and no offense to her writing, but he is so much more than what she could ever put in a book. Yes, he is all of that, with a little something extra on the side."

I couldn't help but laugh and so did many of the other ladies. They were taken aback by Theresa's confession and many still had doubts.

"Hey, Theresa," one lady stood to ask. "Whatever happened to Steven?"

"Steven is history and never will I involve myself with a man like that again."

I could tell that Theresa's experience with Jaylin had her looking at relationships a little differently. Definitely, what one man won't do another one will.

"On the count of three ladies, repeat after me," I said, waving. "Bye Steven!"

The ladies in the room yelled out loudly. "Bye Steven!"

"And hello, Jaylin," one woman said. She stood and walked up to the front as well. Everybody watched as she stood next to me and Theresa, admitting that Jaylin had allowed her into his world, too. "My name is Giana Monroe and I'm addicted to Jaylin Rogers."

"You're not alone," somebody shouted. "But, what's your story?" Once again, we all got comfortable in our seats, tuning into Giana's every word...

No Regrets

Giana Monroe

The day I met Jaylin Jerome Rogers was the day my life changed forever. My day started out like any Saturday during the fall football season, with me heading over to North Carolina Central University to perform my duties as part of the medical staff for the NCCU football team. I was a bit more excited than usual because it was the last Saturday in October, which meant three things; Central's Homecoming, an awesome halftime show and great food. When I pulled into the university's parking lot at 12:30 pm, I was eagerly met by my colleague, and best friend, Dr. Lamar Turner. I worked with Lamar at his sports medicine clinic, Turner Sports Medicine and Physical Therapy located in Durham, North Carolina. We were part of a team of doctors who served as the sports medicine staff for Central.

"Dr. Turner," I said, giving him a big hug. "You look well-rested. I guess that conference in Miami Beach did you a world of good. Look at you coming back here all tanned and whatnot. I'm still mad at you for going without me," I said, pretending to pout.

Lamar hugged me backed and laughed. "Come on Dr. Monroe. I can't help it if you're the low person on the totem pole. Somebody had to work. Besides, I did leave you in charge, didn't I?" he teased, a huge grin on his face. Lamar and I had become friends from the moment I started working for him. Our paths had crossed occasionally during my Sports Medicine fellowship at the University of North Carolina–Chapel Hill, so when he was looking to add another physician to his rapidly growing practice, I was at the top of his list.

"So Lamar, tell me about your trip to Miami," I sing-songed, playfully poking him in the ribs. "Did you do anything you shouldn't have?"

We began to walk towards the home team's bench area to meet up with the rest of the sports medicine team. A food stand was nearby so we stopped to get a quick bite to eat.

"Let's just say I had a really, really, REALLY good time in Miami," Lamar bragged.

I paid for the food, and passed a sandwich and a drink to Lamar. "That's all I get? No details? You usually tell me everything," I said pretending to look hurt.

"Come on now, don't go acting like that. You know I'm gonna tell you, but later. There's way too much to tell you now, and besides, I'd rather tell you over drinks," Lamar said, finishing up his sandwich. "I will tell you this much; I owe my good time to an old friend of mine. We went to college together, and funny enough, I ran into him down in Miami. He lives down there now."

"I see. How come I've never heard about this fun-loving friend of yours before now?"

"We haven't talked much since college. I ran into Jaylin when I was taking a run on the beach, and it was like old times. My last two nights there he took me to all the South Beach hotspots. Like I said, I'll tell you all about it later. Actually, he's coming to the game. I wanted to return the favor for his hospitality, so I invited him here for Homecoming weekend. I'll introduce you two after the game. We're supposed to hang out later on, and you're more than welcome to come along. That way, we can all hang out, you'll get to meet one of my boys, and I can tell you about the trip. You in?"

I put my hands on my hips. "Oh, I wouldn't miss this for anything. A chance to meet one of your old friends AND get the dirt on you; I am so there!"

The game and halftime show were great, as usual, with Central coming out on top beating Edward Waters 53-22. The sports medicine team met for our post-game meeting and injury report, then Lamar and I headed out. As we walked towards our cars, I noticed someone coming towards us, and let me just say he was fine! Scratch that, I mean drop dead gorgeous! The light-skinned brotha coming our way had curly black hair, nice kissable lips, a mustache and goatee that were on point, and as he got closer, I noticed he had the most piercing grey eyes. This week had been unseasonably warm, so nobody had a jacket on, including the gorgeous guy in front me. He had on a red Lacoste polo shirt and a pair of expensive-looking blue jeans. The outfit definitely showed off his body, which was magnificent. I couldn't help but notice the blinged out Rolex on his wrist, and the pair of Nike Hyperdunk 2010 Men's Basketball shoes on his feet. The whole outfit screamed, "I have money, and I like to spend it!"

When the exceedingly attractive man finally reached us, he and Lamar gave each other dap, and Lamar made introductions. "Dr. Giana Denize Monroe, meet Jaylin Jerome Rogers, the friend I was telling you about."

Jaylin extended his hand to me. "Lamar has told me a lot about you, but he neglected to mention how fine you are."

This man was obviously throwing me a line, but I still felt myself blushing nonetheless. "Thank you. I'm sorry, but Lamar has told me very little about you," I responded, taking Jaylin's hand and looking over at Lamar. Jaylin was blatantly looking me up and down. It may have been my imagination, but I felt as if he was undressing me with his eyes. Even though I was working a sporting event, I still felt the need to look good, simply because you never know who you might meet. My locks were curled in ringlets and hung down to my shoulders. I really didn't wear makeup just because I didn't like it, and didn't really need it. Not that I needed validation, but I received plenty of compliments from men on my looks. My NCCU sports medicine shirt and my beige khakis hugged my body well enough to show off my slender curves.

"Why get second hand information when you can get it directly from the source?" Jaylin queried, as he continued to hold my hand. "Anything you want to know about me, and I do mean anything, just ask."

Jaylin was clearly working me, but since I hadn't flirted with a man since forever, I decided to play along. "Anything at all, huh? I just may take you up on that, Mr. Rogers."

"It's Jaylin to my friends, and I certainly hope so. Please tell me you're hanging out with us tonight. I'd be very disappointed if you didn't."

"Okay Jaylin. And yes, I will be hanging out with you guys tonight. Like I told Lamar, I wouldn't miss this for anything. I'm looking forward to hearing all the dirt you have on Lamar...and hearing a lot more about you." Yeah I know, it was a bit much, but I was enjoying Jaylin's and my tête à tête verbal exchange.

"Excuse me, but would you two like to be alone, because I can leave," Lamar teased.

Jaylin and I let go of each other's hand as Lamar interrupted us. "Man, can't you see I'm trying to get to know the lady better?" Jaylin was talking to Lamar, but was looking directly at me.

Lamar started to walk back towards the parking lot. "Jay, you can do that later. It's not like you won't see her tonight."

"Alright, sounds like a plan. Speaking of, where are we going?" Jaylin asked.

"I'm not sure yet, but no worries. Wherever we go, you'll have a good time."

We reached Jaylin's rented 2011 Mercedes-Benz CLS63 AMG 4-Door Coupe first. His choice of car confirmed my first impression of him; he liked to spend money. "No doubt. I always enjoy myself," Jaylin quipped as he deactivated the car's alarm. "Lamar, just hit me up when you have a location." He and Lamar shook hands, then Jaylin turned to me. "Giana, I'll see you later," he replied, taking my hand and kissing it.

"See you later, Jaylin." With that, Jaylin was off, and Lamar and I headed to our own vehicles. "So that's who you were with in Miami," I said, watching as Jaylin's car tore out of the parking lot.

"Yep, that's Jaylin," Lamar replied, just as his cell phone began to ring. He took the call, and looked none too happy when he finished.

Once I got to my car, I leaned up against it. "What's wrong Lamar?"

"I need to cover another football game tonight. One of the doctors called out sick, and I'm next in line on the coverage schedule," Lamar stated, annoyance in his voice.

"Sorry to hear that. Guess you'll have to cancel your plans with Jaylin, huh?"

"Yeah. I really hate to do that since I invited him here, unless..." Lamar was giving me an all too familiar look.

"Oh no Lamar!" I exclaimed, shaking my head from side to side. "I am NOT entertaining your friend for you."

"Come on Giana, please," Lamar begged. "I promised him a good time, and Jaylin already thinks you're hanging out with us anyway. I'll just let him know that it'll be the two of you. I'll owe you big time."

"Lamar, I just met the guy. I don't know anything about him, except that he's your friend, and he's a big flirt." I stood with my hands on my hips.

"And you, Giana, were flirting right back. Don't try to deny it," he countered.

"Okay I won't deny it, but flirting with him for a few short minutes, and spending a few hours alone with him are two different things entirely."

"From where I was standing, you two were getting along just fine without me. Giana, do me this one little favor, okay?"

If it weren't for the fact that Lamar was my best friend, I would have easily said no, but since he was, I decided to take one for the team. And the fact that Jaylin was an attractive man didn't hurt either. "Fine, I'll do it, but you really owe me for this, and I intend to collect my friend." Then I had another thought. "Lamar, you haven't picked out somewhere for us to go."

He contemplated for a moment. "Go to The Republic at eight o'clock." The Republic Bar & Lounge was on West Main Street in Durham. It was a hot spot for urban sophisticates to get together, relax, and unwind. Saturday night was International Party night, and the DJ played international, house, and chillout music. "I'll reserve the V.I.P. spot as usual. Use your corporate card for expenses, and have a good time on me," he continued, beaming.

"Ya darn right it's gonna be on you," I laughed. I will be at The Republic at eight o'clock."

Lamar opened my car door and I climbed in. "Thank you Giana," he replied, leaning in to kiss me on the cheek.

21

I rolled my eyes at him, closing my car door, and rolling down the window. "Umm hmm. You just be sure to hold up your end of the bargain when I'm ready to call in my marker. " With that said, I drove off.

Once I arrived at my 2500 square foot, 3 bedroom, 2.5 bathroom Chapel Hill condo, I immediately started looking for something to wear. I knew how Lamar dressed when he went out, decked out from head to toe in designer clothes. Based on what I had seen earlier, I could only assume that Jaylin was the same way. I pulled out a pair of black lace Victoria's Secret boyshorts from my dresser drawer, then I checked The Weather Channel to see what the overnight temperature was going to be. Since the evening low was supposed to be in the low seventies, I settled on a Victoria's Secret black halter dress with an asymmetric hem and a pair of Collin Stewart four-and-a-half inch black strappy heels with silver accents. Even though I didn't wear heels often, I did have a thing for buying them. I figured now was as good a time as any to put my money to good use.

As I was laying my clothes out on the bed, Lamar sent a text, letting me know that everything at The Republic was all set, and that Jaylin would meet me there at 8:00 pm. I took a quick shower, moisturized my café mocha skin with cocoa butter and shea butter lotion, and got dressed. I put on a little eyeliner, some lip gloss, and some Pink Sugar scented body oil, and then checked myself out in the full length mirror in my bedroom. I liked what I saw. Although I was only 5'3", I was 5'7 ½" with my heels. My little black dress hugged my petite frame perfectly, and my dark brown curled locks hung down around my shoulders. Satisfied with my appearance, I grabbed my keys and purse, and I headed out the door.

It didn't take me long to arrive at The Republic. As soon as I opened the door, I heard the music pumping, as well as lively conversation and laughter from patrons. I walked to the back of the lounge towards the V.I.P. section, where I knew Jaylin would be. He was sitting on one of the black soft leather couches in a dimly lit area of the V.I.P. section. When I saw him, I was floored. He was without a doubt the handsomest man in that place. The man looked like sheer perfection in a Zenga charcoal birdseye wool 2-

22

button 'Fit Mila' suit with flat front trousers and a Z Zenga black stretch poplin dress shirt. His outfit was completed by a pair of gray Z Zenga moccasins. Jaylin's attire seemed to make his grey eyes stand out even more.

Not surprisingly, women were shamelessly vying for Jaylin's attention. Some of them were so thirsty, I was surprised they weren't throwing their panties at him. Since the V.I.P. section was a reserved area, it was off limits to most of them. Jaylin stood up as I approached him.

As I walked up to him, I noticed some of his admirers were giving me the evil eye, which I found rather entertaining. "Hi Jaylin. You're looking very handsome."

"Damn, that's all I get? I thought we were friends. Can I at least get a hug?" he replied.

"I'm sorry, Jaylin, and yes we are friends," I laughed.

I walked the few steps to him, intent on giving him a quick hug, but he had other ideas. Before I knew it, both of his arms were around my waist, and he pulled me into a tight embrace. So tight, in fact, that I could feel the hardness of his muscular chest and the hardness in his pants pressed against my body. That, along with the fact that he smelled really good, did something to me. He placed a soft kiss on my cheek, then whispered in my ear, "I forgive you, but don't let it happen again. You clean up nicely, Dr. Monroe, very, very sexy."

Under most circumstances I would have felt very uncomfortable with someone I hardly knew invading my personal space and speaking to me the way Jaylin did, but I didn't feel that way in the least bit with him. Part of the reason was because I took extreme pleasure in watching the reactions on the faces of Jaylin's groupies. The other part was I was flattered because he was undeniably the hottest guy in the place, and I had his undivided attention. "Why thank you Jaylin," I responded, looking into his hypnotic grey eyes.

After what seemed like forever, Jaylin finally released me from his grip. "What are you drinking?"

I thought about it for a second, and told him I wanted a mimosa. Jaylin waved down a server and ordered my drink, Remy for himself, and then he sat down on the sofa next to me. "So, I guess it's just the two of us tonight," I said, suddenly feeling at a loss for words, which was rare for me.

"Fine by me," Jaylin replied. "I'd rather get to know you better one-on-one anyway. "

I shook my head and smiled. "Earlier you said Lamar told you a lot about me. How much more could you need to know?"

"I'm sure there's a whole lot I don't know about you. For instance, I don't know if your man knows you're here with me tonight. I wouldn't want him rolling up in here starting no shit."

"There's no chance of that, considering I'm single at the moment," I verbalized, figuring that was his way of finding out if I was in a relationship.

"Good. That's very good news," he replied, moving a little closer to me.

"And why is that?"

"Because now I know you have no reason to rush off tonight."

"I have no intentions of rushing off."

"Glad to hear it. Now why is it that you don't have a man?"

"Honestly," I started, just as our drinks arrived, "I broke up with my boyfriend of five years six months ago, so I haven't really been looking. Besides, work has been keeping me pretty busy, so I don't think about it much."

Taking a swig of his Remy, Jaylin asked, "You've been single for six months, and nobody's tried to get at you?"

"I never said that. Yeah some have tried, I just haven't been interested in any of them," I said, finishing my first drink. "But enough about me, tell me about you."

"What do you want to know?"

"Are you in a relationship?" Since he basically asked me, I decided there was no harm in me asking the same.

Jaylin polished off his drink and signaled to the server again. "Yeah, but we're not together right now. It's...complicated."

The tone in his voice said that I needed to leave the topic alone, and I would...for now. "Okay, so changing the subject, what do you like to do for fun?"

"I like to do a lot of things, but making new friends is my specialty," he said.

The server took our orders, with me ordering Moscato D'Asti this time around, and Jaylin again ordering Remy. "When you say new friends, I take it you mean of the female persuasion," I teased. "Jaylin, are you always such a flirt?"

"It depends."

"Depends on what?"

"It depends on who the lady is. And baby, you're no slouch yourself."

I feigned shock. "Why, Jaylin, are you accusing me of flirting with you?"

"Hell no, I'm not accusing you. I'm just outright saying it. You were flirting with me just as hard as I was flirting with you," he laughed.

After the server handed us our second round of drinks, I replied with a snicker, "Alright, I'll admit it. I haven't done it in such a long time and I just wanted to make sure I still knew how."

"What, has it been that long since you've flirted with a man?"

I took a sip of my Moscato before responding. "Yes, it has. I didn't do it during my relationship, and I haven't really flirted since the break up, so it's been about five and a half years. "

"Interesting?"

"And what is so interesting about that?" My curiosity was piqued.

"Because of all the men you could have flirted with," he said between gulps of his drink. "You chose me. I get the impression that you like me, Giana."

I couldn't help but to laugh. I knew exactly what he meant by that statement, but I decided to play it another way. "Why of course I like you. I find you rather amusing."

"Woman stop bullshitting, you know exactly what I mean."

"Oh, you mean LIKE you, as in I'm attracted to you," I kidded. "Maybe a little."

Jaylin set his now-empty glass on a side table and ordered another round for us. "Why only just a little?"

"Because as much as you think I might like you, I've noticed certain things about you."

"So what is it you think you know about me, Doc?"

The look Jaylin gave me challenged me to either speak up or shut up, and I was definitely not shutting up.

Looking Jaylin squarely in the eyes, I answered, "Since you did say we were friends, I'm going to be completely honest with you. From what I can tell, you're a player, a very smooth talking one, but a player nonetheless. Don't get me wrong, you're a very handsome and charismatic man, and some, possibly many, women may fall under your spell. However, in my opinion, you are very transparent."

Jaylin moved a little closer to me, lifting my chin with his finger. "What you call transparent, I call it keepin' it real. The ladies know where I stand from the jump. And as far as me being a player, I can't help it if they know what time it is and still want to be a part of Jaylin's world."

"Jaylin's world? I take it this is your world, and we all just live in it."

"You said it, I didn't," was his smug reply.

I moved away from Jaylin as our drinks arrived. "Yes, but you didn't disagree with me either, which tells me you like to have things your way."

"Damn right I do," he said, raising his glass. "So, Giana, since you haven't dated in six months does that mean you haven't had sex?"

"Man, that's rather forward of you, considering we just met."

"We met a few hours ago, and we are adults here, so are you going to answer the question or not?"

"Why do you want to know?"

Jaylin shrugged. "Just curious."

"You mean nosey," I countered. "But I will answer your question. No I haven't been with anybody in six months."

"Hold up, you really ain't had no dick in six months? Damn! The only way I wouldn't be getting no pussy would be if I was dead, and maybe not even then." Jaylin was finding my plight extremely comical.

"Dang, you have a potty mouth," I joked. "Glad you're finding this funny. And, the reason I haven't had sex in six months is because I'm not seeing anybody at the moment," I noted.

"And? What does seeing anybody have to do with it?"

"For me, it has everything to do with it. I would like to be in a relationship before I have sex again."

"If everybody thought like that nobody would be fucking," Jaylin laughed.

I rolled my eyes. "Jaylin, I'm not a fan of casual sex, and I don't do one-night stands, okay? Is there something wrong with that?"

"Are you telling me you never hooked up with somebody just for the hell of it?"

I gave a loud sigh. "No, I'm not saying that. I've had a couple of hook ups, as you put it, but they weren't good experiences for me. The only thing I got out of them was regrets. And as far as having a one-night stand, I've never had one before."

"Maybe you should have one. At least with a one-night stand, if the sex is bad, you don't have to worry about seeing that person again. The way I see it, if the pussy is whack, I ain't coming back! Now if it's good, that's a different story."

"You have such a way with words," I said, shaking my head.

"Giana, when was the last time you had *good* sex?"

I couldn't believe I was actually having this conversation with him, but oddly I felt relaxed enough talking with Jaylin. Maybe it was the alcohol. Nah, who was I fooling, the drinks I had were like water to me. I sat there for a minute, and truth be told, I couldn't remember when last I had *good* sex, which was really sad when you think about it. "Actually, I'm not sure."

"What do you mean you're not sure? You only broke up with your ex six months ago, or was sex with him really that bad?"

I sat back on the couch, crossing my arms in front of me. "It was okay."

"Just okay? You were with him for five years, and it was just okay? What was wrong with him?"

He sure asked a whole lot of questions. "I don't even know if I should tell you," I remarked, a little apprehensive.

"Tell me. I just want to know why you would put up with whack-ass sex for five years, that's all."

"Okay fine, but if you laugh I swear I am going to hurt you, badly."

"Is that a promise or a threat?" The look in Jaylin's eyes said that he hoped I meant what I said.

"Alright already," I laughed. "There's really not that much to tell. My ex-boyfriend had this little problem..."

"He had a small dick?" Jaylin interrupted.

"No actually he was very, uh, very well-endowed," I said, feeling a little embarrassed now.

"Head game was lousy?"

"It was okay, nothing to brag about, but that wasn't the main problem." I felt the heat rising in my face.

"So what then, was he a two-minute man?"

"Actually it was more like...thirty seconds," I said, barely loud enough for him to hear because I was uncomfortable.

Between the two of us, there was an almost deafening silence for a few seconds, until finally Jaylin broke out laughing so loudly people were looking in our direction. Needless to say, I wasn't too happy with him at that moment. "Okay, are you done now?" I asked, visibly irritated.

Jaylin was still laughing like it was the most hilarious thing ever. "Hell no I'm not finished. That is some of the funniest shit I ever heard! Thirty seconds ain't even enough time for me to get my dick wet! And you put up with that shit for five years?"

"Yes, Jaylin, I did."

"Why in the hell would you do that?"

"I don't think you'd understand," I remarked, my annoyance with his questions apparent.

But Jaylin wouldn't let the subject go. "Try me."

"Because I loved him, and it wasn't all about sex with us."

"Sounds to me like it wasn't about sex at all. Did you even get off when y'all had sex?"

"Sometimes I did, sometimes I didn't," I replied, becoming exasperated.

"Do you want to know what I think?" Jaylin asked. I was pretty sure it was a rhetorical question.

On a loud exhale, I replied, "No, but I'm sure you're going to tell me anyway."

"You're right, and I'm probably going to piss you off by saying this, but since we're keeping it real, here's my take. You may have loved your ex, but I don't think that's the only reason you stayed with him for so long. I think you felt sorry for the brotha because he sucked in bed, and you didn't want to hurt his feelings by kicking him to the curb. You sacrificed your own pleasure just to make him happy."

"Thank you for that colorful psychological commentary, Dr. Phil, but you don't know me, and please don't presume that you do." Problem was Jaylin was right. I did stay with my ex all that time because I didn't want to hurt him. I mean, he was a good guy and I did love him, but I also believed that my breaking up with him just because the sex wasn't up to par seemed, well, shallow. When I actually did end the relationship, it had very little to do with sex, and a whole lot to do with the fact that I couldn't see myself spending the rest of my life with him because of other issues we had.

Jaylin continued his unsolicited assessment. "Sorry, baby, but your ex was slackin' on the job. If the dick wasn't gettin' the job done, his face should've been in the pussy all day long. No woman should ever leave a man's bed unsatisfied, especially a woman as fine as you are. If I was him, I would have done whatever was necessary to please my woman." I wanted to be mad at Jaylin for grilling me the way he did, but after what he just said I found it difficult to remain angry.

"Thanks, but can we please just change the subject now?" I had had enough of this discussion. "I am definitely ready for another drink," I voiced. The mimosa and two Moscatos I drank did little, if nothing, in the way of a buzz for me, and I needed something a little stronger. "Order me a kamikaze, please."

Once Jaylin got the server's attention, he ordered drinks for both of us. I needed a breather, so I grabbed my purse and stood up, intent on heading to the ladies' room. "Will you excuse me for a minute?"

Jaylin stood and queried, "Are you alright, baby?"

I put on the biggest fake smile I could muster. "I'm fine. I just have to go to the ladies' room." I turned and headed off in that direction. I wasn't really good at covering up my feelings, so I knew Jaylin could tell I was lying, but at that point I really didn't care. Once I reached the ladies' room, I stepped inside, closing and locking the door behind me. I leaned against the door, took a deep breath, and closed my eyes for a second, reflecting on what Jaylin had said. I wanted to hate him for being so observant and on point, especially for someone who just met me a few hours prior, but I couldn't. Couldn't fault the man for being honest, no matter how crude and unwanted his honesty was. If anything, I was disappointed with myself for staying so long in a situation that I could, and should, have ended years ago.

But I was done with my pity party. I was determined to enjoy the rest of my evening. I got myself together and walked back over to where Jaylin was sitting. He stood up, again, as I reached him. I noticed he had taken off his suit jacket and had laid it neatly on the back of the couch. Jaylin looked good without that jacket, really, really good. We both sat down, and he handed me my drink. "Thank you," was all I could muster to say at that moment.

Jaylin and I sat in silence for a few minutes. I still felt a little unsettled by what he said earlier. The DJ was ending a house music set and started playing reggae music. I was wrapped up in my own thoughts when I heard Jaylin call my name. "Giana."

"Yes."

"Dance with me," he said, his hand held out to me as he got to his feet.

I had to get out of my own head, and took Jaylin's offer as a much-needed diversion. I took his hand and stood up. We could have walked over to the dance floor, but instead we stayed right where we were. Jaylin put his arms around my waist, and I put mine around his neck. He pulled me close to him, my body flush with his. We started to move in rhythm to Maxi Priest's Art of Seduction. I loved reggae music, possibly because I have island roots in my blood. Problem with dancing to it is it usually requires intimate contact, something I wasn't comfortable with when it came to dancing with a stranger. Some men took it as an opportunity to feel you up or try to have sex with you through your clothes. But I didn't mind with Jaylin, despite the fact that I felt his hard-on pressing against me.

Jaylin was a good dancer. He actually knew how to move his hips to the music. Some men didn't. The way he was pressed against me, his penis was rubbing against my clitoris, and I felt myself getting wet. I was trying to keep my mind on the music, but it was becoming a task. Luckily, Jaylin started talking. "You haven't really said anything since you came out of the bathroom. You mad at me because of what I said earlier?"

I looked up into his beautiful grey eyes. "No, I'm not mad. Thing is, you were right about everything. I just don't like admitting it to myself, that's all, let alone talk about."

"Okay, let's talk about something else then. So you really ain't had no dick in six months?" Jaylin asked again.

I laughed despite myself. "We've already established that, but just to reiterate, no I have not had sex in six long months."

The song changed to "Give It to Her" by Tanto Metro and Devante. Gee great. This music was not helping at all. Jaylin shifted his position so that his penis was now not only stroking my clit, but my already wet folds as well. It felt so good I bit my lip to keep from moaning. "Let me get this straight, no dick in six months, but in reality no GOOD dick for five and a half years."

"Can you make my sex life sound any more depressing?" I asked, leaving one of my arms around his neck, and placing a hand on his chest. I placed my head on his shoulder because I didn't want him looking in my face and seeing how much I was enjoying this little dance of ours. I knew it was just a dance, but I hadn't felt anything like this in a really long time. My walls were having a dance party of their own, and try as I might, I couldn't make them stop.

"Sure I can, but I won't. Instead, let's think of a way we can make it better."

I knew where this was going. And as if on cue, the next song said it all. It was Sean Paul with Keyshia Cole belting out "When You Gonna Give It Up to Me." The way Jaylin was working me, I

31

felt like I was going to have an orgasm any second. I couldn't let that happen. I freed myself from his grasp, and turned around, backing myself up to him. I took a deep breath, and continued dancing, grinding my round derrière against Jaylin's rock hard penis. "What exactly did you have in mind?"

"You, me, and my hotel room for the rest of the night. Baby, I guarantee it'll be much, much longer than thirty seconds. I'll make it a night you won't ever forget," Jaylin said into my ear, his soft lips brushing against it. His hands found their way down my thighs, pulling me even closer to him.

"Awfully smug aren't you?"

"Not smug, confident. Confident enough to know that I can give you exactly what you want and need," he replied, turning me back around to face him.

Smug, confident, or whatever you want to call it, this man was really getting to me. I was almost ready to give in to him; almost, but not quite. "I don't know Jaylin, I want to, but..."

"But what? What are you afraid of?" he questioned, looking me squarely in the eyes.

"I'm not afraid of anything." I lied. I was afraid. Afraid of what Jaylin would think of me if I slept with him tonight, that I would have major regrets, and that I wouldn't respect myself in the morning.

"Then if you're not afraid, why are you depriving yourself of something you want? Tell you what; I'll give you a few minutes to think about it while I go to the men's room. When I get back, I'll ask you what you've decided. I hope your answer is yes." Jaylin released me from his grip, and made his way towards the men's room.

No pressure there! I had all of maybe five minutes to decide whether or not I was going to have a one-night stand with a man I had just met a few hours ago. Five minutes to decide if I would go for one night of pleasure or go home with all this pent up sexual energy. What a choice! I sat down, contemplating my next move.

After what seemed like the shortest few minutes in history, Jaylin came back over to where I was and sat next to me. "So, Giana, are we going to do this or not? Your move."

I took a deep breath, and gave him my answer. I simply said, "Yes." From that moment on, I had decided to drop all my misgivings and let nature take its course.

A smile crossed Jaylin's face. "Are you sure?"

"I'm sure. Once I settle up this bill, let's go, before I change my mind." Not that I would have changed my mind at that point, but he didn't need to know that.

"Tabs already taken care of," he said. Without another word, Jaylin grabbed his jacket and my hand and we exited the building. He walked me to my 2010 blue graphite metallic Volkswagen Jetta TDI. I deactivated my car's alarm, and Jaylin opened the door.

"What hotel are you staying at?" I asked.

"The Siena Hotel in Chapel Hill."

"Really? The Siena Hotel is only a few minutes from my house. You can follow me there to drop off my car and I need to pick up a few things."

Jaylin agreed and followed me to my condo. I quickly ran upstairs to my bedroom, going between my walk-in closet and bathroom, packing an overnight bag with toiletries and some clothes. I was about to walk back downstairs when I realized I had almost forgotten the most important reason for stopping home in the first place. I ran back into the bathroom, looked in a drawer, and pulled out a box of unopened extra large condoms. I made a habit of buying them for my ex and me. Needless to say, this box had been sitting around for a minute. I checked the expiration date, and once I saw they were still usable, I threw them in my bag, and took off for the stairs.

Once I turned off the lights, I reset the alarm via the front door keypad, and exited through the front door. After I locked up, I walked towards Jaylin's car, which he was leaning up against, arms folded across his muscular chest. "What took you so long? I was beginning to think you changed your mind," he smirked, taking my bag from me and opening the passenger's side door.

"Impatient much Jaylin?"

"Possibly," he said, shooting me a megawatt smile. I got inside, and he closed the door. Once he placed my bag in the trunk, he got into the car, and drove the short distance to The Siena Hotel. When he pulled up to the hotel, I couldn't believe how beautiful it was. In the very front of the hotel was a lighted 4-tiered fountain surrounded by neatly trimmed hedges. The hotel itself was a four story off-white brick building with off-white columns and a red awning at the entrance.

Jaylin parked the car, grabbed my bag out of the trunk, and opened my door for me. As we walked towards the hotel entrance, I remarked, "All this time living right near this place, and I never really paid attention to it. It's really nice."

"If you think this is nice, wait until you see the inside," Jaylin stated. He wasn't lying. When I stepped inside, The Siena definitely had the look and feel of a world-class luxury boutique hotel with European-style furniture and antiques, Italian marble floors, and majestic columns decorating the brightly lit lobby. And to think, I lived right down the road from all this!

Jaylin and I walked to the elevator, which luckily for us, was already on the first floor. We stepped inside, and he pressed the button for the fourth floor. When the doors closed, I turned around and leaned against the elevator wall. Jaylin boxed me in, pressed his body against mine, looked me in the eyes, and said, "Last chance to change your mind, baby. Once we get inside that room, it's you and me for the rest of the night."

"No chance of that Jaylin. I'm in it for however long it takes," I said, returning his gaze. When the elevator doors opened, Jaylin backed up, and stepped out, with me following. We walked down a long hallway, stopping once we reached the last room at the end of the hall.

Jaylin took his keycard out of his pocket, and opened the door. When he let me enter the room first, I realized that it was obviously a suite. I had to stop for a second to admire the surroundings. The first thing I noticed was the large sitting and dining areas. To the left of those were the French doors leading to a private balcony. To the right of the sitting area was an alcove leading to a huge king size bed.

I was in such awe of the room that Jaylin had to get my attention. "I take it you like the room," he said.

"I definitely like the room. I might have to check in here one night just because," I replied.

"Nothing wrong with that. Do you want something to drink?" he asked, as he took off his suit jacket and shoes, placing them in the closet.

"A bottle of water, if you have one." I had had enough alcohol for the night, and needed to keep a clear head.

Jaylin placed my bag on a chair, and got me a bottle of water. "Make yourself comfortable. I'll be back in a minute." He walked into what I assumed was the bathroom.

I took my shoes off and also placed them in the closet. When I did, I noticed how orderly everything was arranged. And I thought I was a neat freak! I made short work of that bottle of water, then removed my bag off of the chair and placed it on the bed. I took out the box of condoms, and placed them on a nightstand. I then took out something more comfortable to change into.

Jaylin finally came out of the bathroom, and when he did, my jaw almost dropped to the floor. The only thing he had on was a pair of black boxer briefs. All I can say is that man's body was a marvel to behold! Nothing but pure muscle for days! My eyes traveled up and down his body, and settled on the massive bulge in his underwear. My walls started having that dance party again, and I had to pull my eyes away. "See something you like?" Jaylin queried with lust in his expression. I'm pretty sure he saw the same look on my face.

"Absolutely." I bit my lip. "Hold that thought though. I'll be right back," I said, taking my clothes and bag with me into the bathroom.

Jaylin walked to the closet with his clothes. "Alright, but hurry up. Don't make me come in there and get you."

"Wouldn't dream of it," I said, closing the bathroom door. I quickly shed my dress and lace boyshorts, put some lotion on my body, and donned my Victoria's Secret Sexy Little Things red sheer babydoll with matching bikini. If I was going to do this, I was going to do it right. I threw my clothes in my bag, and opened the door. I couldn't have been in the bathroom for more than two minutes, but there he was standing by the door leaning against the wall in all his sexiness. "Now, I know I didn't take that long," I said, dropping my bag in front of the nightstand.

"No you didn't, but I'm not a patient man." Jaylin was giving me the same look I gave him not five minutes ago. I was glad I worked out regularly and kept it tight otherwise I might have felt insecure at that very moment.

"You see something you like?" I asked.

"You're damn right I do," he replied as he grabbed me by my arm and pulled me to him. "Damn, you are really short," he teased.

"Yeah well, good things come in small packages," I replied, standing on my tiptoes and putting my arms around his neck. Before I was able to get out another word, Jaylin's lips were on mine. His lips were so soft and tasted so good. His tongue entered my mouth, while his hands explored my body. From my locks all the way down to my shapely rear, his hands were everywhere.

I braced myself and jumped, wrapping my legs around his waist. Jaylin traveled the short distance to the bed, and lowered us both down onto it. His tongue continued to explore my mouth as one of his hands moved down to my shaved kitty. His fingers stroked my wetness through my panties causing an involuntary moan to escape my lips into his mouth. Jaylin's hand found its way into my bikinis. His thumb began caressing my already swollen clit, as he inserted one finger between my soaked womanhood. My back arched as his finger delved deep inside me.

"It has been a long time hasn't it?" Jaylin remarked, my juices saturating his fingers. "Damn shame you letting all this good pussy go to waste. Let's see what you taste like." He reached behind me, untying the satin ribbon to my teddy, and lifting it off of my body. His lips moved down to my neck, while he fondled my 34-B cup breasts in his hands. He brought both of my breasts together and teased my nipples with his tongue, then closed his mouth over them, sucking on them. When he finally released my wet nipples, he kissed down my torso to my belly ring, stopping long enough to remark, "Somebody has a little bit of bad girl in her."

"Oh, you have no idea," I said, as he removed my panties.

"No, but I'm damn sure gonna find out, starting with seeing how this juicy pussy tastes."

Jaylin had a filthy mouth, but right now I was turned on by it. He pushed my legs apart, positioned himself, then plunged in. His tongue brushed against my clit, sending shivers throughout my body. I moaned out and held on tightly to the pillow behind my head as he continued to flick his tongue. The more I moaned, the faster his tongue went. He placed his mouth over my bud and gently sucked on it. What Jaylin was doing to me was about to have me lose my mind. He then moved to my drenched pleasure palace plunging his tongue inside of me. I placed my hand on top of his head, my fingers running through his curly black hair, my hips moving in rhythm with his tongue thrusts. Jaylin must have sensed I was close to reaching my peak, because he grabbed me by my thighs and pulled me closer to him. My whole body began to shake as I started to climax, and Jaylin slurped up my nectar. He didn't stop until I was finished. When I did, he kissed his way up my body all the way to my lips, my essence on his mouth and tongue.

"Sweet and juicy, just how I like it," Jaylin said, pressing his throbbing member against me. "Was it good for you?"

"Very, very good," I said with a huge grin on my face. "So good in fact, I owe you one. Lie down."

"I see the bad girl is coming out to play, right? Ain't nothing wrong with that." Jaylin removed his underwear, and when I saw how long and thick his penis was, I was awestruck. He had what one of my girlfriends would call a BFBPD, big fat black pretty dick, the type that you didn't mind putting your mouth on.

"You tell me if the bad girl showed up, after I'm done," I replied, taking Jaylin's package in my hands. I lightly stroked him up and down from shaft to tip. Jaylin was lying with his hands behind his head and his eyes closed, a slight smile on his face. I lowered my mouth onto his engorged head, my tongue circling around it. Gradually, I took more of him into my mouth until his phallus hit an end point at the back of my throat. But I couldn't go out like a sucker. Let me rephrase that, I was no quitter. I intended to handle all of him. I relaxed my throat muscles, and hoped that my gag reflex wouldn't kick in. Slowly more of him entered my mouth, sliding down my throat. Once I had all of Jaylin in my mouth, I sped up my movements, working my tongue and tightening my mouth around him at the same time. I felt Jaylin's hand on my head, as he began thrusting upward. I continued to slide my mouth from his shaft to tip, Jaylin's words, "I love how you're sucking this dick," encouraged me to continue. His penis expanded even more, telling me he was about to come. Instead of pulling up, I kept going. The tight suction from my mouth brought him to an orgasm, and the release of his warm fluid down my throat turned me on. After I had swallowed the last of his seed, I slowly removed him from my mouth.

"Damn, baby, that was definitely a bad girl move right there. You did promise back at the club you'd hurt me."

"I did, didn't I? Yeah well that's what you get for laughing at me earlier," I grinned, climbing on top of him.

Jaylin put his arm around my waist and flipped both of us over. "Now that the preliminaries are over, are you ready for these nine plus inches?" I thought Jaylin would need a breather after what I just did, but the man was still hard as a steel rod and raring to go.

That nine plus inches sounded a little intimidating, especially since I hadn't been with anyone in six months. But I wanted Jaylin badly, and was ready, willing, and able to take all he had to give. "Anytime you are."

That was all Jaylin needed to hear. He positioned himself at my opening, centimeters away from making contact when I stopped him. "Jaylin wait. I forgot something."

"What?"

I reached over to the nightstand, and pulled a condom out of the box. I tried to hand it to Jaylin, but he wasn't having it. "Come on, baby. Sometimes I hate wearing those fuckin' things. It's probably not even the right size."

"For your information, these are extra large, so they should fit just fine. Besides, you know what they say...no glove, no love. I know this is your world and all, and you're used to having things your way, but not this time."

From the frown on his face, I knew Jaylin wasn't happy about being told to wear a condom, but if I also read him correctly, he wanted the sex more, so he'd tolerate it. I called that one, because he said, "Fine, but if you want me to wear it, you put it on me."

Without hesitation, I opened the condom, and rolled it down on all nine plus inches. "See, Jaylin, perfect fit," I said, a triumphant smile crossing my face.

"Whatever," was all he said. Jaylin lowered himself on top of me, and as I braced for impact, he entered me slowly. It was at that moment that I realized I had no idea what I was getting into, or rather what I was letting get into me. He wasn't even halfway in, and I felt like I was being split in two. "Damn this pussy tight," he said, still not having penetrated me completely. "Your ex definitely was not doing his muthafucking job."

Although Jaylin wasn't being rough, I still felt quite a bit of pain as he tried to go deeper, and on a reflex, I tensed up. He obviously knew it because he said, "Giana, I need you to relax." Relax? Easy for him to say. It wasn't my fault he was hung like a Triple Crown winner. He took one of my already hard nipples into his mouth, his tongue teasing it, I guess trying to distract me, but it was working. I started to relax, allowing Jaylin to push further inside me. Once most of the pain was gone, he was slow stroking me, giving me all nine plus inches, hitting my G spot, A spot, and spots that probably didn't even have names, so we'll just call them X, Y, and Z.

"This is what a real man feels like, baby, and if you haven't noticed, it's been a lot longer than thirty seconds."

"Shut...up... Jaylin," I replied between moans, starting to match him thrust for thrust.

"Make me," he said, driving harder and faster into me.

"Plan to." And I would, but only after I stopped having an orgasm so intense I thought my head would explode. Jaylin was pummeling my G spot, and the more he did, the more I came. By the time it was over, I could barely speak.

"You were saying Giana?" Jaylin slowed up his pace, giving me time to catch my breath. "You gonna make me shut up or what?" He climbed off of me and laid back, a self-satisfied look on his face.

"In a minute." I was still coming down from my sexual high.

"Do you really want to make me shut up?" Jaylin inquired a mischievous grin on his handsome face.

"I'd love to. What are you suggesting?" I rolled over onto my side and propped myself up on one arm.

"I'm suggesting you sit that sweet pussy on my face."

He didn't have to tell me twice. Hey, whatever Jaylin wants, Jaylin gets, right? I quickly lowered myself onto his waiting tongue, and proceeded to shut him up. Jaylin wrapped his arms around my thighs keeping me on lock. He snaked his tongue inside me as I rode his face. The way he was licking and sucking it only took a few minutes before I was spraying his mouth and tongue for a second time. It was then that I decided that Jaylin was a coochie connoisseur, the king of cunnilingus.

I climbed off of him, ready to go for round two, but this time I was ready to take control of the situation. I took off Jaylin's condom and put a new one on him. I mounted him slowly, trying to accommodate his nine plus inches. He held onto my waist as I slid up and down. He drove so deep into me I felt it all the way up my spine. I then brought my legs around, placing my feet up near Jaylin's chest, and my hands behind me for balance. I moved my hips back and forth, working him like a pro. I felt him swell inside me, which told me he was going to come soon. I moved my legs back, placed my hands on his chest, and rode him like I was a jockey and he was a prized stallion. We moved at a frenzied pace, until finally, I came all over him. My walls tightened around Jaylin, siphoning everything from him as he released. By the time we finished, we were both breathing hard. I laid my head on Jaylin's damp chest, feeling exhausted yet exhilarated at the same time.

Jaylin let out a quiet laugh. "What's so funny?" I questioned.

"Giana, you are a freak, and I mean that in a good way. Who would have guessed the Doc had a wild side?"

I giggled. "The wild side only came out because of all those naughty things you said and did to me."

"And you liked every one of those things, didn't you?"

"Yes I did, very much." I rolled off of Jaylin and took a much needed stretch. I used muscles that I had forgotten I even had. I lay down on my stomach and placed my head on my hands. Feeling a little tired, I closed my eyes.

Jaylin ran his fingers down my back, and then lightly squeezed my butt. "Good, because I am not done with you yet."

My eyes shot open, and I raised my head up. "Come again?"

"Oh you most certainly will, again, again, and again. Don't forget, you said I can take it anyway I wanted it." Jaylin took me by my hand and helped me off of the bed. Needless to say, I did not get to sleep like I anticipated. In fact, I didn't get any sleep at all. Jaylin most certainly took me anyway he wanted me. From the couch to the desk to the dining room table, we were all over that room. And oh yeah, let's not forget about the balcony. Actually, that was my idea. Hey, I figured if I was going to let my freak flag fly, let it fly high. Jaylin and I were at it for hours, and before I knew it, he was arranging for a late check-out because it was already two o'clock in the afternoon.

Jaylin's flight wasn't until seven thirty, so we figured we had plenty of time to relax a bit, order room service, and shower. I was happy about that, because it dawned on me that I hadn't eaten anything in over twenty-four hours, and I was starving. We looked over the menu and Jaylin ended up ordering pan roasted flat iron steak with spring vegetables and local new potatoes. I ordered whole wheat pancakes with roasted bananas, vanilla, walnuts, and pure maple syrup. We also ordered a carafe of orange juice and some extra ice. The ice was for me. I needed to make an ice pack because when it was all said and done, my coochie was so sore I could barely sit down.

When the food arrived, we pulled the cart into the room next to the bed. Jaylin sat down and sat me down between his legs. I made the ice pack and placed it on a towel between my legs. "Sorry, baby, but that tends to happen when you get with me," he said, tearing into his food.

"No need to apologize, it was all good. Nothing this ice pack and a lot of ibuprofen won't cure," I chuckled, downing my pancakes and sipping my orange juice.

"Any regrets?" Jaylin asked.

"Huh?"

"You said before that the hook-ups you had weren't good experiences and you only ended up with regrets. Any now?"

I turned around and looked at Jaylin. "Honestly, not one single solitary regret."

Jaylin raised one eyebrow. "Even though it was a one-night stand?"

"Yes, even though it was a one-night stand. I can't say I would have another one, but this one was definitely worth me breaking my own rule." I finished my pancakes, and laid my plate on the room service cart. Removing my ice pack, I said, "I'm going to take a shower."

"I'll join you," Jaylin said, his hand finding its way inside my robe, caressing one of my nipples. "We still have plenty of time before I have to get to the airport." He moved my locks away from my neck, and placed his lips on it.

"As much as I would enjoy that, we are out of condoms, so unless you're just going to keep me company, you might want to stay out here." Jaylin was breaking down my resistant fast, so I slowly got up and walked towards the bathroom.

"Well, go handle your business," Jaylin said, waving me on, picking up the remote, and turning on the big screen television.

As I walked to the bathroom, I noticed something on the floor between the bed and the nightstand. I reached down to pick it up, a smirk on my face. Standing in the bathroom doorway, I said, "Jaylin, on second thought, you sure you don't want to join me?"

"Hell no!" he yelled, keeping his eyes on the television. "I ain't getting none, so carry your pretty ass on and take your shower already."

I acted disappointment. "Oh well, it was worth a try," I sighed. "Too bad this unopened condom is going to go to waste though." I took off my robe, and held up the condom. Once Jaylin finally looked in my direction, a broad smile crossed his face. Jaylin got up off the bed, walked over to me, slid out of his robe, and had me in the shower in no time flat. I opened the condom and slid it on to his penis. Jaylin lifted me up by my waist. I wrapped my legs around him, and I once again impaled myself on his nine plus inches. Yeah, I knew I'd pay for it later, but for what little time Jaylin and I had left, I was going to enjoy every last second.

By the time Jaylin dropped me off at home, it was four thirty, which still gave him plenty of time to get to the airport, considering Raleigh-Durham International Airport, or RDU for short, was less than thirty minutes away and traffic to the airport was generally light. Since we had some time, we sat in his rental and talked for a few minutes.

I wanted to continue the discussion that we were having at the club, and I figured it was now or never. "Jaylin, I know I didn't press you last night when you told me you and your lady weren't together right now, but now I'm asking."

"Like I told you, it's complicated," he said, sitting back in his seat. "Let's just say some changes need to be made before we get back together, and believe me we will get back together."

"Was what we did last night the type of complication that caused you two to be separated in the first place? I'm not judging or anything, I'm just curious."

"You mean nosey," he said. "But yeah, that's part of it."

"Look, I'm not trying to get all in your personal business, but since you were all in mine, and you did say we were friends, I'm just wondering about something. You said that you and your lady will get back together, right? At the risk of upsetting you, how's that going to happen if you're with other women?"

"I'm not upset. Honestly, I'm waiting for my lady to decide what she wants to do. Once she does, I'll handle it from there."

"I have one more question, and then I'll leave it alone. Do you think she could be taking so long because she knows what you're doing? Don't you think she might make up her mind sooner if you stopped?"

"Giana, that's two questions and it's not that simple. But no matter what, we'll work it out one way or another."

"Okay, I'll take that as my cue to drop the subject, again. Last thing I'll say is this, things may seem complicated, and I'm only an outsider looking in, but Jaylin, in my humble opinion you can probably make them a lot less complicated. I'm done now, and I hope you two do work it out. After all, you're not such a bad guy. A bit rude, somewhat pushy, and you have a foul mouth, but you're still okay in my book," I said, smiling at him. "Anyway, you better get going. You shouldn't have any problem at the airport, but you can never be too sure."

Jaylin got out of the car and grabbed my bag out of the trunk. I had a little trouble getting out of the car, so he helped me out. I heard him snicker as we walked to the door. "What's so amusing?" I asked, turning around to face him.

"You're walking funny."

"And whose fault is that?" I asked, opening my front door and deactivating the alarm.

"I take full credit for that. That just means I was doing my job, unlike your ex," Jaylin said, handing me my bag.

"You just can't let that go, can you?" I grinned, dropping my bag inside the door. "Time for you to go now. I had a really good time." I gave Jaylin a hug and kiss on the cheek.

"Me too," he said, reciprocating in kind. "Bye, Giana."

"Goodbye, Jaylin." I closed and locked the door behind me, and headed for the kitchen to get a bottle of water and some more ice. I tossed the ice into a Zip Lock bag, and went upstairs to my bedroom. I was exhausted and really needed a nap, and the sooner I got it, the better. Once I grabbed a towel and 600 milligrams of ibuprofen from the bathroom, I fell back onto my bed. It took me a while to get settled, and just as I was about to get comfortable, my cell phone vibrated on my hip. It was from Jaylin:

Hey Giana,
Made it to the airport. Waiting at the gate. Had a great time last night...this morning...and this afternoon. Get some rest because I know you need it. And don't forget that ice pack. Stay sweet.
All love, Jay Baby

I just shook my head, laughed, and put my cell phone on the nightstand. So there you have it. Jaylin Jerome Rogers had shown me the best night, morning, and afternoon ever. He gave me something that even though I thought I didn't want it, I obviously needed it. That consisted of a few hours of unbridled passion with a man who made me feel comfortable enough to explore my sexuality in ways I never even dared to imagine. He also gave me some brutal honesty, something most people won't give you, even if you've known them forever. For that, I actually considered Jaylin a friend. I only hoped I gave him the same. One thing I knew for sure, I didn't regret one single solitary minute I spent in Jaylin's world.

The End

Book Club Meeting...

We had been attentively listening to Giana's story. I, myself, had learned a thing or two about sacrificing my own pleasures for the sake of a man. Been there, done that. Several of the other women in the audience chimed in, too, and one stood to ask Giana a question.

"I was touched by your story, but more so by the feeling of Jaylin's hands," she chuckled. "You say that you don't have any regrets, but was it more of the pleasure he gave you that impressed you the most, or the fact that he kicked down some knowledge to you about your ex?"

"Honestly," Giana said. "One doesn't triumph the other. It was both, and after he left, I felt fulfilled in many ways. In pain, but fulfilled."

"Do you still need an icepack?" Another lady shouted. "That was some steamy sex the two of you had and I'm just wondering if you ever recovered?"

Many people laughed and so did Giana. "It was days before I felt 'normal' again, but that BFBPD was a force to be reckoned with."

"Giana, you say that you were against having one-night stands. What was the one thing about Jaylin that made you give in to him?"

"When he pressed that nine against her clit at the club," one woman said. "Hell, that would have done it for me, too, and I would have dashed out of there so fast that if you blinked, you would have missed me."

Many others agreed, but Giana gave her reason. "I mean, that definitely got me going, but truthfully, it was his conversation that got me. Jaylin is a very intelligent man and I was extremely impressed by him. The way he took the time to figure me out, then

46

giving me a little insight on some things about my ex was appreciated. I guess the only thing that disappointed me was the issue with the condom. I was surprised that he really didn't want to go there."

All of the ladies were nodding their heads. "If a man doesn't want to use one," I said. "Then, don't waste your time with him. Giana did the right thing, but do you think that maybe Jaylin was testing you to see if you would make him use one? Some men do try to see where your head is, and that could have very well been the case with Jaylin."

Giana shrugged. "Can't really say, but as along as I took the initiative to protect myself, I'm happy about that."

There wasn't one person who disagreed, and even though this was a book club meeting, we spent a few minutes discussing the importance of safe sex. That prompted another woman to step forward, and she introduced herself as Tonja.

"I...I know this may come as a surprise to everyone, but then again, maybe not. I had an opportunity to spend one night with Jaylin, but it turned out to be an experience that I will never, ever forget!"

I invited Tonja to come up front to tell us her story. It wasn't long before me and the other ladies were grabbing our stomachs and laughing out extremely loud....

Double Trouble

Tonja Tate

Who said big girls didn't know how to have fun!!?? For the record, we do. Just because more meat covered my bones, it didn't mean that a man like Jaylin Jerome Rogers wouldn't be attracted to me.

See, it all started the other day, when I was minding my own business, working my daily boring job at Barnes & Noble. Every once in a while, a sexy ass man would stroll through, but none compared to this one. I was walking around the store, assisting customers with books and there he was. He was tall, had a head full of healthy looking natural curls and a body that caused me to tear into my lips. Almost immediately, I could hear my pussy saying...*girl, it's been a long time. I need some relief!* It had been one year to be exact, so I knew what kind of relief my *girl* needed. Then, in what seemed like slow motion, he headed my way with swagga in his walk. The suit that he wore fit his frame to a capital T and those grey eyes had me already turning flips. At 5'8", I looked up as he stood next to me.

"Excuse me," he said. "But, uh, do you work here?"

"Yes, I do. Can I help you with something?"

He softly rubbed his goatee, as if he were in thought. "Yes, I...I'm trying to find a good book for a friend. What would you recommend?"

I had the perfect book for Jaylin, and when I asked him to follow me, he did. Knowing that he was close behind me, I put my 220lbs of sexy meat in motion. My hips swayed from side to side and I even bent down in front of him to pick up a tiny piece of white paper. Of course, he bumped into me, and "accidentally" ran right into my ass. He held my waist, as I pretended to slightly lose my balance.

"Are you all right?" he asked.

I stood, showing stability. "Sorry about that. Gotta keep the store clean, you know?"

"I feel you on that. I'm a stickler when it comes to keeping things clean, too."

It was nice to know we already had something in common. Then again, I made a mental note to wash those dirty dishes that were at home in the sink.

I continued down the book filled aisle, then pulled out one of our bestsellers and gave it to him.

"Here you go. Whoever your friend is, she or he would love this book."

"Naughty," he said, reading and observing the book cover. He didn't even read the back, but he asked me to tell him what it was about.

"Trust me, you'll love it. The whole series revolves around a playa, his drama and the women who can't get enough of him. I tell you the character is sex-zy and the sex in that book will set your drawls on fire."

His brows rose. "The character sounds like someone I know. I'll check it out and I'm sure my friend will like it too. Thanks for your help, uh...what did you say your name was?"

"Tonja," I said. But he could call me whatever he wanted to...Baby Cakes, Sugga, Sweetheart, Dick Ryder, Pussy Popper...even a fat bitch if he wanted to. I had to get his phone number and he wasn't leaving until I did.

"Okay, Tonja. My name is Jaylin. Jaylin Rogers and I appreciate your assistance. For your troubles, I wondered if I could, you know...take you out sometime?"

My high cheekbones rose higher than expected, but hell, by the look in my thirsty eyes he already knew I was interested. "Sure," I said. "I do have a better suggestion, though. I cook a mean pot roast, so why don't you let me cook you dinner? Let's say my place at seven and I assure you that it will be the best meal you've ever had."

Jaylin studied me with his inquisitive grey eyes, before giving me an answer. "I would love for you to cook dinner for me. Sounds like a plan, Tonja, and if you'd give me your address, I'll see you around seven. Just a lil F.Y.I., I'm meeting with a friend of mine at eleven. I wouldn't want to rush the evening, but it's too late for me to change plans."

"No problem and dinner should be waaaaaay over by then."

I gave Jaylin my address and he punched it into his BlackBerry. I watched as he paid for three of the books in The Naughty Series and waved before he left the store.

For the next few hours, I couldn't get a darn thing done. I planned out the night with Jaylin in my head, and by five o'clock, I tore out of the parking lot, rushing home to get dinner started. The only thing that I had intended on serving tonight was my own meat and a pot roast couldn't even compare. I washed up real good, moisturized my brown skinned body with lotion, then sprayed on several dashes of my Dark Kiss fragrance from Bath & Body. My red tinted curly locs were already in order, so I didn't have to do nothing to my hair. I was feeling pretty darn good about this, but I couldn't decide what I wanted to wear. One of my sexy pieces of lingerie would be a bit too much, so for now, I settled for my pink silk pajama pants and buttoned down shirt that matched. It was simple, but I didn't want to go overboard.

Now that I had me together, I had to get my love nest together. I fluffed the zebra striped cotton pillows on my queen bed and straightened the hot pink silk sheets. My bed always made a squeaky noise when I sat on it, but I wiggled it around, just to make sure the sound wouldn't be too embarrassing. Thank God, it wasn't. Next, I went into the closet to find my white bear rug, then laid it on the floor, just in case we wanted to sip some blackberry wine and have a quick chat. My room was definitely coming together, and after I dimmed the lights, I plugged in my silver disco ball that had white spinning lights. Perfect! Then again, not quite. The room was missing one thing and that was my stripper pole. I hadn't pulled that thing out in a while, but this would be the perfect opportunity for me to, you know, kind of strut my stuff. I got the pole out of the closet as well, lightly blowing off some of the dust that was settled around it. I propped up the pole in front of my bed, securing it from top to bottom. Just to make sure it was sturdy, I took a slow spin around, immediately realizing that I had lost my touch. Damn, I thought while spinning around and trying to get my rhythm. Maybe some music would help, but as soon as I headed for my CD collection, the doorbell rang. I wiped some of the dust from my silk pajamas, then slid into my tall white pumps before pulling on the door to open it.

"Heyyy," I said, opening the door wider so Mr. Sexy could come in. He looked even better than he did at the bookstore, and since he'd removed his suit jacket, I could see just how well his body was put together, even underneath the passion purple shirt he wore. My pussy started jumping up and down, like a bitch who had just won the lottery. *Go, Tonja, it's your birthday, it's your birthday, it's your birthday...Enough already. Shut up, please!*

Jaylin swaggered in, bringing along a fragrance that made me sniff behind him. I quickly gained my composure, and before I made another move, I had to tell him about my change in plans.

"I am so sorry about this, Jaylin, but my pot roast didn't turn out like I wanted it to. I hope you don't mind, and if that means trouble for me, I'm willing to accept my punishment."

He stood in the foyer with a blank expression on his face. His hand eased into his pocket and he let out a deep frustrating sigh. He then glanced at his shimmering Rolex watch. "I told my friend to pick me up at eleven. I haven't eaten anything all day, and you know what, baby, I'm real, real hungry. If we ain't gon' eat, what else do you have in mind?"

My pussy immediately chimed in...*you're blowing it, girl. Go get that man a Twinkie and be done with it!*

"I...I thought we could see what's up with this attraction that we seem have for one another. I could always find you a little something to eat, later."

My words brought a tiny smile to his face, and when I took his hand, he followed me down the hallway to my bedroom. As soon as we entered, his eyes got big as baseballs. Well, not that big, but he carefully studied the room.

"Uh, that's what's up. Just tell me where you want...need me to be."

I directed Jaylin over to the bed, and as soon as he sat on it, it squeaked. Loudly. He didn't seem to trip, so neither did I.

"If you don't mind," I said. "I want to do a lil dance for you, okay?"

Jaylin shifted himself around on the bed to get comfortable. He wiggled his tie and nodded his head. I guess that was my cue to get this show on the road. I hurried to my CD collection, deciding to play some of the songs I'd been listening to for the last several days. Waiting for the song to start, I held the pole and kept my eyes locked with Jaylin's. The fast beat started, but unfortunately, it was an old Richard Simmons workout CD, yelling for me to kick up my legs fifty times. Jaylin smirked and touched the trimmed hair on his chin.

"Sorry about that," I said, hurrying to change the music. "I've been working out for the last few days and I thought..."

"Take your time and I'm ready whenever you are."

Yes, I was ready, and this time, I let the music start before I made my move on the pole. "It's Time For The Percolator" rang out loudly from my box speakers and I started to pop my body along with the song.

Jaylin covered his mouth, blushing his ass off. I wasn't sure if he liked the music or not, but I did. I got into my groove and turned circles around the pole. I was spinning so fast, that I could feel cool breeze hitting me. Then, I slowed it down for Jaylin. He seemed to be all into it, and when I lifted my leg to do a split against the pole, I saw him lick across his lips.

"You know, that position would look so much better if you'd take off your clothes. I think you're sexy as hell, but it's hard to get a vision of what I'll be working with."

He was right, the clothes had to go. Yes, I was a big girl, but I had curves in all of the right places. I stepped out of my clothes, wearing nothing but my white pumps and a black thong that was swallowed by my fat ass cheeks. "Time For The Percolator" wrapped up and "There's Some Hoe's In This House" kicked in. I wiggled my shoulders and snapped my fingers to the beat. Hell, Jaylin started

52

snapping his fingers, too, and when his leather sharp shoes tapped on the floor, I joined in. I stomped my pump, hitting the floor hard, but to the beat. I was in business and by the way he stared at my ass, I could tell he liked it. I pressed my backside against the pole, then bent over to let the pole separate my crack. My cheeks sat along both sides of the steel pole, and I popped my ass to make it clap. I could only imagine the view Jaylin was getting.

"Umph, umph, umph," he said. "Work that pussy...ass, baby, work it!"

I was cheesing my butt off, and he hadn't seen nothing just yet. I stood, sliding my backside against the pole and slowly squatted down to the floor. On my way back up, I bent over again, then swung my legs around the pole to get to the other side. From the front this time, I squatted down again, opening my legs wide while holding my hands on my shaky knees. Jaylin's eyes were focused between my legs like a razor beam and one by one, he started to unbutton his shirt.

"Move the string on your thong aside. Let me take a look at that pussy."

I pulled the slippery wet string aside, proudly showing off my neatly waxed slit. I could almost see my coochie smiling at him and the way she was throbbing, I knew she was pleased. Right now, that bitch had nothing to say. I eased up from the floor, circling the pole again, as the song was coming to an end. This time when I spun around, the pole wobbled. Next thing I knew, that sucker had cracked into one...two pieces.

"Damn," I shouted, trying not to lose my balance. I did, only because the heel of my shoe had the nerve to break when I came down hard on it.

Jaylin had already jumped up to help me, and while holding me with one arm, he wiped down his face with the other.

"Go ahead," I smirked. "I know you want to laugh, don't you?"

He muffled his lips, holding on for as long as he could. Only a slight snicker came out, and his dimples were too sexy. "I...uh, I really don't know what to say about that. Next time, leave the aluminum poles at the store."

I looked at the pole as if it had attacked me. "I thought it was made of steel. Screw it."

"Nah, let me screw it. Now, let's cut with the dancing and get this party started, for real."

He didn't have to tell me twice, but the pussy hater was back again. *I hope you get this shit right and how could you make a fool of us like that? You just embarrassed the hell out of us and you got one more chance to get this right. If he leaves, I'm going to go find a sexually active woman who knows what the fuck she's doing. Obviously, you don't!*

"Shut up," I said out loudly while making my way over to the bed.

"Come again," Jaylin said, frowning and thinking I was talking to him.

"Nothing. I was just thinking about something, that's all."

I scooted back on the squeaky mattress, watching Jaylin as he removed my shoe with the broken heel. He tossed it aside, then tossed the other shoe as well. While keeping his flirting eyes on me, he got undressed. I could already tell he was working with something when he'd bumped into me earlier, but...*bitch, close your mouth and quit acting like you ain't never seen no big dick before!* The hater just wouldn't leave me along, but with Jaylin packaged up like he was, *she* was about to be in big trouble, not me.

From the sight of him putting a condom over his long hanging hard tubular instrument, I opened my legs and invited him to shove it in as far as it would go. Before he even got to it, he bit at my thong with his pearly white teeth and clinched them tight. Like a growling tiger, he ripped off my thong and let it drop to the floor. I had myself a Tarzan man, and knowing that we were about to enter his jungle, that excited me even more. He massaged the tip of his head and I could already see the pre-cum coming. Seconds later, he moved between my legs, and almost immediately my pussy held a tight grip on his shaft. No, his instrument didn't get too far.

"Wha...what the hell!" I strained to say. "Who...what women have you been putting that darn thing into? No, way, baby...this is a wrap!"

My pussy was too busy choking, and she couldn't say anything. *That's what you get for being greedy*, I thought, and was somewhat unsympathetic. I was sure that *she* felt like I did, though, and enough was enough.

"Just relax," Jaylin said in a seductive tone. "I'm going to take it easy. I promise."

The only reason I was willing to give this a try was because he was one sexy ass man. With his clothes off, his body was carved to perfection. I rubbed my hands on his body, while trying to cope with the excruciating pain. Don't get me wrong, I'd had sex with plenty of men, but nothing this big and juicy had ever entered me.

For the next several minutes, Jaylin took his time. He sucked down my neck, tickled my nipples with his velvety tongue and planted juicy kisses on my lips. His dick was partially in me and I could tell because his mid section never touched my thighs.

"Is that better," he said.

"Yes, better, but not too much more, all right?"

Jaylin said not a word and I could tell by the impatient look in his eyes that he couldn't wait to slam his whole piece of meat into me. While giving the other parts of my body so much pleasure, he tried to throw me off. I felt my pussy breaking open, as he inched further inside. My breathing became more intense and I could feel my juices overflowing. Couldn't believe how wet and super sticky I was, and when I reached down to play with his balls, it was game over. He went in further, tearing up my gut with each thrust.

"You shouldn't have done that," he said through strained words.

I could feel how tense he was, and I guess that playing with his loaded sacks was the key to weakening him. Even so, I couldn't move! The circling of my hips had come to a halt and my mouth dropped wide open.

"Out," I yelled. "I want this...this *thing* out of me, now!"

Jaylin didn't move, but he kissed my cheek. "Damn, baby. Why you tripping? I'm already in there now and I promise you that, from this moment on, I will take it real slow."

Without giving the order, he proceeded. His rhythm was very slow, and his hips were turning in short lingering circles. I was down with what he was doing and so was my pussy. *She* was with it and had made that clear to me. *Girl, give this man a standing ovation.*

Applause!! Applause!! This shit feels too good and you'd better not get rid of him anytime soon.

I hadn't intended to, especially since he had pulled out of me and had gone down low. His tongue lapped against my fire walls, giving me nothing but pure pleasure. I swear his whole face was wet from my juices spraying him, and as he made me come again, I watched him wipe away the drippings from his chin.

"Now, that was an orgasm. That pussy showing out for me and that's how you do it."

Jaylin had given me much pleasure and it was time for me to add my two cents. I laid him back on the bed, and recognizing how sensitive his balls were, I started sucking on those. My mouth was full, but not as full as it was when I slipped that nine of his into my mouth. I gagged, even let out a few coughs.

"Be easy," he said, holding his dick in his hand, protecting it from me.

"Okay, sexy. Let me try this again."

I tackled Jaylin's instrument as best as I could, focusing on the sides of his shaft more than anything. Wasn't no sense in me trying to deep throat him, and the truth of the matter was, my throat just wasn't that deep. My performance was satisfying to him, though, and his moaning and groaning made me aware.

"That's it," he whimpered. "Keep that tongue of yours right there."

My tongue was licking the slit on his head, while my hand massaged his balls. His hands were in action, too, and as he rubbed down my backside, he fingers crept into my pussy from the back. I could barely stay focused on what I was doing, or for that matter, keep still. Jaylin had some mean finger fucking skills and when his thumb flicked my clit, it was all over with. My whole body shut down, and I drew my attention away from his shaft. He grabbed the back of my head, keeping it steady and in place so I could continue.

"See that shit through, baby, and finish what the fuck you started. Do not give up on me yet!"

Damn, okay. His aggressiveness turned me the hell on! I got mine, and he definitely got his. We shouted out together and the hourly long session had us sprawled out on the bed, gasping for the exotic air that filled the room.

"That was good," Jaylin said while softly rubbing his chest. I couldn't even find the right words to say about what had just happened and even my pussy was now speechless. We all lay silently for a while, then Jaylin had the audacity to roll over on me again.

"Uh, what are you doing?" I asked.

He held himself up over me, using the muscles in his strong arms to stay up. "What does it look like I'm doing? I know you don't think we're done after just one hour."

"I don't know about you, but I'm done. The dick was good...great, but my kitty is in need of back up. I couldn't go another minute, and if you don't mind me asking, what woman in her right mind can hang with you?"

Jaylin shrugged. "Not many, only a few. But, I'll be easy..."

I chopped off his words, slightly pushing his shoulders back. "No! Not again. Leave your number on the dresser and I'll be happy to call you in about a week, maybe two."

Jaylin held that blank look on his face again, then got up. It wasn't long before he got dressed, and when he looked at his watch, he said that his ride would be there in five minutes. We stood by the front door, waiting.

"Maybe it was a good thing that you wouldn't let me finish up. I'm sure it would have made me late."

By now, I was feeling a little horny again and the thought of him leaving saddened me. Maybe it was a mistake, not going a few more rounds with him, but he said he'd call whenever he made his way back to St. Louis. Lord knows how long that would be, and I could already see the frown on my pussy's face. As I was in deep thought about not seeing him again, the doorbell rang. Jaylin moved aside so I could open the door and when I did, oh my God!! I felt like one lucky bitch and the man who was standing on my porch was just as gorgeous as Jaylin was. I couldn't get no words to come out of my mouth and Jaylin moved me aside, again, to let in his friend.

"Shane this is Tonja," Jaylin said, making the introduction.

Shane took my hand, placing his thick lips on top to kiss it. "What's up, big sexy," he said.

I was still down for the count and couldn't snap out of it. *Round two, Bitch, it's time for round two!! Hooray!!*

Now, she need to go somewhere and sit down, I thought of my coochie who just didn't know better. Then again, maybe *she* did.

"Nice to meet you, Shane, and I hate that you have to rush out of here with Monster Dick. I would love for you to stay so we could get better acquainted, but I understand if you can't."

Shane and Jaylin looked at each other and I was so surprised when Shane reached in his pocket and tossed Jaylin his keys. "Leave the rental car at the airport," he said to Jaylin. "I'll pick it up later and have a safe trip back home."

Jaylin nodded and twirled the key around on his finger. "All I'm gon' say is watch out for the pole and the teeth are a little sharp. Other than that, it's all good."

I slightly cut my wicked eyes at Jaylin and watched as he made his way out the door. Yes, I knew I could only have Jaylin for one night, but it was good to know that I could have Shane for as many of nights as I wanted to. He followed me to my bedroom and I turned around before we made our way inside. "If you don't mind me asking, Shane, but...how many inches did you say you were?"

He showed the measurements with his hands. "About that long," he smiled. So did I.

"Yes, I can definitely work with that so come on!"

I pulled him into my bedroom by his silk tie and slammed the door.

The End

Book Club Meeting...

By now, the entire room was bursting with laughter. I could barely speak and Tonja continued to go on and on about her adventurous evening with Jaylin.

"Tonja, did you have any problem handling Shane?" someone asked. "And if my memory serves me correctly, in *Naughty by Nature*, Scorpio Valentino said that Shane had better oral skills than Jaylin. Was her statement correct?"

"To answer your first question, I had no problem whatsoever handling Shane. Jaylin had loosened up everything a bit and Shane fit right in." Many covered their mouths as Tonja was simply telling it like it was. "As for their oral performances, and you didn't hear this from me, but Scorpio was correct when she said Shane's oral skills were better. It was something about his tongue that worked wonders."

Tonja's confirmation brought about more discussions about Shane and Jaylin. Many of the women appreciated Shane's character and some preferred him over Jaylin. Like Tonja, many had dibs on both. I couldn't help but ask if she ever got her stripper pole fixed, or did she buy another one.

She tossed her hand back and shook her head. "I threw that darn thing in the trash. Now, I did get me another one and I'm waiting for Jaylin to come back over so I can really show him a thing or two."

One lady inquired about Tonja's inabilities to handle Jaylin and we delved into a discussion about what was considered "too big". Many of us agreed that nine inches was pushing it, but then again, it really depended on what each individual woman could handle. Some said that twelve inches wasn't enough, and I was like...more power to them. We continued on, until a woman named

Chyna gave her input about how much a virgin could or couldn't handle. For her, Jaylin was too much.

"Did she say Jaylin?" one woman whispered, but loud enough for us to hear her.

"Yes, Jaylin," Chyna said, making her way up front. "And I guess it's my turn to tell everyone how it all went down."

It seemed as if Jaylin had been real busy, and I was starting to get worried. I guess later on would reveal why, but for now, I sat back and listened to what Chyna had to say...

Shai's Lounge

Shai

I was standing behind the crowded bar, watching the bartenders take care of my patrons. I had opened up Shai's Lounge about four months ago in Miami, Florida, and the place was packed almost every single night. I busted my ass to make sure Shai's Lounge was the best place to come, especially on Friday and Saturday nights, when we were always filled to capacity. See, this was my dream and being raised in foster care all my life, I had to look out for myself. My mother passed away while giving birth to me and lord knows where my sperm donor was at. His absence made me very cautious of men, and the one thing my foster mother always told me was, "Chyna, never allow any man to control you, don't allow any man to steal your happiness, and never expect them to provide for you." She made sure I understood her words, and she would always tell me that as pretty as I was, I was destined to break plenty of hearts. When Mama Jean died, it was the most horrendous day of my life. I was graduating from Harvard, and apparently, at the same time my name was being called to get my diploma, Mama Jean had had a heart attack. Life without her would never be the same, but what I didn't know, though, was she had left everything to me. No one knew that she had plenty of money stashed away, but all of it belonged to me. I used the money wisely, and the first thing that I did was invest. Second, I opened up Shai's Lounge and I had so much more that I wanted to do. For a Puerto Rican and Asian woman, with no mother or father, I felt as if I had something to prove. Thus far, I was well on my way to becoming the successful businesswoman I always knew I could be.

61

You could barely hear anything over the loud talking and R&B music that echoed throughout the lounge. The dance floor was crowded and so was the small stage that was purposely used during karaoke night. The entire place was dim, but with the blue and white spinning lights, it was easy to see who was there. I squinted, noticing a man that had been hitting on me for the past several months. He was sitting at a booth with his friend, drinking as if it were going out of style. His name was Jaylin, and he was a regular at Shai's Lounge. The women in Shai's were super crazy about him, but none of them knew his story like I did. As a matter of fact, our past history was very similar. The first day he'd told me a little about his past, I was shocked because it reminded me so much of mine. I very well understood why his marriage was on the rocks, and I knew why a man like him had difficulties being faithful. Like me, he was selfish and it was his way or no way. The focus was on me, myself and I and what another person wanted, or desired, in no way mattered. Yeah, I got that vibe from him, too, and when he tried to hook up with me, I was skeptical. He'd given me his phone number to call him, but I didn't. He always made advances towards me, but I kept my distance. I wasn't sure if hooking up with someone who had so much in common as me, if it was a good thing or not. Then, about a month ago, I let my guards down. I went on several dates with Jaylin, and surprisingly, I'd had a good time. He was *different* and was not the womanizer that I pegged him out to be. He didn't mind spending his money on me, and I didn't mind returning the favor. That all came to a screeching halt, when he broke the news to me about him being married. Said that he and his wife were separated, but he intended for them to work things out. I was so glad that I hadn't given up the goods, and I continued to keep my virgin status. I was twenty-seven years old, and hadn't quite found the right man yet. Making money was my priority, and needless to say, dick had to wait. A serious relationship wasn't even on the menu and I wasn't sure if or when I would ever feel differently.

One of the customers sitting at the bar had gotten sloppy drunk and was starting to make a scene. My bartender, Vinny, turned to look at me, and I had to make a move. I used my fingers to pull my jet black bone straight hair to one side. It rested on my shoulder that was bare, due to the half mini dress I wore that cut across my chest. In my high black heels, I came from around the bar and stood next to the overly intoxicated man. I touched his back and moved the full glass of Grey Goose from in front of him.

"Sir, I'm going to call a taxi for you. I think you've had enough and my bartenders won't be serving you anymore alcohol tonight."

"Well I'll be damned," he slurred, trying to stand straight up but couldn't. He staggered backwards, tucking his sloppy shirt into his wrinkled baggy pants. When he fell face first to the floor, my bouncer, Leroy, came to his aid.

"Come on, man," he said, helping the man off the floor. "Let's go."

The man placed his arm around Leroy's shoulder, belching out loudly. I thought he was going to vomit, so I hurried to move aside. Leroy was every bit of three hundred plus pounds, so escorting the man to the door was no problem at all. I watched as they went to the door, then asked Vinny to call the man a cab. Vinny nodded, doing as he was told.

Seconds later, I turned and bumped into Jaylin's best friend, Shane. He often came into Shai's with Jaylin and you rarely saw one of them without the other. Now, he was a sight for sore eyes, too, but just like with Jaylin, there were way too many women involved.

"What's up, Chyna?" Shane asked. "I saw that you had some problems over here."

"Yeah, but nothing I can't handle. We get that all the time."

"I'm sure you do," he said, looking me over. I swear him and Jaylin could dress casual as ever and still look dynamite in whatever. Shane's jeans and t-shirt was simple, but he still managed to turn plenty of heads. "You look nice," he said. "And that red silk mini you got on doing justice."

Of course his compliment made me blush, but he didn't have to tell me something I already knew. "Thanks, Shane. But, uh, can I get you anything?"

"Nah. I was just swooping by to hit up the restroom. You may wanna go check with Jay, though, and I'm sure he can think of something you can give him."

Shane knew that Jaylin and I had been on a few dates, and when his eyes turned in the direction of the booth where they were sitting, my eyes followed. Jaylin was relaxing at a booth with six scantly dressed women surrounding him. They were laughing and sipping from the several bottles of wine that sat chilled in ice buckets on the table. Jaylin seemed elated by the attention, and when he noticed me looking in his direction, he lifted his glass and threw back his head. Without responding, I turned to Shane.

"I hope you enjoy the rest of your evening, Shane. If you need anything else, be sure to let me know."

"Will do," he said, stepping away to the restroom.

I asked Vinny to give me a bottle of Remy, and after he handed it to me, I sashayed my way over to the booth where Jaylin and his groupies sat. Jaylin saw me strutting his way, and his striking eyes centered on me. The women were moving their chatty mouths, but he paid them no attention. I kept my smile under control at the lustful gaze in his eyes, and knowing that I was the one woman he couldn't have when he wanted to, satisfied me to the fullest. I teased him more by moving my ample hips and showing my toned thighs. For a woman who was only 5'4", I had my shit together. Jaylin knew I did, too, and that's why he couldn't resist me.

"This one is on the house," I said, placing the Remy bottle on the table. "Save some for Shane and don't get too drunk or else I'll have to put you out of here tonight."

A dimple appeared in Jaylin's cheek and he softly touched his goatee. "Excuse me, ladies," he said, looking around the booth. "Give me a second to holla at Chyna."

Some of the women cut their eyes at me, and the others just got up and left. Either way, the booth cleared out and I scooted into the booth with Jaylin.

"Thanks for the Remy," he said. "That was a nice gesture."

"It's the least that I can do for a man who drops big dollars in here. So, don't look at it as me doing you any favors because I gets mine."

"I'm not looking at it that way. I'll just chalk it up as you looking out for me, because you know that I'll always be looking out for you."

I couldn't help but look at his wedding ring that he now wore faithfully. "How can you look out for me and you still have a wife at home? That's bullshit, Jaylin, and you know what? I'm not buying it."

"What does my wife have to do with this? If you really want to know, we're still on shaky ground. I only wear my ring because it attracts more women to me."

He laughed, but I saw no humor in what he'd said. Men. It didn't matter to me either way, and whatever worked for him, so be it. I got ready to exit the booth, especially after seeing two men starting to argue on the dance floor. Jaylin quickly reached for my hand to stop me.

"Hold up," he said. "Why you always breaking out so fast to get away from me? Do I scare you or something?"

I looked at the grip he had on my hand. "No, you don't scare me at all. And the only one who needs to be afraid of anything here is you. The last thing you need is to hook up with a woman like me, only because that one-night stand you want to have may turn into something you in no way bargained for."

"Try me," he fired back. "Allow me that one-night stand, and after that we'll see what's up."

I didn't have time to respond because the confrontation with the two men seemed to get heated. Leroy beat me to the punch, and had already thrown the men outside. Instead of returning to the booth where Jaylin sat, I walked around, mingling with everyone and making sure they were having a decent time. Many of them seemed to be and that's what Shai's Lounge was all about.

Around 3:00 a.m., the crowd started to disperse. I'd had a few drinks and was feeling lightheaded and free. Feeling this way always made me flirt and I was definitely doing so as I sat at the bar next to a man who was also a regular patron.

"Chyna, you know you fine as hell," he complimented. His hand touched my leg and he moved in closer to me, leaving no breathing room whatsoever. "Why don't we go back to my place tonight? I got something good to give you and there hasn't been one woman that's left my bedroom dissatisfied."

My olive green eyes flirted with him and I lowered my eyelids, giving him a pleasurable smile. I hated men who bragged about how well their sex was, and my thing was be about it, don't talk about it. "You know, Shawn, I would love to take you up on that offer, but I'm so afraid that you would disappoint me. Men who always brag on themselves, they normally don't know how to get the job done. My time is very valuable and I'm particular about who I give that time to."

Just then, another voice interrupted. It was Jaylin. "Yes, she is very particular, and I have been trying to get at it for months and still ain't got no play. I'm feeling lucky tonight, though, and since she's already told you no, maybe she'll be willing to tell me yes."

I wasn't happy about Jaylin interrupting my conversation, and it wasn't the first time he'd done it. Besides, I never said anything to the women who hung all over him and how dare he think he had any rights to interfere as if I were his woman.

"Do you mind?" Shawn said to Jaylin. "I was talking to Chyna, not you."

"I don't mind at all, but like I said, don't waste too much time on pursuing her. Being rejected is quite embarrassing and I'm just trying to spare you from what's about to happen in a few minutes."

Jaylin walked away and I saw him go up to Shane and two other men who stood close by. He was so damn blunt and cocky, but I had to admit that it was a turn on. I loved a man with confidence, and one who knew what he wanted, and refused to give up.

Shawn cleared his throat. "Now, where were we?"

I removed his hand away from my leg and it was time for me to break the bad news. "I was just about ready to tell you that I wasn't interested, and if it were left up to me, you'll be going home alone tonight. There are still some women left in here tonight, so don't let me interfere with your search for the next pussy. Good luck with that and I hope you get what it is that you're looking for tonight."

Shawn's face was cracked all over. He jumped to his feet, busting out of the door as if I had offended him. Jaylin seemed pleased by my actions, as after he took a sip from his glass, he granted me a slow wink. I rolled my eyes and went behind the bar. Vinny made me a Cosmopolitan, more vodka than anything. I sipped, burning my chest as the alcohol made its way down. Didn't know if it was my body, or if the inside of Shai's was feeling awfully hot. Beads of sweat formed on my forehead, and I knew I had better cool it with the alcohol. I laid my drink on top of the bar, shifting my curious eyes around the room. Trying to ignore Jaylin wasn't working too well for me, and my search for him stopped when I'd located my prize. I watched him dance and his gradual moves were so on point. I could tell he knew how to fuck and the way he turned his midsection on the woman in front of him, I imagined him doing it to me. I shook my head fast, trying to clear my nasty thoughts. No way in hell did I want to travel down that road with him, simply because I didn't want to give in to what he wanted. Then again, I had to be real with myself. Was it something that I wanted, too?

As Shai's cleared out, only a few people remained. My bartenders were cleaning up, the waiters and waitresses were trying to get their last tips and the DJ had already announced the last song. I'd seen Shane leave about twenty minutes ago, arm in arm with a female by his side. I hadn't seen Jaylin at all, but then I saw him walk out of the restroom with his jacket thrown over his shoulder. He saw me standing by the bar, and decided to take a seat.

"Why haven't you left yet?" I asked, lifting his arm to look at his diamond Rolex. "You know we close in about five minutes."

"I haven't left yet because I'm still waiting for someone."

"And who might that be?"

"You, Chyna. Why don't you stop playing hard to get and do this shit with me, all right?"

"Do what with you Jaylin? What is it that you want from me? I'm not a house and kids...cooking and all of that shit kind of woman. Is that what you're looking for?"

"No, not at all. I'm just looking for a woman who I can have some fun with, that's all."

"You are so full of it. Why don't you go ahead and be honest with me. You want pussy, Jaylin, and fun or no fun, as long as you get it, you'll be satisfied."

He shrugged, seeming somewhat taken aback about my bluntness. "I can get pussy anywhere, but I do have my preferences. I'm not gon' lie and say that I wouldn't love to have sex with you, because I would. This chase you got me on makes me more anxious for you, and if you ever think I'm going to give up, don't count on me doing it anytime soon. So, either we can do this now, or we can save it for another day. Your call."

I knew the alcohol had me talking shit, as well as thinking it. I quickly took matters into my own hands. "If pussy is what you want, then it's what you get. Besides, I'm getting sick of your weak attempts and they're starting to work me."

"Yeah, that's what they all say, Chyna. And as for working you, I haven't done that yet, but I will."

I stood, getting everyone's attention, and asking them to vacate the premises. Shai's cleared out, and before my DJ left, I asked him to put on some continuous music. At this point I didn't give a damn what he played. All I wanted to know is if Jaylin was worth losing my virginity to. Would this experience be a memorable one, or would I walk away having regrets. I wasn't sure, but as the music played, I moved over to the dance floor and stood in the middle of the floor. Jaylin laid his jacket on the barstool, then made his way towards me. I hated to admit how fine he was and sexiness oozed from his pores. The button down gray shirt that he wore clung to his muscles that bulged from it. The shirt matched his eyes and they could be seen behind his lightly tinted sunglasses.

As soon as he reached the dance floor, he slid his arm around my waist. He left no breathing room between us, and with my five inch heels on, I could feel his hardness poke at my pussy. My arms fell on his shoulders, and as we slowly moved to R. Kelly's latest hits, I twirled my fingers in the back of Jaylin's curly hair.

"Now, this ain't so bad, is it?" he asked.

"One song, Jaylin, and then I'm all yours. I have to tell you something, though, and I want you to listen to me, okay?"

"I'm all ears. Speak."

"I've never given myself to any man before. There's something about you that I can't shake and I want you to be my first. Do not hurt me, and do your best to make it the best sex ever. I expect nothing less and I want to leave here with memories that I'll never forget. Afterward, I don't want to see you in Shai's Lounge again. I don't want you to call me, and you won't have to worry about me calling you. I'm not interested in having drama with any females around here, nor do I expect to have any drama with your wife. As long as we're on the same page, I'm ready whenever you are."

"Almost. But let me say something to you as well. I'm delighted to be your first, and you have my word that I will give this my all. Good memories...absolutely. You don't have to worry about any drama, and if you are asking me never to return to your establishment, then I have no choice other than to honor your request. I am definitely on the same page as you, and after you give me what I want, fun or no fun, I'm out. I assure you that no phone calls will be made, and as far as I'm concerned, consider the chase over."

I removed my arms from Jaylin's shoulders and backed away from him. My hand went on my hip. "Already...mission accomplished, huh?"

"Not just yet," he said, removing his crisp shirt. He dropped it behind him and his pants soon hit the floor. I couldn't believe the size of that thing he was holding in his hand, stroking to make it harder. Lord knows I wanted to break out and run! Just what had I gotten myself into and there wasn't a chance in hell that I would let something like that split into my virgin pussy. My eyes stayed focused on his growing muscle, and I wasn't sure if it was my blurred vision that was making it seem extra, extra thick and long.

"I, uh...maybe we should—

"Should what?" Jaylin asked, coming closer to me. He gripped the back of my head, bringing his lips to mine. They were soft as ever, and as he lightly turned his tongue in my mouth, I shut my fluttering eyes, enjoying the sweet taste. Moments later, I felt my dress being lowered to my ankles and I stepped out of it. I tossed my heels aside and still in my Victoria's Secret satin purple bra and panties, I followed Jaylin over to the karaoke stage. He sat me on top of the stage, while standing between my legs. His hands roamed along my thighs and when he touched my crotch, I widened my legs.

Our lips stayed locked together, and he pulled my panties aside, sinking his fingers into me. A prickling feeling rushed from the tips of my toes, straight to my pussy, sending off shock waves. I couldn't believe how wet I was from the soft touch of his fingers, and that was just the beginning. I lifted my ass from the stage, and Jaylin removed my panties. He tossed them aside, then placed my legs on his shoulders.

"Lay back," he said, obviously noticing my hesitation. "I want you to relax, all right?"

I lay back on my elbows, and when Jaylin's tongue slithered into me like a slippery snake, I quickly tightened my stomach and held my breath. I wanted to burst out a loud ear popping scream, but instead, I started to take deep breaths. His tongue was so deep and the fast fluttering felt like a tickle. I closed my eyes, starting to tear into my own hair. When that didn't do me justice, I jerked forward and pulled at his hair. The tighter I pulled the speed of his tongue increased.

"Ohhh, shit!" I yelled. "What in the fuck are you doing?"

Jaylin didn't answer. That was, not until I let out an oozing orgasm that sprayed right into his mouth. He licked around his lips and sucked the tips of his fingers.

"Now, that's one sweet ass pussy right there. You know better holding back on me like that and I told you that you'd have to pay."

I wasn't sure what that meant, but Jaylin made his way onto the stage with me. He kneeled between my legs, and unloosened the snap on my bra from the front. My breasts wobbled a bit and he started to squeeze them with his hands. He leaned in, sucking one then moving to the other. As his tongue turned circles on my nipples, he reached down and positioned his dick to enter me. I felt my coochie widen, and as his dick pushed into me, my whole body became tense.

"I'm going slow, so release your grip from my hips," he whispered. "Real slow, but I need for you to loosen those pussy muscles and work with me, okay?"

I nodded and relaxed my legs and tight muscles so he could go in further. He could feel my body quivering underneath his, but to soothe the feeling, he softly rubbed my legs, then clinched my hands with his. I shut my eyes, holding back the water that had rushed to them. The feel of him was painful, yet so damn satisfying. I muffled my lips to stay silent, and Jaylin helped me along when he covered my mouth with his. Kissing him helped ease the pain that was becoming less unbearable.

"See, I told you you had nothing to be afraid of. And with a tight soaked pussy like this, we may have to renege on some of the things we said earlier. I may need to get at this again."

I had no response, because the sex he put down had me enjoying him more than I ever thought I would. Sign, sealed and delivered...he'd made his mark on, I assumed, another virgin's pussy. Slowly, but surely, he found home plate and his strokes were smooth as ever. Then all of a sudden, everything took a slight turn. Jaylin sped up his pace and the feel of his fat dick drove me crazy!

"Metemelo, doblame y metemelo. Ven y cógeme! (Fuck me, bend me over and fuck me. Come on and fuck me)," I cried out.

"That's right, baby. It's whatever you say. Bring that ass to me."

I turned on my stomach, using a rail in front of me to hold on to. Jaylin pushed his dick into me from behind, forcing himself all the way inside. He held my hips while slamming into me and I could feel his heavy sacks banging against my tight swollen pussy. I was so wet and the gushing of my juices made music in the room. The sound added fuel to our fire, and I was hot all over. My pussy was getting a true workout, and in an effort to ease some of the pain, I reached back and pulled my ass cheeks apart. The tip of his head touched my anal hole and I feared that he would enter. No way would I be able to muster that kind of pain, but all he did was toy around with it. He then smacked my ass, squeezing large chunks of it and turning it in circles.

"That is one pretty mutha right there. Beautiful ass...just beautiful."

Jaylin quickly found out that I preferred it rough and he beat my pussy good. As his nine was in me again, he did not hold back. The stage floor was covered with my liquids and my trembling legs could barely keep still. I screamed, moaned, even shouted for some relief, but Jaylin kept his word and honored my previous wishes.

"You told me to fuck you, so that's what I'm doing," he said.

Yes, indeed, he was. And when I came, I came so hard that I spit his dick from my pussy. I took no time to regroup and grabbed at his package again because I was still very hungry for it.

"Ay, Papi! Dame'n el culo! Si, Mas Duro! He sido muy mala! (Harder, beat my ass, I've been bad)," I shouted.

"I know," he said with a grin on his face. "That's why I'm punishing you."

I wanted to punish him too, so I removed his dripping wet nine from inside of me, then placed it into my mouth. I sucked him dry, and as he watched me, my eyes stayed locked with his. Finally, his breathing increased and those sexy grey eyes rolled back. I smiled, knowing that I satisfied him, as well as he had satisfied me. I thought it was time to wrap this up, but that didn't happen. Jaylin put me on top of him, and his fingers worked wonders with my clit. As he stimulated my hotspot, I gazed up at the turning blue and white lights. Yes, this would definitely be a night that I'd never forget and I sure as hell would rethink if I ever wanted to see him again. As another orgasm neared, my answer to that question was...a definite yes!!

The End

Book Club Meeting...

Before I could say a word, one lady shouted, "Girl, he wore you out!" Chyna didn't deny it, but she admitted to giving him a run for his money.

"It took me a while to get my rhythm," she confessed. "But with a man like Jaylin, you have to put up or shut up. Showing fear will get you nowhere and I quickly learned that. He started off real gentle, though, and we gradually made it to a point of no return. For a first time experience, I couldn't have chosen a better man to be with."

The same lady asked, "Have you had anyone comparable to him since then? And the bigger question is did you hear from him again?"

"Unfortunately, I haven't had sex like that again, but I'm not giving up. I haven't spoken to Jaylin since then because he has some issues that he needs to resolve with his woman. We talked about her that night, and he got some deep shit going on. I really don't like to interfere in those kinds of situations, so I decided to move on and not look back at what could have been. I doubt that it would have turned out in my favor, but I'm still very grateful for what we shared. Like Giana, I have no regrets."

Giana and Chyna gave each other a high-five. Some of the other ladies started high-fiving too, until one lady stood with her hands on her hips.

"I really don't understand what all the hype is about Jaylin. I read all of your books, Ms. Hampton, but Jaylin rattles my darn nerves. He's rude, he treats women like crap, and no man's sex is that good where it has these women running around like they're clueless. I mean, these are some dumb ass women in those books, and for you to portray them as strong sistas with educations and good heads on their shoulders, you do women of that statue a great disservice. It's almost degrading to some point."

Some women agreed, others waited for a response. "I'm sorry that you feel as if I write stories that degrade black women, but I challenge you to dig deep into my stories and look at the big picture. Many of us have dated men similar to Jaylin and my purpose is for you to get an understanding of where these men generate from. Basically, what does their background tell you about them? Some men aren't capable of loving a woman like she deserves to be loved, and many times it's not completely his fault. You have to know and understand the man you're with. Sometimes, no matter what you do to save your relationship, it won't work because the man is failing to deal with issues that may be suppressed or issues that he's not ready to deal with. Like Nokea does, a woman can love Jaylin all she wants to, but his fix is much deeper than her loving him or her offering him sex. As women, we think that loving a man is enough. I wash, I clean, I cook...I give him all the sex he needs, but he still cheats. The next time you ask yourself why, you must realize that it has little to do with you, but more to do with him. You can do those things all day long and still have the same result. Sometimes, there is no way to prevent yourself from being cheated on, and whether you're a ghetto girl from the streets, or a lawyer in a courtroom, you can find yourself in the same situation with any man. Having an education doesn't make you exempt and neither does being beautiful. My characters are not dumb, they are just everyday ordinary women who, like most women, struggle to figure out why loving a man, sometimes, may not be enough."

The room erupted with questions and comments about what I'd said. I went on about some of my own personal experiences with men and so did some of the other women.

"You have to dig deep into a man's head and pay close attention to what he's all about," Joyce added. "Find out where he's coming from before you make him your baby's daddy, or before you marry him. I approach men like a psychiatrist, seeking every little detail that I can. Therefore, when I had my one night with Jaylin, I found out more about him than I had bargained for."

74

All eyes shot in Joyce's direction, including mine. Now this was taking things too far, and please tell me that she didn't go there with Jaylin. Please....

Pillow Talk

Joyce Hampton

Shopaholic? Maybe. Adorable? Absolutely. Single? You bet and only by choice. Why? Because it was difficult to find a man who could give the same to me, as I would, without one single doubt, give to him. For that reason alone, I was single, yet enjoying my busy-bee life to the fullest! I dated when I wished, had no attachments to anyone, and sex...well, let's just say it's been a while. For now, it wasn't the priority, but going to the mall to get those Jimmy Choo shoes I'd seen last week was. Ever since I'd feasted my eyes upon them, they'd been whirling in my mind. I couldn't even sleep, tossing and turning the night before, waiting for Saturday to come!

On Saturday morning, I threw the covers back, and displayed the biggest smile ever. My seventeen year old daughter was on her way to a friend's house for the entire weekend, and that allowed me to have a day to myself. Sometimes, I needed that. I worked hard, and my career kept me extremely busy. Made enough money to splurge a little on myself sometimes, and that's what I intended to do.

By noon, my daughter was on her way out of the door. I air kissed both of her rosy cheeks and wiggled my fingers in the air, as I watched her and her best friend slowly drive away. Before I could close the door, I heard a loud horn sound. I widened the door, and watched my daughter lower the window.

"Yes," I shouted from the doorway. "Did you forget something?"

"Nope. Just wanted to say that I love you and you'd better not do any shopping without me."

Yes, she knew me all too well, and even though I'd told her that shopping wasn't on my "to do" list, it was. "Love you too, but no need to worry about me today. I will be just fine, and if I see something for you, I'll be sure to get it."

That, of course, caused a smile to grow on her face. She waved again, this time disappearing from my sight.

Within the hour, I was dressed and ready to go. I was the kind of woman who liked to go to the mall dressed as if I were going to a nightclub. Stilettos were on my feet, tight jeans hugged my curves and a silk blouse was buttoned over my 36 D's. A sheer scarf was tied around my waist like a belt, and my original silver accessories explained why others referred to me as Jazzy Joyce. My short hair was styled in a layered cut and a swoop of bangs rested on my forehead. While looking in the mirror, I smacked my glossed lips together, ready to go get the man I couldn't stop thinking about— Mr. Jimmy Choo.

Plaza Frontenac was just a hop, skip and jump away from my house, and as soon as I swerved into a parking spot, my cell phone rang. I noticed it was my sister calling me, but was skeptical about answering. She'd question me about where I was, or why I didn't ask her to go. I didn't want anyone to know I was about to pay over $900 for a pair of shoes I wanted, so that's why I'd gone alone. Instead of ignoring the call, I answered.

"Yes, Brenda," I said, getting out of the car and heading into Saks Fifth Avenue.

"Where are you?"

"At the nail shop," I lied. "I called to see if you wanted to go, but you didn't answer your phone."

"I saw that I missed your call, but..."

Brenda kept yakking, but I wasn't paying much attention to anything she'd said. As soon as I'd walked through the door, I noticed a man standing in front of a jewelry counter. From the backside, he made my mouth fill with water. My eyes were scanning in on him like an important document and my abrupt pace had slowed. Even my heartbeat started to race and I had to take deep breaths to calm it. No, he had no connection to Jimmy Choo, but from what I could see, he was much more competition.

I quickly cut Brenda off, "Girl, let me call you back. I just spotted my future husband. I think."

She laughed and I hung up. I secretly eased my cell phone into my pocket, and almost at a tip-toeing pace, I moved in to get a closer view. The man rocked a silk powder blue button down shirt that was neatly tucked into black pants that fit his waist perfectly. His tan gave his body a smooth caramel color and I could smell him, as well as big money, from a mile away. I cautiously moved to the other side of the jewelry counter, just to see the front side of my prey. *Good God Almighty*, I thought, while observing his thick curly healthy hair. His goatee dressed his chin like a tailored suit, but as he continued to stare at two necklaces in front of him, I couldn't get the view that I wanted. I lowered my head, skimming my eyes through the jewelry cases at the many expensive items. Many of the prices were too pricy for a person on a budget eyes to see, but for a person willing to splurge, it was right up their alley. Either way, the sales associate didn't know my status, but she cleared her throat, telling me that she would be with me shortly.

"Sure," I said. "Take your time."

Hearing my voice caused the man in the spotlight to look up. Having such a clear view of him staggered me, and if my heart didn't slow down, emergency room here I come. I wanted to faint as his eyes united with mine, even more so when he smiled and demonstrated his dimples. He gave me a nod, and a flirty woman like me could do nothing but nod right back. Still debating on the necklaces in front of him, he slightly spread his legs and folded his arms in front of him. The tips of his fingers touched his chin, and he took slow strokes on his goatee as if he were in deep thought. Almost immediately, I noticed the wedding ring on his finger and the excitement that was building rush out of me. Seeing the ring just about ruined it for me, but when he looked up at me again...not quite.

"Excuse me," he said from a short distance, looking in my direction.

I turned around, making sure there was no one behind me. I then pointed to my chest. "Me? Are you talking to me?"

"Yes. Would you mind helping me out with something?"

Oh, I could do more than that, I thought, already making my way up to him. The exotic cologne he wore made me want to just hand over my black lace panties, but I played it cool. *Get it together, Joyce! Girl, get it together!*

I stood close to him, swallowing hard and hoping that he couldn't see perspiration that was causing my silk blouse to stick to my skin.

"What's up?" I said, quickly glancing at his square-toed leather shoes. A man's shoes were something that always had to be right with me, and yes, this brotha was coming correct! "What can I help you with?"

He touched one of the diamond necklaces, then touched the other. "I'm trying to decide which one of these necklaces I should purchase. Need a woman's opinion and I figured that a woman as classy as yourself would be able to help."

No offense to the woman behind the counter, but he obviously knew class when he saw it. I looked at both of the necklaces, noticing the hefty nine thousand dollar price tag on one, and twelve thousand dollar tag on the other. The highest one did have more diamonds, but the cheaper one was prettier. I cleared my throat and reached for the cheaper necklace to observe it.

"If you don't mind me asking," I inquired. "Who are you getting this for? Wife, mother, sister," I cleared my throat again, "Mistress..."

He blushed, but answered. "Don't know yet. I'll know when I decide which one to buy."

His response let me know the wife wasn't as lucky as I thought she may be. "This one," I said, giving the necklace to him. "I like this one better."

He took the necklace from my hand. "Are you sure?"
"Positive."

"Okay," he said, handing the necklace over to the sales associate. "I'll take this one."

I smiled because he'd chosen the one I suggested. Before I could walk away, he reached for my arm. I swear his touch made me tingle all over and I hoped that my apparent attraction to him wasn't so noticeable.

"Damn, baby. Why you moving so fast? I just wanted to say thanks for your time. It was very much appreciated."

"No problem. And I hope that whoever you give the necklace to, she appreciates it."

"I'm sure she will. No doubt."

He released my arm and I walked off to go find Jimmy.

Just my luck, the sales lady said they didn't have the Jimmy Choo shoes that I wanted in my size. What a disappointment that was. My face fell flat, and as she tried to sell me some of the other shoes, I pouted like a three year old child.

"Can I order them online?" I asked with frustration on the rise. "If so, do you know how long it will take?"

"Sure you can order online, but it may take several weeks before you get them. There is a new collection over there and you may find something in that selection that you like, too."

I hated when sales people tried to talk me into something that I didn't want, but I did take a glance at the other shoes. None compared to the ones I wanted, but I did see a pair that was doable. As I held the shoe in my hand, I inhaled that exotic cologne again, even before he'd said a word. He stood behind me, looking over my shoulder.

"Those are nice," he said, referring to the shoes and not my breasts as I had hoped. "But I suggest that you scrap the shoe search, especially if you can't get the ones that you really want."

I swung around, being closer to him than I was before. "What makes you think I don't really want these?"

"I've seen that look in a woman's eyes many times before. Normally, when a woman has tears in her eyes when she's shopping, that means she's disappointed that she can't find what she wants. The look in your eyes clearly says that you're disappointed."

Obviously, he'd been paying attention to me, like I was him. I put the shoe down, knowing that he was right. "I guess I owe you a thank you, too. And thanks for reminding me that if I can't have what I want, then there is no need to settle."

"None," he said, backing away from me. I guess I'd gotten a little closer without knowing it. "I gotta jet, but it was nice talking to you, uh...what did you say your name was?"

"I didn't say, but it's Joyce."

He nodded and slowly exited the shoe section. "Jaylin," he winked. "Jaylin Rogers. Take care."

"You too."

I watched as Jaylin was out of sight, but definitely not out of mind. Wasn't sure what that connection was all about, but it was one of the most interesting encounters I'd ever had. Something about him had me intrigued and I wasn't sure yet if it was the mere fact that he was FINE AS HELL!!

Whenever I couldn't find what I wanted at the mall, I always searched for something else. Never was it in the same category as what I wanted, so if I couldn't get shoes, I had to go for a purse. The Louis Vuitton store was in my sights, but so were those shiny black leather shoes that covered Jaylin's feet. This time, he was standing in a lingerie store, holding up two pieces of sexy negligee. Just for the hell of it, I poked my head in the door.

"Pssst, Jaylin."

His eyes shot up, and those pearly whites were coming through for me. "If those aren't for you," I teased. "I'd say the black one looks better. The red is too slutty."

He laughed, holding up the red one. "You think? I have pretty good taste, and I think the red one looks better than the black one."

I walked into the store, trying to make my point. "No, go with the black one. Trust me. You can't go wrong with black and all women need a little silk mixed with lace in their lives."

Jaylin looked over both pieces, before dropping the hangers to his side. "You know what? Why...why don't you go try both of these on for me? That way I can decide which one I like best. Can you do that for me?"

No doubt, I was flattered, but there wasn't a chance in hell I would model the negligee in front of him. "You can take my word for it. The black one is the way to go, and unfortunately, I just can't see myself showing the *goods* to someone who is not my man."

"What about to a man who is interested?"

I couldn't help but go there, but he made me. "Interested in who? Couldn't be me, especially with that blinding wedding band on your finger."

"That's fair," he said, raising a brow. "But my interest revolves around taking you to dinner." He reached in his pocket, pulling out a business card and handing it to me. "I'm staying downtown at the Four Seasons. If you're interested in dinner, call me. If not, we both become losers."

I skeptically took the card, but didn't look at it. "Maybe so, Jaylin, but there is something about you that says stand clear. No offense, of course."

"Hey, that's what they all say, but many have changed their minds. I hope you can be persuaded as well."

I was already tongue tied, so I kept my mouth shut. I had his card, and if dinner is what I wanted, I could get it. I left the store, refusing to turn around. Not because I wasn't interested, but because I had done the married man thing before and it didn't pan out. Promised myself that I would never go there again, but saying "never" was like saying I'd never shop again. I knew that in no way was the truth.

Later that day, I sat on my couch, debating what to do. I held Jaylin's business card in my hand, flipping it in circles. The situation itself seemed so harmless, and if a fine ass man wanted to take me to dinner, what was the big deal? The big deal was I knew a man like him could get more than dinner, if he wanted to. I hadn't had sex in quite some time and I pictured myself ripping his clothes off and attacking him. I wondered what he looked like naked, and the way his muscles bulged through his clothes, I could tell his body was nothing to play with. I glanced at the T.V. that was showing nothing but repeats. I ignored the telephone calls that were coming from friends who wanted to talk about nothing. I even hung up on my daughter's father, who seemed delighted that I was home alone on a Saturday night. That thought, in itself, made me dial out on my phone to call Jaylin. When he answered, my stomach rumbled. I touched it, just to calm the queasy feeling inside.

"Jaylin Rogers," he said, again.

I quickly spoke up. "Jaylin, this is Joyce. I met you earlier..."

"I know. Been waiting for your call. Up for dinner or do I dine alone?"

"No need. I would love to meet you for dinner. Where and when?"

"The restaurant at the Four Seasons. If you can, meet me there in an hour. I'll be waiting."

He hung up before I could say another word. I didn't think much of it, and to be honest, his arrogance, as well as confidence, was striking. I did, however, make a phone call to my sisters to let them know where I would be and who I would be with.

I arrived at the Four Seasons, and I could see Jaylin from a distance, standing in front of the restaurant. His cell phone was to his ear, and the distressing expression on his face looked serious. I could tell that drama was lurking on the other end, and when I saw him slightly cut his eyes, it was obvious.

"Look, I gotta go," he shot back at the caller. "No time for the bullshit, baby, and I need for you to quickly decide what in the hell you want to do."

He hung up and quickly turned his attention to me.

"Thanks for not allowing me to dine alone," he said.

"Nah, I couldn't let that happen, could I?"

We both smiled, and were taken to our seats by a waitress.

"What would you like to drink?" she asked us.

"I'll take a diet coke," I said.

"Remy, no ice," Jaylin responded.

"Sir, you'll have to go to the bar to get that. We don't serve alcoholic beverages over here. Only Coke and Pepsi products."

Jaylin cocked his head back and eyeballed the woman as if she'd called him ugly. "What kind of restaurant doesn't serve Remy? If I can't get what I want, then there's no need for me to spend my money here."

"Well, sir, I'm sorry but it's..."

Jaylin ignored the waiter and looked at me. "Joyce, sorry for the inconvenience, but this restaurant doesn't suit my needs. Let's go."

I was stunned that we were leaving over a glass over Remy, but it was his money being spent, not mine. Like a true gentleman, he extended his hand for me to go in front of him and we left. He walked through the Four Seasons with authority, and his swag had plenty of heads turning. It wasn't long before we made a detour to the elevators and when it opened, he allowed me to step on first.

"I'm going to order room service," he said. "You can order anything on the menu that you wish, and I bet you that I'll get my glass of Remy, and then some."

There was no doubt in my mind, and as long as I got my food, as well as an opportunity to scroll my hands down his chest, I was going with the flow.

Jaylin used a card to open the double doors to the suite, and to say it was laid out would be an understatement. Why he even chose to meet me at the restaurant was a waste of time, as I would have been a lot more comfortable dining in the suite with him.

"Have a seat," he said, inviting me to sit on the cream silk chaise that was a few feet away from the bed. He placed his keys and cell phone on a cherry-wood table, then picked up a menu, giving it to me.

"Thank you," I said, flipping it open to see what I wanted. There was an array of foods listed, including a New York Strip steak that I was dying to sink my teeth into. I was also in the mood for a salad, so I opted for both. Dessert would be determined much later. I told Jaylin what I wanted and he picked up the phone to call room service.

"Yes," he said, confirming his order. "And I must tell you that I'm disappointed about my experience with the restaurant today. Even though there may not be an affiliation to the hotel, it was still an inconvenience to me and my guest. Someone stands to be corrected."

He listened in, and when all was said and done, the food that was delivered was on the house. So was the wine, specifically for Mr. Roger's inconvenience, and he was given a free room to come back whenever.

After we finished our meal, Jaylin stood in front of me. He stepped out of his shoes and rolled up the sleeves on his shirt.

"That was good," he said, touching his belly. "Sorry if I gobbled that down, but I hadn't eaten all day."

"You're good," I said, watching him pull the shirt out from down inside of his pants. I swear his waistline was so perfect and the bulge in his pants...there was no word to describe it!

"If you don't mind, I'm just getting comfortable. Would you like anything else, or are you cool?"

He came out of his shirt, exposing his white t-shirt underneath. His body was everything that I imagined it to be, and all I could think was why something this good was happening to me. Then again, I wasn't so sure about that yet.

"I'm fine, Jaylin. Relax and enjoy the conversation."

Jaylin was down to his t-shirt and pants. As he squatted to take a seat in the chair that separated him and me with a table, his phone rang. He sighed when he looked at the caller, but answered.

"Yes," he said. For at least a minute, he said not one word. His distressing expression was on display again, and after a minute or two, the phone was placed back on the table without him commenting on the caller.

"Sorry about that," he said, getting ready to sit again. "Where were we?"

"I was about to suggest that you take a seat on the chaise and me in the chair. The chaise is much more comfortable, and from the phone calls alone, I can tell you need to relax more than me."

He laughed, but didn't decline my offer. We switched seats, and either way, I was comfortable. Jaylin lay back on the chaise, resting his arm across his forehead.

"I'm not going to sleep, Joyce. I'm just thinking, that's all."

"Do you want to share your thoughts? I'm a good listener and some of the men in my life seem to think so as well."

Jaylin turned on his side, but before speaking, he reached for the glass on the table. He took several sips of Remy, then cleared his throat. "Ahhh, better," he said. "So much better." Silence swooped in for a minute, and all he did was stare at me with a glossy look in his eyes.

"What?" I said. "What is it?"

"Nothing." He turned on his back and looked up at the high ceiling. "I just wanted to tell you that I think you're a very attractive woman. And excited as I am to be in your presence right now, I...I just got so much shit on my mind that I can't stay focused."

"I told you that I'm here to listen. Whatever you want to say, say it. Feel free to talk about your wife, kids, mistress, dog, cat...whatever."

He chuckled, but it wasn't long before he began to tell me about his troubles. While Jaylin definitely had it going on from the outside, his inside was all jacked up. According to him, the love of his life had left him and hadn't decided yet if she wanted a divorce. His mistress was a baby mama that he had love for, but in no way could replace his wife. To hide his pain, he'd been traveling from one woman to the next, trying to cope with the possibility of losing the one woman he loved. I could see how torn he was, but having sex with multiple women wasn't the answer. I told him just that.

"I know it's not, but it's almost like a drug. During those intimate moments, I forget about all that is transpiring around me. I'm there, enjoying everything that is taking place. The after effect is what troubles me, and when all is said and done, I'm left alone, trying to cope with the feeling of losing my wife forever."

"If you enjoy sex with multiple women, then why did you get married? I'm not judging you, but I am really surprised that a man like you has a wife. I get the feeling that you can have just about any woman that you want, so why choose just one?"

"Because it's not about being with as many women as I want. I want only one woman, because I love her with everything that I own. I stepped out on our marriage, and another woman got pregnant by me. My wife and I have been unable to settle this and it makes me angry that she's not willing to forgive me. I'm so angry that I'm finding myself doing things that I know only hurts her more. Why? Because she won't give me what I want, and I've always gotten what I want. I'm working on trying to change some of the most unfortunate things about myself, but I don't know if she will allow me that time. I'm aware that she needs to heal from what I've done to her, but I need my wife back. The sooner, the better."

The room got quiet again, only because I realized that like many men, Jaylin had a very selfish mentality. I'm sure he didn't understand how difficult it was for his wife, too, to get back to a marriage that was obviously very broken.

"All I can say to you is give her time. Seems like she's going through the healing process right now, and after what you've done, the least you can do is allow her some time. Eventually, she'll come around and being angry with you can't last forever."

"Time isn't a good thing, because tomorrow is never promised. We don't know what the future holds for us, and wasted time only brings about doubts and regrets."

I agreed with Jaylin on that, too, but he seemed like a man who wasn't open to advice. He just wanted someone to talk to, so I was all ears.

For the next few hours, Jaylin continued on about his wife, who he seemed to genuinely love. He even talked about a dog that he wanted to get for his daughters, and when he spoke of his children, he lit up like a Christmas Tree. From what I gathered, Jaylene, Justin, L.J., and Mackenzie had a wonderful father who loved them dearly.

"They're my life," he said, finally smiling. "It's all about them, and at times, nothing else really matters."

"Not even your wife?" I challenged.

He looked over at me with a momentous expression on his face. "At times, like right now when I'm in a hotel room with a beautiful woman, and feeling beat-down about all that is going on in my life, not even my wife matters."

I wanted to help him escape from his misery, but I knew that having sex with him would only temporarily cure the wound that seemed so deep.

"What are you thinking?" he said. "I'm getting tired of talking and I know you're getting tired of listening."

"Actually, I'm not. I enjoy being in the presence of a handsome man, and whatever I can do to help, let me know."

Jaylin scooted over on the chaise, touching the spot next to him. "You can lay right here, that's what you can do. I promise I won't bite, then again, I must warn you...I'm known for breaking my promises."

"Somehow I knew that already."

I stood and made my way over to Jaylin on the chaise. I lay comfortably on my back, but rested my head on his shoulder. Several pillows were tucked behind us and he continued on with his deep thoughts. Don't know why it seemed as if I'd known this man all of my life, but he made it so easy for me to feel comfortable being next to him.

"So, where do you go from here, Jaylin? When you leave this room, what's the plan?"

"No matter what happens between us, I'm going back home to fight hard for my wife. If I'm somehow able to repair the damage I've done, I will never put us in this situation again. It's been like living in hell, and hell is not where I want to be."

I turned to look at him, and couldn't believe how convincing he was. It wasn't like the Republicans lying, telling America that they would make the economy better. That was considered false pretense. However, I didn't get that feeling from Jaylin and I believed when he said he would do whatever to repair his marriage and not make the same mistake again. In knowing so, I reached up and scrolled my finger down the side of his beautifully sculptured face.

"I really wish you all the best with your marriage, truly I do. But I must also be very honest with myself, too. There is no way in hell that I'm going to let you walk out of that door, before giving me the best sex that I know you can provide. I am down for whatever, and as far as I'm concerned, this is just between me and you."

Jaylin said not another word. His seducing grey eyes dropped to my lips and as he held my face in his hands, my insides screamed for him. The touch of his hands starting to move up and down my legs made me quiver. He squeezed, I squeezed. He pressed, and I pressed harder. Our bodies gave off much heat, and even the pile of our clothes right next to us didn't seem to cool things down. Seeing his naked body excited me even more and as my legs were carefully placed on his broad shoulders, he looked down at me.

"Are you sure you're ready for this?" he asked.

"I'm sure. I just hope you are."

Jaylin turned up the heat, and delivered a Naughty performance that left me sprawled out on the chaise, squinting from the bright sun as it entered the room in the morning. I was still lying naked and barely covered with a soft white sheet. I looked around, already realizing that he was gone. From a distance, I could see the jewelry box on the table with a note on top. I covered myself with the sheet and walked over to read the note. It read:

Thanks for such a wonderful evening Joyce. The moment I saw you, I had a vision of what I had hoped would take place between us. Making it a reality pleased my heart in ways that you will never know, and quite frankly, may never understand. Just for listening to me, I couldn't think of a better woman I'd want to give the necklace to. I hope you like it, even though it wasn't the necklace you'd chosen. To say that I don't take other people's advice would been putting it mildly, as I always do what feels best for me. All love, and I hope you never forget...Jay Baby.

I opened the jewelry box, and sure enough, it wasn't the necklace I had chosen. I could only smile, thinking back to yesterday. Who would have ever thought that Jimmy Choo was my preference, but now, Jaylin Rogers was my addiction.

The End

Book Club Meeting. . .

"Joyce, that was an interesting story and I like how you were able to get Jaylin to spill his guts to you," Chyna said. "I had somewhat of the same experience with him, and I was surprised that he'd told me about his childhood."

"I know," Joyce countered. "He didn't dig that far back, but I appreciated him giving me the scoop about what was going on. The sex we had probably did way more for me than it did for him, but he did seem rather relaxed. Sometimes with men, all they want is for you to lend them your ears. They want to be heard, and we get so ahead of ourselves, thinking that sex is the only thing that matters to them. You have to be willing to bring good conversation to the table and dig deep into what he says. Whether you like what he says or not, an honest man is one that you can definitely appreciate. I love Jaylin on the strength of him being honest."

There wasn't one woman in the room that disagreed. We were all pretty much on the same page with this subject, but the problem was getting men to be honest.

"They'd rather lie and have you believing those lies. Just give me a choice, that way when the chips fall where they may, I have no one to blame but myself. Joyce, before we move on. Why didn't you model that lingerie for Jaylin?" A lady inquired. "His request was harmless to me and I would have strutted my stuff, then made him take me to the hotel room right then and there."

Joyce laughed and she asked the women by a show of hands, how many women would have modeled the lingerie for a man they didn't know. A few hands went up, and when she switched it to if the man was Jaylin, several more hands hit the air.

"I'm sorry, but that would have never worked for me," Joyce said. "I'm not insecure about my body or anything, but that was taking it too far. Besides, if I would have presented myself as being an easy catch, I probably would have never gotten my necklace."

Joyce loosened the top button on her shirt and showed everyone the diamond necklace Jaylin had given to her. Many rushed out of their seats to look at it.

"Beautiful," one lady said, checking it out.

"You are too lucky," another said.

"Tuh," the snippy tone of one woman chiming in said. "All I got was several orgasms from him, but I can't say that I'm mad about that. As I think more about it, no I'm not mad. Never."

Obviously, the woman had something on her mind that she wanted to say. These stories were coming back-to-back and I was starting to believe that we'd be here all night. Everyone took their seats and got ready to listen to Shelyse tell why diamonds were no longer a girl's best friend, cumming was...

Here I Cum
Shelyse Tate

As the raindrops hit the window, all I could think about was the night before. I never thought I would do anything as explicit as I did on a first date. The sexual tension between us was that explosive. I found myself imagining what it would be like to fuck him as soon as he sat down at the table for our date. What would he think or do if I gave him a little taste of me? I was so anxious to get our date moving so I could put my imagination to work.

During dinner, I sat watching him devour his meal. His succulent lips were perfect and I contemplated him using that fiery tongue of his to lick my pussy. Just thinking about it made me clench my legs together to control the throbbing that began. *God, it's getting worse,* I thought, as I eased my hand under the table, wondering if I could ease the tension without him knowing. Just a little further and I would be there. Relieved from my own touch, I released a deep "Ah." Yes, right there. I couldn't wait to have his fingers, tongue and dick introduced to this very spot.

I looked up and caught his eyes staring at me in a seductive trance. They were very addictive, and it made me wonder what he was thinking. Was he as anxious to fuck as I was? Not make love or have sex, because I needed a man like him to FUCK me. I wondered if he was into toys, role play, or bondage? How freaky would he want to get? Anything would be fine with me, as long as it wasn't too painful.

Sitting opposite of Jaylin, I began to feel light feathery touches travel up my leg. At first, I thought it was a bug crawling on me, then I realized it was him. As he stared into my eyes, his foot traveled up my leg and under my dress. It stopped at the doors of my pussy that was so ready to invite him in. I was surprised by his actions and the touch of his toe caused me to jump. He smirked a devilish grin, and through my panties, he began to move his toe in a circular pattern. All I could do was sit stunned as my juices began to flow. I couldn't believe that he was actually toe fucking my love spot and I was enjoying it. My eyes fluttered from his performance, and to arouse me even more, he whispered what he intended to do with me, once we were alone. Just the thought of those things made me widen my legs and move my pussy nearer. It wasn't long before I was about to cum. Yes, right here...right now in a restaurant! Maybe being in a public place was so risqué that it made the orgasm so fiery that my body began to shake. I squeezed my eyes and muffled my lips, wondering how did he know I needed that so badly?

Somehow, we managed to get through dinner without anymore teasing, and after finishing our meal he wiped his mouth and gazed at me from across the table. "Shelyse, are you ready to leave?"

I didn't answer, but my eager look into his eyes provided a response. I picked up my purse and expeditiously made my way out of the restaurant, knowing he would follow. By the time I had reached my Candy Apple Red Naughty Volvo S60, Jaylin had caught up with me in the near empty parking garage. Grabbing my hand, he pulled me towards him and began planting kisses all over my steaming body. First, he used his tongue to trace my lips. Then he began to suck my tongue with such force that it made my *other* lips quiver. I wanted to let out a scream. The intenseness was building again, and I could feel a second orgasm coming my way. To calm myself, I bit his lower lip and that's when he backed me up to the hood of my car. His hand eased up my thighs, and before I knew it, he pulled my panties aside and danced around my insides with his fingers.

"Why...why are you so wet like this?" he whispered between kisses.

"You don't have to ask, do you? It's because of you, baby, only you."

No doubt, he liked my answer. He wrapped my legs around his waist and all I could do was savor the ride. I could feel his hard dick poking at my pussy through his pants. He rubbed my hips, then pulled my dress up and removed my panties to gain better access to what he wanted. Having a clear sight of my pussy, he then unbuttoned his pants, causing them to hit the ground. My eyes popped wide open and my kitty started to purr even more. I couldn't help but reach out to touch his meat.

"Wow," I said, stroking him. "I'm impressed. Long and hard, just how I like it."

He winked. "And I wouldn't serve it to you any other way."

His tool was original and had to be at least nine plus inches long. Damn this was going to be a hell of a ride, I could feel it! Yes, I could, and as soon as his tool busted me wide open, I felt all of it. I slightly backed up from the feeling, causing Jaylin to halt his movements. He held my waist while gazing into my eyes. "Calm those pussy muscles and I won't have no problem getting in. Trust and believe."

I felt at ease with him, and his dick going inside me was like an airplane gliding in for a perfect landing. I tightened my legs just above his ass to receive more of that nine, and then some. At first, I didn't think I was going to be able to handle Jaylin, but I quickly found out a women's body is made for whatever it needs and I needed this. It needed for him to navigate his goods in and out of me, just so I could reach that peak I never reached before. His pace increased and I began to feel pin pricks in my toes. The feeling in my toes proceeded to migrate upward like ants on a sugar cookie. Really, really sweet. The feeling hit my G-spot, and after one more good long stroke, I was on the verge of a major explosion.

"Yes, right there," I gasped, moaned and shouted. "Right...right there!" I coated his shaft with my juices, and jerked forward to tighten my arms around his neck.

Jaylin pecked my cheek, then moved his lips over to my ear. "You want another one? I'm not finished yet, so hang tight." I wasn't sure I could take anymore, but the feel of hard steel, still inside of me, keep me motivated. He pumped my insides slow, and I reached around him, gripping his sexy ass. My nails pressed harder and I couldn't believe that I was about to cum again. My heart raced and I shouted, "Yes!"

"Let's do this together," Jaylin requested while sweating profusely. "I'm almost there, baby, so hold that shit until the last moment."

Since I was ready to cum, the only thing I could think to do was count and hope the end was near. "Right now," he said in a soft tone that weakened my body. "Let it flow."

With the build up of holding it in, and the sexiness of his voice made for a powerful climax. I had to lay back to catch my breath and calm the trembling in my legs. Jaylin rested his sweat filled head on my heaving stomach, and as we both took deep breaths, I wondered what was going to come next. Thinking of what he'd done to me in the restaurant, I knew he had a wild imagination.

As he straightened my dress and buttoned his pants, he looked at me. "Your place or mine?"

"Mine," I quickly said. I couldn't wait to get home to take a shower. "Can I have my panties back?"

"No, these belong to me now." He smiled and tucked them into his pocket. "These sexy purple panties will be something I will always remember you by."

I shrugged, guessing that there was a first time for everything. I never had a man want to keep my panties as a personal trophy, but Jay Baby could have them.

The moment we stepped into my house, I knew this time around I wanted to be the aggressor. First things first...a shower. I left Jaylin to use the guest bathroom, then I went into my bedroom to make sure nothing was out of place before showering. I turned on some warm water for my shower and got two towels out of the cabinet. Using my favorite body gel, White Citrus, I began to wash my curvaceous body. Imagining water running down Jaylin's fine ass made me hurry. I dried off, moistening myself with lotion and perfumed White Citrus products. As I started to put on some sexy red panties, I tossed them aside, changing my mind and figuring that they would come off any way. Instead, I put on a red sheer negligee and it felt good rubbing against my nipples. I wondered what Jaylin had been doing all the time I had been in the shower, and it was now time for me to go see.

Dressed in nothing but his pants, Jaylin had been roaming the living room, hopefully waiting to continue our fuck fest. He picked up a picture of my son, while looking at my multiple awards and degrees. Without noticing me standing there, he finally put the picture back down. I assumed he would question me about it later. He slightly turned his head, and from the corner of his eye he saw me exit the bedroom. Still, he continued his exploration of my home.

"I can tell you love the color purple," he said. Besides my panties, nearly everything in my home was a shade of it.

"Yes I do," I said smiling. Since he was looking at everything so intently, I wondered what he was searching for.

Seeing the large amount of crystal dolphin figurines in varied shapes and sizes, he queried, "Why dolphins?"

"I like them because they seem to be such a gentle creature. I fell in love with them as a kid."

Jaylin nodded and kept looking. The artwork in my house was very extensive. There were paintings, etchings, and sculptures all with an African-American theme. He seemed surprised that I had classical music, along with Luther Vandross, Teena Marie, Kindred, Jill Scott, Jay-Z, and Ludacris. He looked through my CD's then decided to play some Teddy P.

I walked further into the room and stood next to him. "I haven't been a proper hostess. Would you like something to drink? I have wine, juice or ice water."

"Sure. I would love a glass of wine."

I sauntered towards the kitchen, knowing that Jaylin had his eyes on my backside. I considered myself to be a fine woman, and from my long curly tresses, my arched eyebrows, my plump chocolate breasts with nipples protruding like the chocolate kisses candy...to my kissable lips, I knew I had it going on. I was a petite woman, packed with one hell of a punch. I poured Jaylin's wine, then returned to join him in the living room.

"How far do you want to take this," I asked, handing him his glass of wine.

He sipped from the glass and shrugged. "As far as you want to."

"I guess I need to be little more specific. The bed, the floor, the desk or table? Toys, handcuffs, or rope? You name it, I probably have it."

Jaylin rubbed his chin and blushed. "I'm going to let you decide. Do whatever you wish...I'm all yours." He sat his glass on a table, waiting for me to make the next move.

I stepped forward and placed my mouth on his neck, sucking it like it was my favorite dessert. Leaving a passion mark there, I gravitated to his chest. There I sucked and bit his nipples. They were very sensitive, and I could tell he liked my touch from the way he grabbed my hair. As I looked into his passionate grey eyes, I felt the zing of his desire. Unbuckling his belt and unzipping his pants, I stuck my hands in and pushed his underwear and pants down in one swoop. Moving downward, I stuck my tongue in his navel to get a taste of the caramel flavor I was looking at. The more I touched and licked, the harder he pulled on my hair.

I pushed him away as he attempted to grab me. In my house, I was in charge here. I was already on my knees, drawing my hands up his long muscular legs. The soft feathery hair on them felt nice against my hands. His dick began to swell as I drew my lips near. I placed my tongue on the tip of it, ready to taste his cum. My tongue turned circles on his head, and it wasn't long before I had a mouth full. I could feel the tip near the edge of my throat. I had to open wide to accommodate his generously proportioned cock. I started sucking as if it was a Big Stick Popsicle in my mouth, and the harder I sucked, the tighter his grip got on my hair.

"That's it right there, baby. Mmmmmm," he repeated, multiple times. I went to work on him like a professional, and I could feel his dick pulsating. His legs got weak, but I kept at it. "Daaaamn, here I cum!" he strained. I had to quickly decide whether to swallow or to hold his cum in my mouth. Ultimately, that was decided for me as he let out a load. Swallow! Swallow! Swallow!

I licked my wet lips and stood to my feet. My arms rested on his shoulders. "How did you like that?" I asked.

"All I can say is you got skills. You damn sure know how to work that tongue," he said, breathlessly.

"No doubt."

Before I knew it, Jaylin lifted me to his waist. He snatched off my lingerie, and put his dick in me. I gasped at the suddenness of his impact. In that moment, I realized how strong he was. With my legs wrapped around him, and as "Promise" by Ciara played in the background, I moved with the rhythm of the song. The sexiness of the song increased the sexual ambiance. I could only think how many times a person could cum before the body says, "No more!"

In and out, he glided his hard muscle. As the friction increased, Jaylin bit and sucked my nipples. He gave each one a turn, and I knew my nipples were going to be sore from all the action they were getting. The feeling of his tongue whirling around them was causing flashes of fire in my pussy. I held on tight to his neck, trying to stay calm as his monster kept working my coochie over. I felt another orgasm stirring, so I started sucking on his tongue. The closer the orgasm got, the harder I sucked. With so much sucking and pumping going on at once, I became lightheaded. I took a moment to regroup and leaned my head against his handsome face. The stubble from his trimmed beard and goatee was a sensory turn on.

While I had stopped moving, Jaylin hadn't. He wrapped his arms around my thighs, bouncing my body hard against his. With each thrust, my pussy widened. Once again, I was defeated. "I'm cumming, again," I whispered with my eyes shut tightly.

"Go ahead, baby," he ordered.

I tightened my fist, wanting so badly to pound at his buffed chest. "I have never come this much before in my life!"

Jaylin's dick was like a genie that gave away wishes of a perfect fuck! He lowered my legs, then bent me over the arm of the couch. My legs were straddled far apart, and he leaned over me while kissing the back of my neck. His lips pecked down my spine and the feelings was so tantalizing. Nearing the small of my back, I assumed he was going to flip me over to fuck. But I was wrong. He started kissing places where the sun wasn't allowed to shine. Wow was the only word I could come up with to describe my experience with Jaylin. Something told me I was in deep trouble, and that he'd introduce me to many more experiences tonight. He told me he was going to kiss my beautiful ass, but I didn't think he meant that literally. Feeling the tremors from his moans caused my fluids to stir up once again as he licked, kissed, and bit my ass as if it was a favorite dessert.

What Jaylin had been doing to me felt first-class, but it could not take the place of what his nine could do. Feeling him smack it against my ass, I wondered what he was about to do. I lifted my head to look in the mirror that was on a wall in front of us. Watching him carefully, he positioned my cheeks in the right position for him to enter me from behind. He could see the shocked expression on my face, and when I gasped he smiled. "Are you comfortable in this position?"

My first instinct was to say "hell no", only because I liked being in the dominate position and this was a submissive one. But as my body began to accommodate this position, I went with the flow. "Yes, baby, we can try this position. I am willing to try anything once."

The mirror seemed to intensify the desire reverberating from his eyes. "That's good to know because there is one more thing I want to try after this."

What Jay Baby wants, he gets. Like I said, I was down with whatever. Still, in the current position, I felt stuffed. Maybe that was because he was able to push more of himself in me. Seeing him standing in back of me through the mirror was a feast for my ego. Who would have thought this fine ass man would want to dick me down like he had been doing for the past hour. *Hmm, my pussy must be extraordinary,* I thought. It took a pro to toughen up and deal with this kind of beating and I was ready to pat myself on the back. We had been experiencing orgasms, after orgasms...and couldn't seem to get enough.

As music continued to play in the background, Jaylin proceeded to nudge his hips to gain a better position for his device. That wasn't easy to do being as wet as I was. Leaning into me and placing his arms on each side of me gave him more stability. I moaned out loudly as he hit his designated mark. I clenched my toes to control the sensual sensation that was beginning to vibrate through my body. I grabbed the couch pillow to cover the scream that I knew was about to erupt.

"Don't silence yourself," Jaylin said huskily and thrusting faster into my pussy. "I like hearing you scream. It makes the mood more pleasurable. Scream as long and loud as you want."

This time, I held back, but I was going to have couch burns if this position went on any longer. He must have read my mind because the next thing he did was pull out of me. Not for long, though, and as we repositioned ourselves on the couch, he entered me from the back again. I gripped the couch, and as I screamed his name, I wondered if my neighbors could hear? I kept looking at us in the mirror, and with his hand navigating upward towards my breasts I wondered how much I was going to want him again after tonight. He was the best sexual partner I'd ever had. Usually, with my sexual partners it was a wham, bam thank-you-ma'am deal. With Jaylin, it was the appetizer, the meal, the dessert, and the after dinner coffee. It was addicting, and the next man was going to have a hard time satisfying me.

Once Jaylin got his, I called for a time-out. A something...I needed time to catch my breath and gain some sensation back into my legs. I was actually weak from the ongoing sex session, so I lay back on the couch. Jaylin walked away, so I assumed he went to clean himself up. I heard bath water running and contemplated on putting in another CD, but I couldn't move. My eyes faded, and I must have fallen asleep. What seemed like minutes later, I was being carried in his arms.

"Where are you taking me," I asked, securing my arms around his neck.

"I concocted a bubble bath for us."

I was pleased to hear that. We went through my bedroom to enter my bathroom, and I couldn't help but notice the ambiance of the room. Jaylin had turned down the covers on the bed, lit some lavender scented candles, turned on some soft music, and found my stash of handcuffs. Looking at those I wondered what he was planning. Just the thought of what it might be had my pussy turning flips.

"I see you've been busy," I said.

"Yes I have, but before we get busy again, I think you need to relax in some warm water."

We sat in the water and Jaylin positioned me on his lap. I lay back on his chest and snuggling against him felt wonderful. The warm water and bubbles, the lavender scent, and the soft music were relaxing.

"What I know about you, I only know from Facebook. We didn't talk much at the restaurant, or at your place. How about telling me something very few people know about you," he inquired.

I sighed and clinched my hands together with his. "Well...when I was younger, I had a chance to sing professionally but I chickened out. I knew if my mother ever found out that I had auditioned for something like that she would have flipped out. Back then, I cared about what she thought."

"What about now?"

"Now, I intend to do me. Someday I will bring my dreams alive and I hope it will be soon. What about you? What did you want to be growing up?"

"Hmmm. When I was younger, all I wanted to do was make money. I wanted to have my own business and make as much money as I could. If you hang on to your dreams, trust me, all things are possible."

"I couldn't agree more. Now, you know my favorite color is purple, right? What's yours?"

"I don't have a favorite color specifically. My mood decides what color I wear for the day. Today, I wanted to match my eye color so I wore grey."

"Honestly, if you ask me, you would look good in any color."

He blushed and rubbed up and down on my arms. "Thanks, baby. I'm sure you would, too."

His compliment made me smile, and as we listened to soothing music over the radio, I asked him his favorite kind. "I noticed you have an eclectic range of music styles on your book case," he noted. "But I would say my music taste varies. I love jazz when I want to relax, and I listen to Hip Hop when cleaning or driving long distances. Usually, I listen to soft sexy music when a sexual encounter is taking place, as it sets that damn mood."

I squeezed his hand, feeling so comfortable in between his legs. "Why me, Jaylin? Why did you decide to meet with me?"

He jerked his head back. "Why you what?"

"I mean...I would think you would have preferred to have this extravagant rendezvous with someone else."

"Why would you say that? And, why not you is the question?"

"Because I didn't think you'd be attracted to me. When I think about your ideal woman, a beautiful, classy, tall and slim woman comes to mind. As you can see, that's clearly not me."

"Whatever, but you should always be satisfied with who you are. I am very satisfied and I'm damn sure attracted to you. When I saw you walking down the street to greet me, you had me hooked with that beautiful face and figure. I knew this would lead to something special, and as fine as you are, you should never worry about a man's preference."

I snickered, knowing Jaylin was right. "You do wonders for a woman's ego."

"Yes, I know, but I also speak the truth."

"You're also very bold and extremely confident."

He rubbed his goatee. "Am I?"

"Yes, you are that and then some. I don't think bold is the right adjective to describe you and let's just say that you definitely know how to put it out there."

"I would say so, too, but what other adjective would you use?"

I laughed, trying to come up with something. "Sensual. Sensational. Sexy."

"That's three adjectives," he laughed.

"You didn't ask for one, so I gave you three."

"Then sum it up, baby. One word and one word only."

Feeling his dick swell, I reached my hand in the water to touch it. "Stiff," I said.

"Stiff?"

"Yes. Meaning, your dick is as *stiff* as a rod."

"Are you sure?" he said with a smile.

"Yes, I'm positive. Since my sitting on your lap is arousing you, I think I'm going to wash myself and get out so you can calm down."

"Your choice, but you gotta let me wash you up first."

I gave Jaylin a soapy sponge and allowed him to wash me. I thought about the different positions we had tried today. This sexual rollercoaster ride made me wonder when I would be ready to get off and throw in the towel. Though Jaylin seemed to be able to go on and on, due to his incredible stamina, I didn't think I could fuck all night long.

After stepping out of the tub, Jaylin dried both of us before picking me up and carrying me to the bed. While lying beside me, I thought he was ready to go another round. Instead, he turned to me and propped his head up with his hand. "Close your eyes and get some rest. Your body is going to need it, and for the record, I'm not done with you yet." The last thought in my mind, before I closed my eyes, was what could Jaylin come up with better than what he had already presented?

A while later, I had my answer. I slowly cracked my eyes, feeling feathery licks against my feet. Attempting to move my arms, I realized I couldn't. That brought me full wakefulness. My eyes popped open and I called Jaylin's name. He responded with a soft "yes" but I couldn't see him.

I moved my head from side to side, looking at the cuffs. "Umm, I'm not sure if I feel comfortable with being handcuffed. I like to be able to move freely."

"Why do you have handcuffs then?" he said, kneeling between my legs so I could see him. "I was curious and I assumed this was something you were used to."

"You seem to be curious about a lot of things. Now, are you going to uncuff me?"

"No," he said without hesitation. "I like having you like this. Besides, I'm ready for you to start screaming my name again. It's like music to my ears."

Saying nothing else, I watched as he moved to the edge of the bed. I never knew I would like having my toes sucked before Jaylin did it. It started with a massage of my feet. When he was finished with that, he tongued each of my toes. That was foreplay to the ultimate event. He started sucking my baby toe first, saving my big toe for last. As with everything, it seemed, he gave it his all. By the time he got to my big toes, I was ready and willing to do whatever to satisfy the roaring fire that was building in me. This man was a god with that mouth of his. I couldn't wait to have it on my pussy. His tongue, lips and teeth action were to die for.

I moved around, but he grabbed my hips to stop me from wiggling. His hands inched up my legs, and as he kissed them, it inflamed the fire within me. He kissed my calves, and the inside of each thigh before he got to the hotspot I urgently needed him at. I wished he would hurry up, only because my toes were starting to curl. He moved slowly to my vaginal area, teasing the minimal hair on my pussy with his tongue. It slithered inside to get a taste, and that caused me to wiggle even more. He added his fingers to the mix, and I couldn't hold back my screams.

"Where in the hell did you come from Jaylin? I...I can't take this shit anymore!"

"Well, I can," he arrogantly responded, continuing on with his foreplay.

Trying to catch my breath, I bit down hard on my lip. Jaylin played with my nipples and made love to my navel with his tongue. Soft and delicate licks were being placed on it and as his hands rotated my breasts, there was no way to put out this fire. His mouth was fierce. Yeah, I'd said it before, but it was something that needed to be repeated. My body was yearning for more, and when I looked into his eyes, I spoke with the truth.

"I want to feel it again," I whispered. "Put it in me and make me cum again."

"Ask," he said. "And you will receive."

His dick was already near the opening of my slit, but he only put half of it in. His fingers touched my clit and before he started his rotations, he tossed out a question. "Who owns this pussy," he asked. I didn't respond, so he inched further in. I gasped and that's when he leaned his ear in closer to me. "Let me try this again...who owns the pussy?"

I knew he was teasing me, which was so unfair. "Do...don't play with me, Jaylin. Just give me what I want."

My insides expanded more, but he halted his movements. "I'm going to hold out until you tell me who owns this pussy."

I was wet as ever, and it was the wrong time to question me. Besides, why do men ask that stupid question anyway? Every woman knows, at this point, they will say anything to get the job done. The real decision was to tell the truth or tell a lie? Was this really Jaylin's pussy? He really wouldn't know if it was or wasn't, but by the way he had my pussy talking, hell yeah it was his!

As I debated whether or not to tell him my answer, he started to pull out.

"Now, why would you go there?" I asked. "You already know what's up."

Those grey eyes went straight to my heart as he stared at me. "You know what I want to hear. Say it, or let's be done with it." I couldn't believe that he backed up again. He was serious as hell about me saying it. "Say it," he ordered.

"Say what?" He was starting to piss me off and my voice rose to a higher pitch. "Damn it, Jaylin, you own thi...."

Before I could finish, he slammed his dick into me as far as it could go. I squeezed in my stomach and my whole body shuddered. *Oh God, heaven*, I thought. His full package was delightful and I had created one slippery wet mess between my legs. Pumping faster and faster, Jaylin began to sweat. With smells of sex and lavender surrounding us, I quivered with anticipation. I repositioned my legs around his neck, allowing him to gain further access into my pussy that intensified the feel of ecstasy. From the licks of fire echoing through my body, I knew when I came it was going to be a bursting release.

Jaylin was close to completion. I could tell by his sighs and moans as they got louder and louder. I started clenching my pussy with every glide. Since I couldn't touch him with my hands, I begged him to place his lips on mine. He satisfied this sensory need at first, but when he had enough of my lips, he sucked my nipples. Doing so made my tunnel throb and he quickly returned to it.

As hard as he was banging me, I just knew I might be in need of another bed. I was holding onto the headboard so tightly that my fingers were hurting. Starting to cum made me squeeze my legs tighter. I screamed Jaylin's name, and he quickly uncuffed me. He picked me up and we slammed our bodies against each others, as if this would be our last fuck on earth. To have one orgasm was great. To have multiple orgasms within the span of seconds was magical. I wasn't sure I could survive it. Men always think dying while having sex is the best way to go. If this would be what it was like then hell yeah dying like this would be wonderful. Only thing, I wasn't ready to die yet, and I damn sure wanted dick like this forever.

Surging into my body Jaylin whispered, "I will always own this pussy, whether you want to admit it or not. Yeah, I know...you love this dick, don't you? You love to fuck it and suck it! You love when my cum coats your pussy like frosting on a cake. Don't you baby? Don't you!" he shouted with veins showing up in his neck. *Well damn*, I thought. *I guess I do love it.* We screamed together and it pleased me that I was capable of taking him to that level. Many had tried, but many had failed. No doubt, I felt accomplished.

Rolling over me, Jaylin plopped down on the bed. My body was still vibrating, but I turned on my side. I traced from his nose to his beautiful lips.

"I think that's it for me," I confessed. "I can't go another round."

Of course, he boasted. "I probably could go a couple of more rounds, but if you can't, I'm good. What we've been doing sure has filled my tank. This was one explosive encounter and I doubt that I'll ever forget it."

He got off the bed and walked into the bathroom, where he removed his condom. With his back to me, he washed his goods. It wasn't long before his fine ass was stepping back into his clothes and that made me get up to put my robe on. I walked Jaylin to my door, and before he walked out, he turned and kissed me. "Stay sweet," he said, holding my face with his hands. "Never underestimate who you are and always remember whose pussy this really is."

I nodded, and if we never have another night like this, the memories of those lips will forever be burned into my soul. Saying goodbye, Jaylin gave me another peck before walking out the door. *Damn,* I thought. *Fantasies really can come true.*

The End

Book Club Meeting...

The fans were already being passed around the room. "Somebody crack some windows, open the doors or turn up the air conditioner," someone shouted. Now, this definitely wasn't no church, but there were many fans being waved throughout the room and we all needed to cool down after that one. Shelyse's admission to what she and Jaylin had done sparked a thirty minute conversation about the difference between making love, having sex and fucking. By a show of hands, the results were shocking. Many women chose fucking, especially with a man of Jaylin's caliber.

"That's why I was like forget the love thing," Shelyse said. "No need to go there, especially when we don't even love each other. I had some serious needs that day and it felt so good to just...just let it all hang out!"

Many laughed, some left in awe. Either way, nobody could deny that Shelyse and Jaylin had taken steamy sex to a whole new level.

"Hey Shelyse," a woman said. "Is it still Jaylin's pussy or have you found a replacement?"

Shelyse giggled. "Replacement, no. I'm settling right now, but what I'm settling for isn't so bad. Jaylin left his mark on me, but I'm still a little concerned about men who always trying to claim a woman's pussy. You just can't do that, and if it can walk away from you, there's no telling who it will walk to. I'm just saying."

So many agreed and we all felt as if it were so tacky for men to spill those words during sex.

"Normally, it's a turn off for me, but Jaylin was the exception," Shelyse said. "I thought we were about to jump up and start fighting, but when he dipped that potion into my motion, I...I had to change my mind."

I threw my hand back at Shelyse, knowing that she was defeated before it ever got started. Her admission that "Jaylin's dick was like a genie that gave away wishes" was the truth and I was in no way mad at her for making her wish come true.

"I had a wish, too," a lady said, coming all the way from the back row. "I wished that Jaylin wouldn't steal any business away from me, but he took that and then some. Let me tell you that it's a very thin line between love and hate and I learned it the 'HARD' way."

"So, I guess since you put quotes around the word hard, this may have something to do with Jaylin's penis?" I asked.

The woman gave me a devilish grin and introduced herself as Veronique...

There's a Thin Line Between Love and Hate

Veronique

Jaylin Jerome Rogers was considered to be the most successful Investment Broker in Miami, perhaps in the state of Florida. I considered myself to be the female Jaylin Jerome Rogers—arrogant, confident, successful, a body to die for, and sexy as hell. What I want, I get...well, most of the time. Right now, I was pissed off at my competition for charming the panties off one of my richest and most sought after investors and stealing a million dollar real estate deal that should have been mine. Mr. Rogers and I have certainly been down this road before and the bullshit had to end NOW! I sat at my desk, typing away on the keyboard and cursing his ass out in numerous e-mails. I'd even left threatening voice messages on his cell phone, but to no avail. It wasn't until late Friday night that he called me back, and I listened to his demanding voice over the phone.

"Meet me tomorrow, on my yacht," he snapped. "We can discuss what's on your mind, and we need to talk about your emails and threats. I'm not with that shit, and even though I've never met you, I didn't think a woman could get that down and dirty with her choice of words."

"When need be, I can. Just make sure you're there tomorrow and I'll see you soon."

I slammed down the phone and couldn't wait to tell him how I felt about being snubbed by him.

By four o'clock the next day, I was boarding his huge magnificent yacht, the SSLJ that reeked success and money. My anger increased with each step as I checked out the white vessel with navy blue trimmings. It must have been forty feet long and rivaled any cruise ship on the high seas. I had to admit, Mr. Rogers was damn sure living the good life. I had never met him personally, but his reputation preceded him. In the business circle he was known as a fearless and ruthless businessman and a ladies' man. I'd seen pictures of him and they were...aw-ight. I knew of women whose panties got wet at the mention of his name. And the names that they called him: Jay Baby, Cherry Popper, Sugar Monster, Ding Dong Man, Big Daddy, Bedroom Bully, Superman, Mr. Fabulous...well, we'd just have to see about that. Many women say that once you've had his nine plus inches, you are hooked! Me...I admired his intelligence and business savvy, which added to his already millionaire status. He had set the bar high for the rest of us in the business, and that was very impressive. Although we've never met, we do serve some of the same clientele and both of us have reaped the rewards of being very good at what we do. What pissed me off was when he fucking seals the deal in business transactions. I guess when it came to females who wanted to invest their money, if they could get prime property and fringe benefits, so be it. Usually, I wouldn't give a damn who he screwed, because I always got mine however, whenever, and with whomever I wanted...but damn, I wanted to get paid, too!

As I rounded the deck, I collided with this gorgeous, handsome hunk of a man smelling of Issey Miyake. His bedroom grey eyes were to die for, and the white golf shirt he wore hugged his abs and mountain stacked six-pack. His black shorts revealed a bulge that possibly showed he was happy to see me, or was the bulge his actual size? Not to be distracted by his sexiness, I inched back and lifted my finger to his face. "You bastard," I spat. "You fucked my client and stole a deal that should have been mine! I hate you and how dare you take something...anything from me!"

Jaylin rubbed his trimmed goatee, looking at me as if I were crazy. He quickly shot back in a nonchalant manner. "Well, if you say I stole business away from you, then I guess I did. But don't blame me if your business skills are as cold as your sex life. Bring your hot ass in here and let's discuss this."

I followed Jaylin into an immaculately decorated office, while eyeing his jaw dropping backside. I was so sure that I wouldn't get caught up with his looks, but without even knowing it, he was slowly breaking me down. Inside of his office, there was a long cherry-wood table covered in a rich blue velvet fabric. It also included a well-stocked bar, floors covered with soft white carpet and a plasma TV that covered a whole wall. The walls were draped with silky navy blue fabric and framed awards and certificates covered portions of the walls. He quickly turned around, causing us to be very close. So close that when I bumped into the front of him, I felt his dick jump. My pussy started to pop, and before I knew it, I could feel the drip-drops coming down. Jaylin smiled behind the lustful gaze in my eyes, but only cleared his throat. He extended his hand to a nearby leather seat.

"Take a seat," he invited. "Would you like a drink?"

I sat down, doing my best to play hard to get. "Sure. A drink would be nice."

I watched his swagger—tight ass and rippling muscles—move to the bar. He came back with a bottle of Remy and poured us some drinks. I crossed my legs and my black mini dress rose up, revealing my caramelized tanned, sexy legs. I wore no panties, only because I hated to wear them. Jaylin's eyes scanned up my legs, checking out the well put together presentation. He seductively licked his lips from one end to the other. I took a swig from the glass, then placed it on a table. I turned to him, watching as he sat next to me, tossing back his drink.

"Mr. Rogers, don't think your smooth talking, alcohol, and anxious dick can get to me like they do other women. I'm not here to play this game with you and I seriously want some answers."

His calmness fired me up! And so did that damn smirk on his face. "Call me Jaylin, and do away with the Mr. Rogers thing. Also, I'm gon' need you to loosen up, baby, and that tone doesn't suit you. In case you're worried, I won't hurt you, and if I do, I promise to hurt you in a good way." He winked and took a few more swigs from his glass. I sighed, trying to tone down my attitude, just a little.

"So, uh, I gather from what you've said to me, women are talking about me, huh? I'm not surprised; I leave one hell of an impression."

My brows went up and I shrugged. "Well, unfortunately, not a good one with me. I'm so mad at you, I could..."

Jaylin swooped in so fast that I could barely get another word out. He lifted me from the chair by my waist, while thrusting his snake-like tongue in my mouth. Next thing I knew, I was being backed up to the cherry-wood table. His tongue tasted so good, and all I could do was run my fingers through the soft curls in his hair. Things were getting intense, and with one hand, he swept the bottle of Remy, books, and papers to the floor. The loud crash startled neither of us, and he lifted me onto the table. He stared into my eyes, ripping my dress off with one tug. I anxiously pulled his shirt over his head, and scrolled my hands down his carved chest. I pushed his shorts and briefs down, eyeballing his smooth dick that popped out long and throbbing. Hard dick to juicy awaiting pussy, he forced monster dick inside me—all nine plus inches. It felt soo-oo goo–d, I almost cried. His skillful tongue slithered a hot trail down my neck, teased my breasts, and played in my belly button. Still determined to get revenge and take control, I wrestled to mount him. I was able to do so, and looked down at him as I rode him like a jock.

"No you didn't criticize my sex life, did you?" I asked.

"If I did," he moaned, while squeezing his fingertips into my rocking hips. "I now have a change of heart."

I tightened my vaginal walls like a viselike grip around his goods, and arched my back, popping my ass each time I came down on him. The sounds of blistering sex taking place, and our sweaty bodies rocking together, turned us the fuck on! The more we insulted each other and talked dirty, the hornier we became. Our curses turned to moans, groans, and whimpers as we fucked the length of the table...me on top, then him on top, rolling, rolling, rolling until our bodies shuddered and rocked—like the waves rocking the yacht. ~~~~~~~~~~

I took deep exhausting breaths, trying to regain my sanity and remember that I came here to diss Jaylin's ass. I scrambled from his embrace, fell off the table and landed hard. My bitch mode kicked back in, "I still hate you for backstabbing me on that deal."

Jaylin reached for my hand, helping me off the floor. He stood naked in front of me, moving in very close. "I love feisty ass women, I swear I do. As far as the deal goes...do you mean like you've played me so many times before? You really don't want to go there, do you? I guess you didn't think I knew about the underhanded shit you've pulled on me, but a man like me knows everything."

I inched backwards, feeling a bit unsure. "But I...I came so close to landing that deal. Then Jordan met with you and the rest is history."

He touched his goatee, staring at me long and hard. "So, uh, let me get this straight. You assumed that I fucked her and you think that's why the deal turned in my favor? Assumption is a motherfucker and don't assume nothing when it comes to me."

I bit my lip, thinking I'd possibly gotten a few things wrong. "Well, but I..."

Jaylin quickly cut me off. "Baby, that's the problem. You just can't come close to making shit happen, you have to go in for the kill. Like˜ ˜This." He reached for my waist again, and being so close to his body I was caught in a trance.

"Show me, My Dick Master. How is it that I'm supposed to go in for the kill?" I asked.

"I'm showing you right now."

Jaylin had already bent me over the table. He hiked my ass, spread my cheeks, and worked his way in with ease. While giving it to me doggy-style, his hands roamed my body, touching every hotspot that he could find. I put the hound dog into another position, and dropped to my knees. This position was one of my favorites and I suspected he'd never been here before. On all fours, I continuously inched forward across the room with him glued to my ass, never missing a stroke.

"Where in the hell did you learn this?" he panted.

"It's called 'Walking the Dog' and I thought it would be so fitting for you."

He chuckled and playfully barked "Whoof, whoof" while slapping my ass and plunging into me. "I like that and just when I thought you couldn't teach an old dog new tricks," he said.

I stopped the motion and turned to look back at Jaylin. "You're not the only one with skills. And let's just say that we can learn a lot from each other."

We continued on, and when we climaxed together, we took another moment to catch our breaths. Jaylin sat beside me with our backs against the wall. He reached over and clinched my hand with his.

"So, why do you think I fucked my way into landing that deal? Do you really think I just point my dick and squirt my love potion on women to get their business?" he asked matter-of-factly. "I guess the question is would that approach work on you?"

"Never," I shook my head emphatically. "Unless I wanted it to."

Jaylin grabbed his manhood, slowly stroking it up and down. He got on his knees in front of me, and then glided the tip of his head along my lips. I couldn't help myself. I licked the pre-cum from the tip and sucked him into the back of my throat. He gave my mouth the special treatment, and when his body tightened, his cum erupted like an oozing volcano. I moaned out loudly with him, refusing to let one drop hit the floor.

Jaylin reached for my hand. "Follow me," he ordered. We made our way to the stateroom where we continued going at it like two dogs in heat in the oversized canoe-shaped bed. In the sixty-nine position, he licked my sweet nectar...I sucked his dick-cum as we quenched our sexpetite. Once again, our sweaty bodies collapsed and we slept in each others' arms as "Bad Boy" by Luther Vandross played in the background.

The next morning, as Jaylin and I washed each other, he pressed my body against the glass shower and whispered in my ear. "I'm pleased that we had an opportunity to have that conversation you came over here to have. What exactly did you learn?"

"I learned," I said, pressing my naked wetness into him. "Hmmm, let's see. I learned that you can handle business in the bedroom as well as the boardroom."

"And?" he said with his eyes closed, pecking down my neck to my nipples.

"Oh-ooo, right there. Keep your tongue right there, and I, uh, also learned that there's a thin line between love and hate."

"And?" he fired back, sinking his fingers into my wetness.

I sucked in a heap of air. "Um–mmmm, yes. If...if you fucked my client like you fucked me, you deserve that million dollars."

"Two million," he whispered, grazing my kitty with his thumb.

I cocked my head back in awe. "Where did two million come from?"

"One million for the deal and your sweet pussy damn sure made me feel like a million!"

I rolled my eyes, upset because he always knew how to say the right things. "Damn you, Jaylin," I whispered breathlessly. "I could really fall in love with you."

He stopped his motion, taking a second to look in my eyes. "And you know how I feel, too."

He plunged into my waiting inferno, and like all of the other names that were given to him by women, my Dick Master had earned a new award winning reputation. Yes, there was a very thin line between love and hate, but where Jaylin was concerned it was now nothing but love!

The End

Book Club Meeting...

"Go ahead and walk that dog," someone bellowed. "I'm truly hot and bothered by these stories, but Jaylin Rogers is a D-O-double G! Veronique, you should have stood your ground, instead of melting in his hands like putty. Is there anybody willing to show this man that he can not have any woman that he wants? I wish it were me and I know for a fact I would tell him m-fucking no! No you can't have me, not never!"

As expected a few women agreed and we talked about why some women were so willing to satisfy Jaylin's needs, as well as their own needs, than others.

"I don't care what anyone says," Veronique added. "When you get up close and personal with Jaylin, the game changes. It's not necessarily a 'dick thing' and the man knows how to get into your head. He's smooth, he knows exactly what to say and he makes you feel as if it's all about you and him. He can turn a day of misery into a day of joy. He's very respectful and that is why so many women give in to him. Aside from the sex, you can learn a lot about men, just listening to him. His advice is decent, and ever since we got together, I conduct my business in a different way. I always keep my eyes on the prize, and go for the kill right at the end. I definitely get it now, but I really didn't get it before. I do know where some of you women are coming from, but you have to stop viewing everything about him from a straight and narrow point of view."

Many of the other ladies who had already told their stories agreed. They had gotten more than a sexual escapade, too, and all that Jaylin had given was priceless.

"Have you walked any dogs lately, Veronique, or should I say have you had any dogs walk you?"

Veronique laughed out loudly, admitting that her days of walking dogs were over. According to her, she was focused on her new business adventures and so was Mrs. Krisha Robinson.

"I had a business relationship with Jaylin Rogers," Krisha said, already sitting near the front. "Let's just say that things got a bit sticky between me and Jaylin, but we managed to work it out."

I was almost ready for intermission and this thing with Jaylin was starting to worry me more. I was getting tired of defending his actions, and after what Krisha revealed, I was left shaking my head...

Sticky Situation

Krisha Robinson

I spotted him from a distance, eating lunch at The Capital Grille. After the Rib-eye steak sandwich with cheese, he looked stuffed and wiggled his silk tie away from his neck. I watched his sexy lips press against the glass as he drank from it, then he flagged down a waitress. She approached, dropping the receipt stamped PAID on the table. I could see him mouth the words that he hadn't paid for his dinner yet, but the waitress turned in my direction. "It was paid for by the woman at the bar. The one with the purple on," she said, walking away.

I saw him peek around the waitress to take a look, but all I did was smile. He nodded, then dropped a measly quarter on the table. I sure as heck knew why because the waitress had a very snobby attitude and didn't deserve one penny. I guess he was willing to give her way more than her services were worth.

I tilted my glass to my lips to drink, while crossing my long legs. My ass hugged the barstool like it was a best friend, and the lavender skirt I wore stopped mid thigh high. I was a petite woman, but my assets were all in the right place, especially my cleavage that busted through my fitted jacket. By the smell of masculine cologne, I knew he was getting near, so I quickly turned my head and smiled. I wondered if he'd known what I was thinking all throughout lunch, but then again, as wide as his smile was...what had he been thinking?

He took a seat next to me at the bar, and moved his jacket back as he slipped his hand into his pocket. I'd already seen the wedding ring, so I hoped like hell he wasn't trying to disclose it. Without opening his mouth yet, he glanced into my piercing brown eyes and I looked into his grey ones. My throat was a little dry, so I cleared it, then used my hand to swing back my shoulder length brown hair with blonde streaks. I pushed the empty glass away from in front of me and proceeded to kick up a conversation.

"Did you enjoy lunch?" I asked, with my eyes searching all over him. Sexy, sexy, sexy was all I could think to myself.

"Yes, I did, but you didn't have to take care of it for me. Thanks, though, and I would somehow or someway love to repay you."

I surely knew how he could repay me, but when he removed his hand from his pocket, the diamond wedding ring flashed at me.

"You're welcome, but let me think about how I want you to repay me, okay?"

A slow nod followed. "So, uh, do you always come here and buy strangers food?"

"No, not always, but since you were sooo sexy, I had to show you how much I appreciate a man with good looks and pay for your meal. Is there something wrong with that?"

"Nothing is wrong with it, but usually when someone is that nice to me, they want something in return. Tell me what that may be?"

I looked down at the floor, then my eyes shifted to him and said it all. I hoped my thoughts were transmitting for me, just so I didn't have to be blunt about what I really wanted him to do for me. I placed my hand on top of his, then flipped it over. Using the tip of my finger, I made small circles in his palm. "Let's see," I said, wetting my lips. "What is it that I want from you? For starters, what's your name?"

"Jaylin. Jaylin Rogers," he said, looking at what I was circling into his palm. Seconds later, he lifted his head and called for the bartender.

"Jaylin, I'm Krisha Robinson. Nice to meet you."

"Same here." The bartender came over and Jaylin ordered Remy, no ice and also a Long Island Iced Tea for me.

His eyes teased me by trailing down my shapely legs. "So, sexy lady, you only addressed part of my question. I know the only thing that you wanted from me wasn't just a name."

"No, but it's a start. We have to start somewhere, don't we?"

"Absolutely, but we start by you answering my questions, then I'll be willing to answer yours."

The bartender placed the Long Island Tea in front of me and I removed the cherry from it. The tip of my tongue rolled around it, then I quickly sucked it into my mouth, feeling a burst of juices explode. I swear I saw Jaylin's dick jump, and he was definitely tuned in.

"Stop teasing me," he whispered. "I love to be played with, but only in a good way."

"I wasn't teasing you. Besides, since you're married, and I'm married, too, I think its best that we just sit here and talk." I wiggled my fingers in his face, just in case he didn't notice my wedding ring.

He grabbed my hand and lightly squeezed my fingers, covering my ring. "That's not a problem for me, and I have a feeling that you don't care much about my status either. Talking can lead to other things, you know, so let's...talk."

I pulled my hand away and took another swallow from my Long Island Tea. Jaylin's Remy had been put in front of him, and he guzzled it down quickly.

"I have a place not too far from here," I blurted out. "We can go there."

"I have a 3:00 p.m. meeting. Will we be done by then?"

"That depends on you."

I dropped a fifty dollar bill on the bar, insisting that I pay for our drinks. Instead, Jaylin gave the bartender his black card, and after Jaylin paid, we were well on our way.

Walking to our cars, I walked ahead of Jaylin and I could feel his eyes watching me. I couldn't blame him, though, cause my strut was capable of turning plenty of heads. He had some head turning going on, too, and he was dressed in a tailored, probably, Adrian Jules suit, grey-like that matched his eyes. The expensive looking leather shoes he wore gave him the smell of mega money, and his "rich man's" aura increased when he stepped up to a black Mercedes.

"Follow me," I said, walking up to my white Corvette ZR1. I let the top down, and put my hair into a ponytail before I sped off.

121

Twenty minutes later, we pulled up at the Yacht Club at Brickell Apartments. I released my hair from the ponytail, and got out of the car. Jaylin parked right beside me, so I walked over and opened his car door.

"This way Jaylin," I directed. He was only a few steps behind me, talking business over the phone. When we reached the door, I couldn't help but ask what he did for a living.

He removed his sunglasses, checking out the surrounding that I assumed impressed him. "I'm retired," he confessed. "But it doesn't mean that I've stopped making money."

"That must be nice. I wish my husband would retire," I said, opening the door.

My place was decorated in black and white, with splashes of red here and there. It was more modern than anything and black carpet covered the floors. A small forest of plants was growing in one corner, and a huge book case lined with African American literature was against the white walls. A 46 inch flat screen T.V. was mounted on the wall and I had over 200 DVD's neatly stacked on an entertainment center.

"Make yourself comfortable on the couch," I said to Jaylin. "Can I get you something else to drink?"

He removed his jacket and took a seat on the couch. "No thanks. I've had enough to drink already."

I sat next to him on the couch. "Me too. Besides, we didn't come here to do anymore drinking, did we?"

Jaylin eased his arms around me, slowly moving his hand up and down my back. The feel of his touch aroused me and I felt my breasts, of all things, get tight.

"Do you mind if we take this to the bedroom?" I asked.

Jaylin stood and moved aside so I could lead the way.

My bedroom was the best part of the place. It was still flowing with black, white and red colors. The linen on my king bed was black, and there were white and red pillows on top. An even bigger T.V. was mounted on the wall, and a small coffee table with crystal elephants sat in front of two leather chairs. Silk and lacy curtains draped from the windows that displayed an awesome view of the blue ocean. Jaylin walked over to the window, and stood for a moment, gazing outside. He looked to be in deep thought, so I stepped in front of him to get his attention. "How about a nickel for your thoughts?" I asked.

"I thought it was a penny?"

"Pennies sound too cheap and I would pay any amount of money to get into your head."

"You can get into my head for free, especially if you choose the correct one."

"I will. And with those words, it wouldn't surprise me if you could get in the draws of a nun. Your eyes come with benefits, too. They're almost mesmerizing."

Jaylin smirked. "We should start our talk, or I'll be late for my three o'clock meeting."

I took his hand, moving him over to a chair to take a seat. I sat on his lap and put my arms around his broad shoulders. "What do you want to talk about?" I asked.

"About how you're going to let me have my way with you? When I'm done, you can have your way with me."

"You bet I will," I said, standing up in front of him. I didn't have on any panties, and after I hiked up my skirt a bit, I gave Jaylin a glimpse of what he was about to get into. Leaning forward, I pecked down his neck, and rapidly ran my fingers through his curly hair. I stared into those mesmerizing eyes, and started to unbutton his shirt. Exposing his chest, I planted juicy kisses that went down to his belly button.

"Stand for me, please," I asked. He stood up, and I squatted to unbutton his slacks. Along with his boxers, I pulled them down to his ankles. His long ass heavy dick nearly slapped me in the face, but that was perfectly fine with me.

"I had a feeling that I would like what I'd see. Not only are you fine as hell, but you're working with something very extraordinary."

He blushed and touched the tip of his head, massaging it. "You're fine, too, but I'm anxious to see more of what that pussy can do for me."

I nudged my head towards the bed. "Then go sit on the bed and I'll show you."

Jaylin made his way over to the bed, watching me as I unzipped my skirt. I let it fall to the floor, then unbuttoned my blouse, leaving it in a pile next to my feet. I stood before Jaylin with nothing but my bra and shoes on.

"That's nice," he said while stroking himself. "But, uh, can you come help me with this?"

I stepped out of my shoes and made my way over to the bed. My body slithered against Jaylin's and I rested between his legs. His hands roamed on my ass, and I could tell he liked the soft feel of it. In knowing so, I turned around, just so he could get a closer look. I had a scorpion tattooed above my crack with the numbers 11-06 under it. He tapped his dick against my ass and the hardness of it made me eager.

"I'm about to make that scorpion dance," he assured.

"I hope so."

I unhooked my bra, then turned back around to face him. He held my breasts, then rubbed his hands along the sides of my hourglass figure. The only fat I had on me was on my ass. My abs were solid like his, only feminine. I leaned forward, planting more trails of kisses down his chest and stomach. My hands massaged his shaft and when I looked down at it, I started to inspect it. It was definitely to my likings and before tackling it, I took a deep breath, gearing myself to go all in. I sucked in about nine inches, then tightened my throat. My velvety tongue ran along his shaft, then made way to the tip. I purposely sucked him lightly, then the suction of my mouth got stronger and harder. A pleasing moan escaped from Jaylin's mouth and he watched my every move.

"Damn, the way you going at it, it must taste like chicken," he chuckled.

I laughed, pausing for a few seconds. "I don't think I've ever heard that one before, but whatever it is, it damn sure tastes good."

I smiled and immediately got back to the business at hand. While my mouth and tongue worked his head, my hand stroked his pole. My other hand was stroking my kitty, right along with Jaylin's hand. I could feel the juices running between my legs, only because his thick fingers felt like a dick.

"Your mouth is scorching hot and wet," he said, moaning from pure pleasure. "I love how you treating this muthafucka."

His words inspired me to go faster and faster, but he put his hands on my bobbing head to slow me down. That affected me in no way, and I kept on my mission to make him cum.

"Are you ready, Jaylin?"

"Yessss," he barely uttered. His body jolted and his hot lava poured over my hand as it oozed out. Allowing him a few seconds to re-energize, I got off the bed and made my way over to the dresser. I retrieved a condom and used my mouth to roll it down his dick. I straddled his lap, then bent down to whisper in his ear.

"You have to make this good to me, Jaylin."

He reached for the back of my hair and pulled it back so he could see my face. "One less worry...I will."

After much teasing, Jaylin was in a rush to get inside of me. He eased in, causing me to wheeze right away. My pussy was too tight for him, but it was sopping wet, so that helped. It was one very Sticky Situation. I let go of my tight grasp on him, attempting to make the pain a little easier.

"I don't do this often," I admitted. "I have to get used to something this big, so bear with me."

"I understand," Jaylin said, waiting for me to move.

My pace started off gradual, then with the help of his timed movements, it increased. Jaylin put his hands on my hips, starting to plunge faster into me.

"Cette bite es bonne," I spat, knowing that he had no idea what I'd said.

"Yeah, whatever, baby. Just...just keep working that pussy."

I leaned forward, pressing my dime sized nipples against his lips.

"Bite it a little. That's what I said."

He honored my request and took soft bites at my nipples. He laced them with saliva and plucked them too. I moaned repeatedly, while riding him like a slow moving mechanical bull. Jaylin's hardness kept rubbing against my clit, and each time he grazed it, the tingling feeling inside of me took over.

"I'M CUMMING!" I shouted out loud and pulled on the sheets. My muscles clamped down on his dick hard and I was breathless. Tears rushed to my eyes. "Thank you, Jaylin. You don't know how much this means to me."

He looked stunned by my actions. "I...is something wrong?"

"Nothing is wrong. Everything is excellent. I just don't get this kind of treatment everyday and I'm grateful for your efforts. Now it's your turn."

"You should demand this kind of treatment, after all, you're damn sure worth it. Now it's my turn for what?" he skeptically asked, but played with my nipples that were at his face.

"Time for you to have your way with me. Where do you want me?" I asked.

He smiled with glee in his eyes. "I want you bending over that chair."

No questions asked, I bent over the chair and spread my legs far apart. Jaylin stood behind me, but just for the hell of it, I reached down and grabbed my ankles. He went in with force, fucking me from many different angles. My legs were wobbly, but he kept his arm around my waist to keep me in position.

"Oh, yeah, Jay. That feels soooo good."

This time, he moved faster and was hitting his mark hard. I threw my pussy back to him and the rhythm we had was perfect.

"Smack my ass!" I yelled. "Jay, smack my ass hard!"

He smacked my ass hard, then massaged a good chunk of it with his hot hand. I knew my ass had turned red and the scorpion tattooed on my backside was probably doing the Stanky Leg. I looked back to see Jaylin, but his eyes were shut. I closed mine too, and started to speak another language. "Cette bite est bonne. Votre femme a de la chance. Oh hell yeah, baby, fuck me harder!"

Jaylin hit against me so hard that it sounded like we were clapping.

"I'M CUMMING!" I announced again.

He pulled out of me, watching my creamy juices roll down my thighs. I needed a second to drink some wine, regroup...something, but Jaylin turned me around to face him. He picked me up and wrapped my long legs around his waist. He entered me, and wasted no time catching his rhythm.

I was on a serious high, and my eyes rolled so far back in my head, hiding my pupils. My coochie muscles were moving one by one, up and down on his shaft. He grabbed my ass, vigorously moving me towards his thrusts. I had to do something about this to help calm down the intenseness. With my arms on his shoulders, I leaned forward to nibble his ears. "Jaylin, Jaylin, Jaylin. How could you do me like this?" was all I could say.

He walked us over to the bed, carefully laying me down. While still in between my legs, he massaged my breasts together. He sucked my nipples, and his magic stick brought back the action again. Our tongues did a little dance, and even I couldn't believe just how incredible this was. Yes, I was on the verge of coming again. My toes curled and I reached for the sheets.

"Ooooh shit!" I screamed. "Why in the hell have you been so good to me?"

"Cause I like being Naughty," he said, kissing my cheek.

For a while, we laid there in silence. I swerved my fingers down his chest and turned sideways to look at him. "Well, Jaylin, you gave me everything I wanted and needed. Thank you very much and I couldn't have asked for more."

He kissed my forehead. "Same here."

I stood and turned around when I heard him laughing.

"What's so funny?" I asked.

He got up and wrapped his arms around me from behind. His chin dropped to my shoulder and he whispered in my ear. "You have a big ole red handprint on your ass." He had the nerve to smack it again.

"No problem. I guess you had to leave your mark, right?"

"I guess so. But where can I go clean up at? I guess you know I'm already late for my three o'clock meeting."

"You can freshen up in the bathroom down the hall. If I'm not out when you're done, you can let yourself out."

I made my way to one bathroom, while Jaylin went into another. As I washed my body, all I could think about was what had happened. That was some of the best dick I'd had, and unfortunately for me, by the time I came out of the bathroom, Jaylin was gone. I put on my clothes, and hurried to my appointment that I had scheduled with my husband.

When I arrived at my husband's office, he was the only one there. He was considered one of the wealthiest men in Miami, but his sex wasn't worth a damn. What attracted me to him was the fact that money seeped from his pores. Even today, he wore a pinstriped Armani suit, diamond cuff links, and a monogrammed shirt. Black Gators were on his feet and he would never leave home without them.

Since his clients hadn't arrived yet, I went to the restroom. And by the time I made it back, two of his clients had arrived. I peeked in the door, getting the shock of my life. My heart raced and I couldn't believe my eyes. They had to be playing tricks on me. There stood Jaylin and another man, shaking my husband's hand. Seems like I'd gotten myself into another Sticky Situation, but this one may not be as much fun as the one from earlier today.

Instead of entering the room, I stayed outside of the door to listen. "Fellas," my husband said. "I asked my C.O.O. to attend this meeting also, but she went to the restroom. Can we wait about five more minutes?"

"Sure, no problem," the other man responded.

"Can I get either of you anything while we wait?"

"No thank you," Jaylin said.

They took their seats and I was in a panic about what to do. Wasn't sure if Jaylin would say anything or not, but he didn't seem like the type who would put me on blast. Still, I waited for a few more minutes, listening to them talk about sports, cars, stocks and money. I knew my husband would come looking for me soon, so it was now or never. I took a deep breath, and finally made my way into the boardroom. With my red pants suit on, and Gator sandals, I was nervous as hell. My hair was in a neat bun, so I couldn't fidget with it. With all three men's eyes on me, I walked up to William, kissing him on the lips. He held my waist, then pulled back a chair for me.

"Have a seat," he said. "Fellas, this is my C.O.O., and also my wife Krisha Robinson. Babe, this is Shane Alexander and Jaylin Rogers."

"Hello Gentleman," I said, shaking Shane's hand first, then Jaylin's. I felt his finger make a circle in my palm. I smiled, pulling my hand back and returning to the seat next to my husband.

"Well Fellas," I said, opening the folder in front of me. "I have a hair appointment later today, so let's get to work." My husband and Shane dropped their heads to look at their folders. My eyes stayed glued with Jaylin's and when he winked, I winked back. All I couldn't think about was that good dick that he had just plunged into me, and I'm sure that the only thing on his mind right now was my pussy. I just hoped that he wouldn't thank my husband for *it* later.

The End

Book Club Meeting...

Krisha's story turned the tables a little bit, because not only were we discussing a cheating man, but also a cheating woman. Many married women weren't willing to admit that they had skeletons and Krisha was very brave for coming forward.

"I just needed some serious satisfaction," she said. "My husband is a wonderful man, but he doesn't take the time to please me like I need to be pleased. Sometimes, I feel so deprived and when I try to discuss how I feel, it goes in one ear and out the other. He may try something different for a week or two, then we go back to our boring sex life that I'm in no way happy with. I don't want to divorce him, simply because I do love him. A part of me feels guilty for what I did with Jaylin, then again, how can I feel guilty about satisfying myself?"

Several ladies expressed their issues with the exact same thing, and they, too, had cheated on their husbands. Some felt guilty, many didn't.

"These men should learn how to step up to the plate. I don't blame Krisha and she did what she had to do! I mean, men do it all the time, and let a woman fall short in the bedroom and see what he does. I was married for twenty-four years, and the last time I had some good dick was in 1985. One day I woke up and said enough is enough! I got myself a vibrator and we now live happily ever after," one woman admitted.

Everyone laughed and another woman asked Krisha if the scorpion had had any action since Jaylin.

"Not really, but I do have his cell phone number to call him. Being a business partner has great benefits and when I'm in the mood to go at it again, he is just a phone call away. Thing is, he put it on me! I'm good right now, but I won't be for long."

I had rarely known Jaylin to go back for seconds so I had to ask Krisha a question. "Say, Krisha. Do you have it like that where you can pick up the phone and he will come right over?"

"I believe so, Brenda, and he whispered to me that it would be our little secret."

"Yeah, he's good at wanting you to keep his secrets," a woman name La Shaun said out loudly. "But if my pussy could talk, she would tell it all!"

Oh boy, I thought. *Not another one*. This time she wasn't the one who was willing to do the talking, her vagina was...

If My Pussy Could Talk
Tamika Smith

Legs wide lips spread, waiting for Mr. Jaylin Rogers to taste me. As I lay back, I imagined what my pussy would say if she could speak? "Jaylin 'Bad Boy' Rogers come and get me!" is what she would yell.

Thinking back to the first day we met, I was as impatient then as I was now. I was just getting off of work. The elevator was full, so I backed up and waited for the next one. It was always like this on Fridays. Men rushing downstairs to the bar for happy hour, and women rushing out to their hair appointments, or doing some last minute shopping for the weekend. I considered myself to be a patient woman. I rush for no one or nothing, and my take on it was, it will be there when I get there. If not, it wasn't meant for me. *"If you're patient enough, something better will come along,"* Big Mama used to say. So, I stood, waiting for the next elevator, thinking of her words.

Exiting one of the conference rooms was my boss, Mr. Bourke, and his stock broker. They walked towards me, waiting for the elevator as well. They seemed to be in a deep conversation, allowing me a little time to glance over Mr. Stock Broker. From head to toe, this man was breathtaking. From the jet black curls on his head, to the silver grey eyes that you could lose your soul looking into, he was fabulous. He had the skin complexion of honey. As I looked at his wide shoulders, I knew he was a man of fitness. The way he was wearing a black Armani suit, I could tell it was tailored specifically for his body. I appreciated how the green shirt and tie brought out the fun and adventure to his suit. He was like a...a god and I couldn't stop staring.

The elevator doors opened, and I was the first to step in. Mr. Bourke and his stock broker followed, and the elevator quickly lit up with panty-dropping cologne. There wasn't a chance in hell Mr. Bourke was wearing it, and that addictive smell belonged to Mr. Sexy alone. As I stood in front of the two men, I could see them watching me from the corner of my eye. Almost immediately, Mr. Bourke spoke up, "Ms. Smith, how are you this evening?"

"Fine, Sir, and you?" I replied.

"I'm great, now that my stocks are doing well." He turned to his stock broker to introduce him. "This is my good friend and stock broker, Jaylin Rogers."

Damn, I thought. *What a sexy name for a fine ass man.* I extended my hand to shake his.

"Jaylin," Mr. Bourke continued. "This is our new realtor on board here at Bourke's Real Estate, La Shaun Smith."

I shook Jaylin's hand, looking into his soul stealing grey eyes. "Hello, Mr. Rogers, nice to meet you."

"The pleasure is all mine," he said in a deep and very masculine voice. Just hearing his voice made me trickle in my panties and I hadn't even released his hand yet. Finally, I did.

"Ms. Smith, would you be interested in speaking to someone about your investments?" Jaylin asked.

"I'm not sure, Mr. Rogers," I replied. Maybe not investments, but I surely had something else better in mind.

He reached into his pocket and I couldn't help but notice the diamond filled Rolex on his wrist. "Please call me Jaylin and leave the 'Sir' for Mr. Bourke." He patted the old man on the back and they both laughed.

"If you change your mind," he said, handing the card to me. "Or if you need *assistance* with anything else, here's my card. Feel free to call me."

I took his card, and he gave my hand a swiping touch. A dimple formed on his cheek and something about the whole exchange got me pretty hyped. The elevator doors opened and when the air hit me, it was like a slap on the face, telling me to snap out of it. I had to get out of there, because my body was doing things that it hadn't done in quite some time.

"Gentlemen, have a nice weekend," I rushed to say. Not waiting for a response, I walked away with a throbbing pussy. Just when I thought I was coming down from my high, I heard someone call my name. I turned, and only a few feet away stood Jaylin. For a second, I just had to stare and check out his swag. The way he walked...he strutted as if he owned the earth. Hell, the universe for that matter and he was so damn sexy. I swear, the closer he got to me, the wetter my panties got. By the time he reached me, I could feel the built up excitement running down my legs.

"Yes," I said, playing down my attraction to him. "Can I help you with something?"

He licked his lips and ran his fingers over his trimmed goatee. "I...I was wondering if you didn't have any plans for this evening, if I could take you to dinner?"

I was overly thrilled about his invitation, but I looked at my watch and smiled. "I have only known you for what five...maybe ten minutes and you're asking me to go on a date?"

He shrugged. "And? Yes, La Shaun, I'm asking you to go on a date. Correct me if I'm wrong, but I'm feeling a little something between us and I would love to see what it leads to."

He was so close to me that the fragrance of his cologne played with my nostrils. "You're right, Jaylin, and I'm feeling something, too. I would love to share an evening with you and I'm so glad you asked."

Jaylin followed me to the parking lot and I unlocked the door to my black Audi A8. Dressed in a loose miniskirt, I bent over to grab one of my business cards. The further I reached, the higher my skirt rose. I figured Jaylin's eyes were on me, so I wiggled my ass just a little bit more. Once I figured he'd seen enough, I stood and pressed my hands over my ass to fix my skirt.

"Red is one of my favorite colors," he said. I blushed because I knew he was talking about my red g-string.

"I'll have to remember that." I placed the card in his hand. "I guess I will see you around eight?"

He put the card in his pocket. "Sounds like a plan."

Jaylin moseyed away and I already knew tonight was going to be one hell of a night. I drove home with a serious smile on my face and when I got home, I couldn't stop thinking about what the night had in store for me. Going into my bedroom, I turned on my IPod and let Adina Howard play. I stepped out of my Dereon suit, swaying my hips to the beat of "Nasty Grind." I was wondering if Mr. Rogers was a freak. Would he like to watch me play with my pussy or would his eyes watch as I gave him head? *Oh, yes, I would love to show him my nasty grind,* I thought. I couldn't believe I was thinking about this man to this extent, especially since I didn't even know him.

"Sex Me" by R. Kelly was blasting loud through the speakers and I went into the bathroom. It was like the music was reading my mind. I stepped into the shower, playing with my nipples while the warm water sprayed on them. All I could think of was Jaylin's tongue teasing my hotspots. My hands eased between my legs, searching for my swollen clit. I closed my eyes, thinking of him and all that he could possibly do for me. *Oooooo, yes, Daddy, right there.* The rotations of my fingers felt so good, and it was only a matter of time before I was about to cum. *Yes, Daddy, harder...harder!* Ring! Ring! Ring! My eyes shot open and I was so disappointed that the phone had brought me back to reality. I realized that it wasn't Jaylin turning his thick fingers inside of me, but it was me, giving my own self much pleasure.

Shit! I thought, covering myself with a towel and stepping out of the shower. *A sister needs some dick bad.* I snatched up the phone, upset at the person who continued to call.

"Hello," I snapped.

"Say, baby. This is Jaylin. Just calling to see if we're still on for tonight?"

Hell yes we were, but I didn't want to scream it to the world. Instead, I remained calm with a warming smile on my face. "I just stepped out of the shower, but..."

"It looks like I caught you at the right time then."

Shit if you only knew! Did I just say that out loud? I hoped not. "Yes you did catch me at the right time."

"Good. Then we can get this date started now, if you'd like?"

"I would like that, but truth be told, our date started when I was in the shower. Let's just say you were satisfying me beyond my

135

wildest dream and I was very...overly pleased." I couldn't believe I was talking to him like this. I had never rushed at anything, and here I was talking about sexing a man I had just met today.

"Well, baby, let me wrap up some business and I'll be there in about an hour."

"Okay and I'll be waiting."

Hanging up the phone with my pussy humming from hearing his voice, I returned to the bathroom. I kept debating with myself, questioning if I really wanted to have sex with a man I had just met. I thought long and hard, and thinking about it only made me hornier.

"Fuck it," I said, throwing my hands up in the air. "I'm about to turn this date and the man that I now know as Jaylin upside down."

I had a little under an hour to turn my bedroom into a sex haven. I knew this would be a date of a lifetime, so I had to give him something to remember me by. That would include my Double D's, my phat ass and luscious sweet tunnel that would taste like the sweetest thing he'd ever known. Oh, yes, he would come back for more and I'd make sure of that!

With my bedroom done, music programmed, chocolate covered strawberries and whip cream on the nightstand...champagne chilling, and lights dimmed, I would say I was ready. I was debating on if I should put on some clothes or stay naked. I decided on an appealing black and red baby doll nightie that I had just purchased from Fredrick's of Hollywood. While looking in the mirror, I sat on the bed, putting on strawberries and cream lotion. I knew Jaylin would love my perky breasts and appreciate my small waistline and mouth watering thighs. When I stood to check out the final package, my doorbell rang. My heart jumped to my stomach, and I admit that I had a few butterflies. No sooner than I opened the door, those butterflies flew out the window. There stood Jaylin, looking like he was straight off the cover of GQ Magazine. All I could think was... *yeah, we're fucking tonight!*

With a sexy grin, he moseyed in. "Love the nightie and it damn sure looks good on you."

They say patience is virtue, but just looking at him, I wanted to strip him down and start fucking him right away. Never had I been this impatient to screw somebody. He saw the keen look in my eyes and already knew dinner wouldn't be on the menu tonight.

"So, uh, I guess we're not having dinner, right?" he asked.

I gave him a wink and wandered back to my bedroom, hoping he would follow. He did. Once we were in my room, my arms fell on his shoulders. "If you don't mind, I thought we could skip dinner and go straight to dessert."

With his eyes secured with mine, he backed up and started to remove his jacket. I could see his biceps coming through his shirt and his body was picture perfect. I couldn't resist swirling my hands down his washboard abs, and the feel of him made me seal my eyes. I felt his butter-soft lips touch mine and his tongue tasted superior. My eyes opened and I slowly traced his lips with my tongue. I felt his hands inching up my nightie, but he was in for a surprise, because I didn't have on any panties. All he touched was bare ass, and that caused him to pace me backwards towards the bed.

"Damn, baby, I need to taste you right now," he whispered and carefully laid me on the bed.

"Well, Daddy, wait no more. Go ahead and taste it!"

Easing up my nightie, I could feel Jaylin's hands on my thighs, to my stomach. The way he caressed my breasts, I was ready to explode. Still, I wanted more.

"Jaylin, please hurry. My swelling lips are begging to be touched by your tongue, and I can't wait much longer."

With the sexiest smile ever, he parted my legs and dropped to his knees. "I love when a woman begs for it. That shit turns me the fuck on."

I couldn't believe I was begging for this man to satisfy me. I had learned when it came to Jaylin, my patience was gone. Once I felt his cool breath blowing on my clit, I knew ecstasy was on its way. My pussy was throbbing in one succulent lick, causing me to clinch the silk sheets. "Oh, Jay, that feels so good, Daddy, don't stop. Please don't stop."

He wanted me to beg, so I did. As he continued to feast up on me, I could feel my first orgasm coming down. "Yes, Daddy, right there! Don't stop, gotdamn-it that's my spot! I'm about to cuumm!!

A tingling feeling rocked my entire body. The more he slurped my interior walls, the more I came undone. I came with so much force I had the bed shuddering. Never have I had an orgasm so intense and Jaylin's tongue was ferocious!

"Are you ready for part two?" he asked.

Hell, if part two was anything like this, then hell yeah! He rose from the floor to take off his pants and immediately my pussy felt withdrawals. I wanted him so bad. I was a fiend, needing my fix and Jaylin was my drug. When he took off his belt, I could see the rising bulge. Daddy was packing a load, and if my pussy could speak she would say, "come and get me Daddy."

Jaylin let his pants and boxers fall to the ground, then he put his wallet and condoms on the nightstand. He lay on the bed and it was my turn to have him climbing the walls. Jay Baby looked like a god lying in my bed. His smooth honey skin felt like silk, and being able to hold his monstrous dick in my hand was priceless.

"Baby, close your eyes and enjoy," I suggested, straddling him. I began at the top of his head with kisses, his curls so soft I could smell his shampoo. I made my way down to his ears, whispering promises I knew I would keep. "This pussy is yours...however you want it, you can have it...whatever Jay Baby wants, he gets."

He let out a moan, so sexually charged that I knew he liked my choice of words. Moving my way to his neck, I licked and sucked feather lightly. His manly fragrance began to stimulate me.

"Move forward, baby," he said. I moved forward, sitting on his upper chest. "No, you're not close enough."

I shrugged. Wha...what exactly do you want me to do?"

"I want you to sit that sweet muthafucking pussy on my lips so I can have another taste."

Well, damn. Didn't he just suck it? Seeing his dick long and hard made me too hungry for it. I wanted to see how far it could dip into me, as well as sample it with my mouth. For now, I didn't honor Jaylin's request. I made my way down south, hoping that he wouldn't trip.

"Daddy, you already had your way with me. Now it's my turn to have my way with you."

"That will never happen," he boasted. "But I'm damn sure going to watch you try."

Before he could say another word to me, I put his package in my mouth. The feel of it being pushed into my mouth was challenging. I had to pull back some and catch my breath. I began to lick and caress his manhood with ease. Loving the groaning sounds he was making, I went a little further by adding his balls to the mix. Jaylin lifted his head and pulled at my hair.

"Shit! What are you doing to me?" he inquired. Giving no response, I continued to give his balls pleasure. "Baby, you're going to make me cum and I'm not ready for that."

I wasn't ready for him to cum either, as we definitely had the whole night ahead of us. I stood and grabbed a condom from the nightstand. I ripped it open and applied it with my mouth. My pussy was screaming to feel him and it neared satisfaction when I straddled his lap. He positioned his muscle, and as I carefully slid down on him, I could feel my interior wet walls squeezing him. We sighed from the electrical feeling and it was time for us to put in the extra labor. Never had I been so impatient for a man when it came to sex, but Jaylin "Bad Boy" Rogers was turning my world inside out, and upside down. Needless to say, we fucked, and screwed and sucked...the entire night away!

The End

Book Club Meeting . . .

"I'm exhausted," I said, dropping back in my seat. "And Jaylin should be, too. LaShaun it seems as if you made the investment that you were looking for and I hope it paid off."

"In a major way," she smiled. "I'm back to being patient again, but that was one day that everything turned into a rush-rush situation for me. My coochie couldn't get enough of that man, and *she's* still talking about him."

"Mine would be too," a lady yelled and chuckled. "But Ms. Hampton I have a question for you. LaShaun mentioned masturbation in her story, but I don't see you writing much about it in yours. If the women can't get Jaylin to act right, why not show some scenes where the women seek pleasure from themselves? Personally, I love to please myself and can't no one do it better than me. Passion Parties...Doctor Johns, I'm into all of that stuff. I love being creative and appreciate authors like Zane who encourage women to be free and explore their inner freak."

Many ladies clapped and concurred with what the woman had said. I did, too, but there was something about me that she needed to know. "I love and respect all that Zane does and she's a very unique author that no one can duplicate. She broke down barriers so that writers like me can feel comfortable writing what we do, but I have a different approach to writing than she does. As for masturbation, the truth is I can't write about something I don't know about. Honestly, I couldn't even tell you where to begin, and masturbation is one subject I am clueless on. I don't get it and I don't see how I can go about pleasing my own self. Don't think I'm crazy, please, but I just can't see a vibrator doing anything for me."

"What?" one lady shouted. "You mean to tell me you be writing allllll that freaky stuff in those books and you are clueless about masturbation? I don't believe that, Ms. Hampton, and with Jaylin constantly in your thoughts, I don't see how that's possible."

"I have no problem speaking the truth, and are there any women in the audience who are as clueless about this subject as I am?" Very few women raised their hands, and the others talked to us about how much *action* we were missing out on. I guess you had to be willing to explore things that you didn't know much about, but there wasn't no telling when I would get to that point. The conversation went on for a while and LaShaun had even given us a few pointers. I took notes, after all, we were here learning from each other. So much that when another lady stepped forward, giving advice on riding, we thought she was speaking about her motorcycle. Instead, she was referencing Jaylin. My worries were growing by the minute, as Taji admitted to giving Jaylin the ride of his life....

Ride' em

Taji Hines-Kirby

When Taji pulled up to the annual Ruff Ryders event in St Louis, in the middle of August, the temperature must have been 100 degrees. With all of her riding equipment on, the temp felt well over 115 degrees. Taji pulled her MV Augusta F4CC powder blue custom made Suzuki GSX-R motorcycle into an empty parking spot, noticing two gentlemen standing at a vendor booth. The attractive men were checking out different types and newer models of bikes. Taji thought as she walked away, *I will have to make sure I stop at the vendor booth before leaving today.* When she removed her helmet, her long flowing curls fell down her back and a few fell in front of her face. Her skin was kissed with just the right amount of sun, making her look even more like the black and Dominican female that she was.

Curious, she looked back at the two gentlemen she'd noticed before, observing that they had moved closer to her bike. She could tell they were fascinated by it. She finished her water, deciding to go back and talk to them. Looking the men over from head to toe, Taji noticed that the taller of the two men was one of the finest men she had seen in a long time.

"Hello," she said smiling, as she walked up to the men. She addressed the one who had her attention.

Surprised, Jaylin turned to her. "I'm Jaylin. Jaylin Rogers. But, uh, am I in your way?"

Taji's grin got wider, as she noticed how much finer the man was closer up. "As a matter of fact, you are in my way."

Jaylin placed one hand on his chest, the other hand in the air. "I apologize, Miss Lady. My bad." He studied Taji's frame that was a work of art, liking what was in his view. "I assume this is your bike?"

Taji slightly grinned and flirted with her alluring eyes. "Yes, that is my bike. Why do you ask? Would you like for me to teach you how to ride it?"

Not to be outdone, Jaylin looked over at his friend, Shane, and tapped his arm. "Man, she wants to give me lessons on how to *ride* a motorcycle. What do you think about that?"

Shane shrugged. "I don't think you can go wrong with that. I say go ahead and give it a try."

Jaylin looked back at Taji, touching the goatee that fit his chin well. "Naw baby, no lessons, but I'll tell you what. Maybe I can teach you a few other things about riding."

"I don't think there is much more that you can teach a professional."

Jaylin was quick to respond. "Oh, so you're a *professional* motorcycle rider, huh? Well if you are a professional, then I think I would have heard of you before. And before I forget to ask, what is your name?"

Taji extended her hand. "It's a pleasure to meet you, Jaylin. My name is Taji and my rewards and trophies speak for themselves."

Jaylin shook Taji's hand and nodded. "I see. What else are you a professional at?"

"I'm a Sports and Entertainment attorney in Los Angles. According to my clients, they say I handle my profession very well."

Jaylin responded with a raised eyebrow, "I'm impressed. Would it be possible for me to take you out later for a drink, dinner, movie or a ride?"

Taji sighed, and even though she was a bit tired, she definitely didn't want to let an opportunity like this one pass her by. Then again, she knew that without much rest, she wouldn't be good company. "I've had a very long day, Jaylin, and I wouldn't be very good company tonight. So, maybe some other time, and it was nice meeting you."

Taji walked away, leaving Jaylin to wonder about a sexy woman he for surely wanted to see again.

The next morning, Taji went for a sweat dripping jog. After showering, she looked into the mirror, more than satisfied with her hour glass figure. She had jogged every morning, and for a thirty-four year old, she was more than satisfied with everything about her. She had the looks of a supermodel, and her 5ft. 7in. frame had curves in all of the right places. Her hair was charcoal black with golden bronze highlights, and her caramel skin was smooth as butter. Her eyes were slightly slanted, and almost looked as if she had some Asian in her family. Needless to say, she was packaged up very well, and had worked hard at perfecting her looks.

When Taji arrived at her father's house for lunch the next day, she whispered in her mother Sabana's ear, "Does Dad have a clue about his surprise birthday party tonight?"

Her mother looked at Taji, putting her finger on her lips to shush her so her dad wouldn't hear them talking. "Not a clue," she whispered.

Later that night, the house was all set for Taji's father's 60th surprise birthday party. When her father walked in, everyone yelled, "SURPRISE!!" His face lit up with joy, especially after seeing his family and some of his colleagues he hadn't seen in years, either because they had retired or moved away to practice another branch of the law. Surprisingly, and unbeknownst to Taji, Jaylin was standing out by the pool in the backyard, taking a business call. Shane was also there, chatting with some old friends that had also known Taji's father. Like always, Jaylin was dressed to impress in a Brooks Brothers suit and shiny black leather shoes. His cologne lit up the area, causing several of the women to take double...triple looks. With all of the attention, he was guaranteed a piece of pussy that night.

Taji had two glasses of white wine, and by the third glass, she had loosened up a bit. She strutted down the t-staircase, wearing a fitted cream colored dress that exposed her bare back. A pair of Christian Louboutin heels matched her dress perfectly. When Jaylin finished his call, he noticed Taji standing with her back towards him. His grey eyes zoned in on her backside, and his tongue rolled from one side of his lips to the other as he licked them. *Damn,* he thought, noticing right away that it was the woman he had come in contact with yesterday. *I refuse to let her get away from me tonight,* he thought.

Jaylin went up to Taji, taking a closer look to confirm that it was really her. "Long time no see, Miss Lady," he said, with a flute wine glass in his hand. He sipped from the glass, hoping that Taji's taste would be sweeter than the wine.

Taji smiled a nonchalant smile, but inside she was grinning wide. They spoke briefly, but flirted with each other throughout the night.

By one o'clock in the morning, the party had wrapped up, and everyone vacated the premises, including Taji's parents. Jaylin, however, was waiting to pounce on his prey. Taji sat out by the pool, looking as if she were in deep thought. When Jaylin walked up to her, all he could say was, "it looks like you have something heavy on your mind."

"No, not at all," she replied, untruthfully. "But would you still like to have that drink with me?"

"Absolutely. I thought you'd never ask."

Jaylin sat in one of the lawn chairs, watching Taji as she walked away to get his drink. Almost instantly, his dick got hard just from checking her out in her white bikini that she had changed into. Her cleavage was so inviting and the way her plump ass poked out of her bottoms, he was in a trance.

Taji turned, noticing the gaze in his eyes. "I forgot to ask. What are you drinking?"

"Remy, no ice."

Moments later, Taji came back with a glass of wine for her and a shot of Remy for Jaylin. They talked, laughed, and yet again, flirted with each other for hours. Neither realized that it was after 3:00 a.m., and they were glad to be alone. Being tipsy, and the mix of good jazz music by Ken Ford, helped set the mood. Anyone would have thought they were a couple by how comfortable they looked with each other.

"I need to go inside for a minute," Taji said, excusing herself.

"Hurry," was all Jaylin could say. He was more than ready to take things to the next level.

When Taji came back out, she had on a more revealing bikini that showed off her voluptuous body that Jaylin had been thinking about all night. Taji sauntered by him, diving into the pool. The water splashed, and when she came up, she rubbed back her long wet hair, looking at Jaylin.

"Aren't you coming in?" she asked seductively with her eyes, and not necessarily her mouth.

Jaylin sat on the lawn chair, definitely ready for some action. Still, he was in a teasing mood. "Not yet, baby. You seem to be having a really good time without me. Maybe I should pass."

Taji shrugged and got ready to swim away. "Suit yourself."

The next time Taji came up for air, she had taken off her bikini top and threw it at Jaylin. Still, he sat composed and unfazed. Taji got out of the pool, working her hips and going up to him. She straddled him on the lawn chair, moving her face very close to his. As they eyed each other's lips, she pecked his and ran her finger along the side of his face.

"You are a very handsome man. I've had my eyes on you since the Ruff Ryders event and couldn't stop thinking about you last night."

"I usually have that kind of affect on women and what you said doesn't surprise me."

"Really?" Taji said, paying no mind to his arrogance. She leaned forward, guiding Jaylin's hands to grip her ass cheeks and giving him a lengthy kiss that seemed to last forever. She then rested her arms on his shoulders, and moved her hips in slow circles. While grinding down on him, she felt what seemed like a mammoth dick through his slacks. He became anxious and she could tell by the lustful look in his eyes.

"I seem to have an affect on many men, in the same way you do women."

Jaylin stuck his fingers in between her legs, moving the crotch section of her bikini bottoms to the side. His fingers polished her clit, which made her jump with excitement. Seeing her so aroused, Jaylin kept manipulating her clit and then stuck his finger into her pussy to stir her wetness. Taji let out a light moan, letting Jaylin know that her pussy was ready for him to enter it. She backed away from his finger fucking festivities and stood up.

"I'm getting back into the pool. Are you coming?" she asked.

Jaylin stood, removing all of his clothes. He eased into the crystal clear water, moving face-to-face with Taji. The look into each other's eyes was powerful, but Taji waited for Jaylin to make the next move. He wrapped her legs around his waist and entered her already wet pussy. Round one wrapped up quickly, and before Round two got started, Taji got out of the pool and sashayed to the bar. She got them more drinks and sat down on the edge of the pool so they could finish their conversation. The conversation didn't last for long because Jaylin had opened her legs again. Her beautifully shaven slit was fully exposed, leaving him in a trance. Taji lifted Jaylin's chin, breaking his lustful stares between her legs.

"What?" she said. "Why are you looking like you've never seen a pussy before?"

"Oh, I've seen plenty before, but I'm looking because I can tell that you really take care of yourself. I like that."

Taji laughed and splashed water in his face. She then lay back on the ground near the edge of the pool. Jaylin got out and laid a towel on the ground so he could relax on it. He pulled Taji on top of him and she gave him a heart racing ride that made his body weaken. She rode him while looking into his eyes and watching them roll to the back of his head. Even backwards, while leaning back with her hands rested on his chest, she gave him pleasure. The scenery for him was priceless, and as she grinded her pussy on him, he looked defeated.

"Daaaamn, baby," he panted. "You gon break my dick in half, riding it so tough like that. Take it eeeeasy."

Taji ignored Jaylin's request and continued to work him over. Minutes later, they moved over to a chair. Jaylin stood behind Taji with one of her hands stretched behind his head. She massaged his wet curls, and using both of his hands he cuffed her breasts, massaging them. She trembled all over, especially when he lowered his hands and fingered her pussy. Her soaking wetness proved that she was ready to go at it again, but he told her to put her heels back on so they could be the same height.

"Whyyy?" she moaned, enjoying his tantalizing touch.

"Because I want to have a perfect shot at that pussy for the next round."

Taji asked no more questions and stepped into her heels. Jaylin bent her slightly over from behind, and as flexible as Taji was, she held onto her ankles. At first, Jaylin was taking it easy on her, giving her slow and long strokes that reached the depths of her tunnel. Then, when she started to throw it back at him, it made him speed up his motion. Her bouncy curls fell and moved with each push that he gave her. He looked down at her heart shaped ass, giving it a slight tap. While watching it move, he bent over and whispered in her ear, "Is this one of your professions, too?"

Taji let out a chuckle, "I'll let you be the judge of that, Mister."

Within the next hour, they were beyond exhausted. Jaylin embraced Taji, holding her tightly in his arms as they lay together on a lawn chair. "How long will you be here in St. Louis?" he asked.

Taji lifted his wrist, looking at his watch. "I only have four more hours until I have to catch my plane back to Los Angeles."

"Well, I guess that means you have to get some sleep before you leave."

"If I go to sleep, I will surely miss my flight. Can I ask you for a favor?"

"Sure, you can ask me anything."

"Will you take me to the airport this morning?"

"I will do better than that. How about I wet that pussy one more time before you go, buy you breakfast, and then take you to the airport? I'll even wait with you, until your flight takes off."

We laughed, but I knew Jaylin was serious. "You are such a gentleman. I'm going to take you up on that offer."

"Somehow, I knew you would."

Taji and Jaylin continued their festivities inside. She ran a hot bath for herself and asked Jaylin if he would join her. There was no way for him to decline such an offer, especially from a woman who had put it on him like Taji had. Before they got in the tub, Taji stood in front of the mirror, putting her thick curly hair in a ponytail. Jaylin watched, noticing a tattoo on her hip that read ACE.

"Is ACE your boyfriend?" he asked.

Taji quickly spun around to answer him, "It's a little late for you to be asking if I have a boyfriend, don't you think? Besides, ACE is the name of my motorcycle."

Jaylin nodded and studied her naked body. "You are a very beautiful woman. I hope that when we get done with all of this fucking, I'll be able to see you again."

Taji pressed her body against his. "You can be sure of that and I'm looking forward to hearing from you again."

They kissed, and Jaylin picked her up, sitting her on the edge of the bathroom sink. He held her legs apart, while she braced herself for impact on the sink. Wanting another taste of Taji, he stuck his index and middle fingers inside of her moist hole, then pulled out. Licking his sticky fingers clean, he closed his eyes. "Sweet," he said, whispering in her ear. "Your pussy tastes like honey."

Jaylin turned into full-on-fuck mode, pounding Taji's pussy like sex was the last thing to do on earth. He gave her as much as she could take, causing her to feel every deep thrust that he brought her way. After awhile, she couldn't take it anymore. She almost succumbed to the feel of him, and when her legs began to throb, he knew that he was close to completing his mission.

"Jay Baby," she panted. "Please hold me tight and fuck me harder because I'm about to cum." Jaylin pulled back, watching the glaze that covered the tip of his dick as he rubbed against her clit in slow firm circles. They looked on with a high level of enthusiasm. The head-teasing was so intense for Taji, her entire frame tingled. The sensation made sweat beads form on her forehead, and as she lifted her ass slightly up off the sink, she circled her hips to make him enter her.

Jaylin was teasing her so well, making her eyes roll to the back of her head like he'd done earlier by the pool. He whispered to her, "Do you want me to put it back inside of your pussy? Tell

Daddy that you want my madness back inside of your sweet pussy, Taji? Tell me, baby, and I will give it back to you."

Taji let out a small scream and did what she needed to do to get him to give it back to her. "What Daddy wants, Daddy gets. Please give it back to me...I need it so badly right now."

Jaylin went in deeper, causing Taji to struggle to catch her breath. "Ok baby," he said. "Go ahead and give it to me. Show me how well you can coat my entire dick with your cream."

Taji grabbed him around the neck and tightly wrapped her legs around his back. They climaxed together, leaving both of them breathless. They soon calmed down, took a bath together, had breakfast and made their way to the airport. As they rode to the airport, Jaylin asked if he could visit Taji in a few weeks because he would be in L.A. on business.

"Of course you can. I would love to show you around and give you a lesson on how to handle my Augusta F4CC."

Jaylin put his hand to his chest, "That sounds like a plan. I would be honored for you to give me more lessons on how you 'ride' and this has been one hell of an experience."

Taji playfully hit him on the arm, "I was talking about the motorcycle, not how I rode you. But you're right...this has been an experience that I will never forget."

The End

Book Club Meeting . . .

Listening to Taji's story brought about an interesting discussion about preferred positions.

"Doggy-style," several ladies shouted.

"No, a six-nine position is the way to go!"

"I'd like to be walked like a dog like Veronique, but Jaylin could have me any way he wished."

Many felt the same, but like Taji, there were a lot of riders in the room. Many of these women said that being in that position allowed them to take control.

"It lets me know that I'm running the show," Taji said. "And it's so satisfying to watch a man lose himself in that position. You get to see those faces that he doesn't want you to see, and I love when a man comes in that position. If he's on top, trust me, many men will drop their heads to shield their faces. Now, I'm usually down for whatever, and seeing Jaylin's eyes roll to the back of his head was exciting."

"I'm with you Taji," someone said, hand raised high. "But I can't get with having sex in the water. Never had sex before in no swimming pool, and please explain to me how you can feel yourself being wet?"

I wanted to know the answer to that question as well, and even though I'd thought about sex in pools, tubs, oceans...I'd never gone there. "You can't really feel yourself being wet," Taji added. "And the only thing you should concern yourself with feeling is the man going inside of you. It takes a man like Jaylin to make you feel it, and I can't stress enough how many orgasms rang out that night."

"You may have had plenty of orgasms, but not nearly as many as me. In the famous words of a wise man, trust and believe!"

I slapped my forehead, this time rubbing it. It was time to make a phone call to Jaylin, but before I did, I listened to what a woman, Kellie, had to say. Jaylin didn't have to go there, did he...

Orgasms Galore

Kellie Kelly

It was one of those days, so I called my girls and told them to pack up because we were about to take a trip to our favorite resort. When we arrived at The Four Seasons Hotel & Resort, I noticed a tall and sexy handsome gentleman, with eyes so spellbinding, that if you looked into them too long, you were sure to undress piece by piece. I wanted to approach him, but decided that now wasn't the appropriate time.

Later that day, I sat by the poolside with my girls, sipping on drinks and talking about a party we had gone to a few weeks back. While Sheila was giving us the scoop about a man she'd met, I looked over her shoulder, noticing Mr. Sexy again. This time, he was swimming in the pool. His body had a deep California tan, and as the water rushed down it, I swear I wanted to scream. Instead, I leaned over to my girl, Angel, and whispered in her ear. "I'll be right back, okay? I think I see somebody I know."

She tried to see who it was, but I didn't immediately go up to the man. I watched as he left the pool and sat back on one of the lounging chairs. Muscles were bulging from his arms and his stomach was ripped! I imagined my lips pecking down his stomach, and even a little lower. Keeping my eyes on him, I sat at the mini-bar for a moment, then moved over to a lounging chair in front of it. Wearing a black bikini, I started to rub sunscreen on my toned arms and legs. Minutes later, I was interrupted by a waiter.

"Excuse me, but the gentleman on the other side of the pool would like to know what you're drinking, and if he could come over and apply the sunscreen for you?"

I lowered my sunglasses, peering over them. By this time, Mr. Sexy was already coming my way with two other gentlemen with him. The waiter whispered something to the man, and he kept his eyes on me while nodding his head. Next thing I knew, he was standing in front of me. My palms were now sweating and having him so close to me made me jittery. Not only that, but my pussy was beating a mile a minute. I was already soaking wet in my seat and he hadn't even touched me yet. *Damn,* I thought. *He is even finer close up!*

He took a seat in the chair next to mine, and his friends walked in another direction. "What's up?" he said. "My name is Jaylin. Jaylin Rogers."

I wanted to tell him that he could call me Mrs. Rogers, but instead, I told him my name was Kellie.

"Say, Kellie, I guess you didn't have time to respond to the waiter, but I wanted to know if you needed some help with your sunscreen. If you'd like something to drink, I can work that out for you, too."

I gave the sunscreen tube to him and smiled. "I'm not in the mood for another drink right now, but feel free to rub the sunscreen wherever you'd like to."

I turned my back to Jaylin, allowing him to rub the sunscreen all over my backside. Making sure that he got every spot, I laid on my stomach just so he could get a glimpse of my curves.

"Nice," he complimented while rubbing the sunscreen on my butt cheeks. "You must do a lot of working out."

His touch felt so spectacular that my eyes were fading by the minute. I rested my head on my hands. "Let's just say that I work out enough, but I assure you that it's nothing compared to what you must do. I can't tell you the last time I've seen a man's body as cut and perfected as yours."

"Yes, I do a lot of working out, especially in the bedroom."

Surprised? No. "Now, why doesn't that surprise me? I was going to suggest the same thing about you."

We talked for about another hour or so, before Jaylin turned our conversation in another direction.

"Do you have any plans for this evening, and how long are you staying at the resort?"

"Only a few days. Like I said, I'm here with some friends, and we already have some other things scheduled."

"But, you would have the time of your life with me. Why don't you tell your girls that you will see them tomorrow, because from this moment on, I'm kidnapping you."

I laughed. His invitation didn't sound like a bad idea. "Jaylin, I'm from the Show-Me-State and it's better for you to show me, than tell me."

"I agree and that makes two of us. I'm from the Lou, too, and I'm all about showing you whatever it is that you're willing to see."

I stood and Jaylin's eyes dropped low. As he sat staring in front of me, I lifted his chin. "My room number is 318. Be there at seven o'clock and don't be late."

Around 5:00 p.m., I was in my room and had just gotten out of the shower. My phone rang, and when I answered it, it was Jaylin.

"There's been a slight change in plans," he said.

I sighed, feeling a bit disappointed because I could feel the bullshit coming. Just as I got ready to sit on the bed and hear his excuse, there was a knock on my door.

"Hold on," I said, lying the phone down and making my way to the door. When I opened it, Jaylin was standing there with a red rose in his hand.

"I like to catch a woman off guard and surprise her. Are you going to invite me in?"

I widened the door, but tightened the top of the white soft towel that was wrapped around my naked body.

Casually dressed in heavy starched jeans and an Ed Hardy white t-shirt, he stepped inside. His eyes were covered with tinted sunglasses and he removed them. "I hope I didn't catch you at a bad time," he said.

"Not really, but I was just getting ready to go down to the sauna for a while."

"Why don't you wait to do that until later? I promise I'll make it well worth the wait."

"You'd better," I demanded, closing the door and taking the rose from his hand. "Thank you for the rose. Go ahead and make yourself comfortable over there on the couch. I need to put on some clothes."

"Are you sure you want to do that? I'm kind of feeling what you have on right now, and I must say, you look very sexy."

I smiled, as he was definitely a charmer. "I know, but the clothes work better for me right now."

I got dressed, and we headed out for a night on the town. At first, we went to see *Takers* at the movies, then dinner followed. We talked as if we'd known each other for years and if I'd told someone that I'd just met Jaylin today, no one would have believed me. Jaylin was a very smart man and I was impressed by everything about him. He seemed to enjoy my company as well, and as the night winded down, we stopped at a cozy spot that played R&B and jazz. We had a few drinks, and then walked arm in arm back to the resort.

"I had a really nice time," I confessed, resting my head against Jaylin's strong arm. "Thanks for inviting me to go out with you. I know my girls are upset with me, but I'm sure they understand."

"Yes, it was nice and the night is just getting started."

While in the elevator, things got a little steamy. We started to kiss and Jaylin backed me up to the mirror covered walls. His hands swayed along my hips and he grinded his hardness against me. I unbuttoned his jeans and reached my hand deep down inside of them, touching his rock solid ass. It was soft, though, and I had a very tight grip on it. My dress inched up, and he pulled at my lace panties, ripping them away from my sweaty skin.

"Turn around," he said between our deep kisses, but I didn't want to let his juicy lips go. From the thought of what was about to enter me, I then turned around. Jaylin hit the stop button on the elevator, then moved my legs apart with his feet. As my naked ass was in his sights, he secured his arm around my waist. His lips pecked down the side of my neck and his hand dropped low to my pussy. His fingers fondled me from the front, and when I bent over, his dick entered me from the back. I felt so fulfilled...stuffed more like it. My pussy was so gushy and wet, you could hear it talking sweet melodies to him.

"I love the sound of that," Jaylin said. "Has our time together been worth it so far?"

I was barely able to say one word, but I did scream out, "Yes...hell yes!"

My ass was bent far over and Jaylin was giving it everything he had. His long strokes had me going crazy and if I squeezed my fists any tighter, I was sure to break my perfectly polished nails. It wasn't long before I had an orgasm and he came too.

"I had a feeling this pussy would be everything that I needed it to be, but let's get the hell off of this elevator and finish up in your room."

I was all for it, and as the elevator started to move, I lowered my dress. Jaylin tucked that big dick of his back into his jeans, but it wouldn't stay there for long. As soon as we got back to my room, Jaylin removed my black and white off the shoulder mini dress, right after I closed the door. I removed his shirt and pulled his jeans down to the floor. He tossed his clothes into a chair, and as I was bending over, trying to unfasten my stilettos, Jaylin asked me to leave them on.

"Stay in that position," he ordered. "And hold your ankles—tight."

I had no problem doing as he'd asked, because Jaylin knew what the hell he was doing. Every inch of him thrilled me, and you best believe that all of it was deep within me. So deep that I massaged my achy stomach and tightened my eyes from his hard, yet rhythmic stroking.

From one position to the next, we traveled from the couch to the table, from the table to the bed, from the bed to the floor, from the floor to the balcony. Orgasm after orgasm rang out and I couldn't believe that I wasn't ready to call it quits. I couldn't decipher who was the naughtiest, him or me? Had to be...both of us because the dirty words that we spewed could be heard in the attached rooms.

"Damn this good pussy, baby. You in this muthafucking room breaking a brotha down!"

"It's this big ass dick, Jaylin. I love this dick and you've got to give me more of it!"

"All you have to do is ask, and...you know the rest."

Jaylin had me his way for a while, then I ordered him on the bed. I took care of his nine plus inches, slurping him up with a variety of juicy fruits in my mouth and cold chunks of ice. He loved every bit of it, and the naughtier I got, the more turned on he became. He busted one hell of a nut, but I didn't let any of his fluids go to waste. It took a while for him to regain his strength, but when he did, we wound up in the sauna where the naughtiness was happening all over again.

This time, Jaylin laid me down on the bench and gently kissed the insides of my burning thighs. His tongue swiped across my kitty, and obviously liking how it tasted, his tongue traveled further inside of me. To no surprise, Jaylin made the kitty purr with three to four more orgasms. Every time I tried to back away from the feeling, he would pull me back to him. He dined on me for a while, leaving no leftovers whatsoever. Finally, I had my chance to stand over him as he lay on the bench. I did a straight split down on his steel pole, riding him like only I could do it. He came, I came, and then we came together. I don't know who had the most orgasms that night, but both of us were damn sure satisfied.

At nearly three o'clock in the morning, we chilled in Jaylin's suite watching movies. I almost hated that our time together was coming to an end, and I hadn't had this much fun in a long time. I lay close to him in bed with my head resting comfortably on his chest. My bottom half was covered with a sheer black thong, and my breasts were bare. Jaylin didn't have on anything and his hand was behind his head. Several pillows were propped behind us, making us very comfortable.

"So, where do we go from here?" I asked while squeezing my arms around his chest.

"Don't know. You tell me."

"I know it may be a little too late to ask this, but are you with someone or married?"

"Both."

"Good answer. And I wish you would have said something earlier. Besides, where is your wedding ring?"

"Sometimes off, many times on. I'm having some issues right now, but if I had told you that I was married, would it had made the difference?"

I shrugged. "Maybe. Can't really say, but at least I know where we stand going forward. I guess I'd better enjoy this while it lasts."

I got off the bed, deciding to do a little dance for Jaylin. At a time like this, my stripper pole would come in handy. Since I didn't have it with me, I put on a show without it. I turned on "Sex Room" by Luda, then stood in front of Jaylin, swaying my curvy hips from left to right. As I moved right to left, his eyes did not blink. My arms crossed behind my head, raising my already perky breasts even higher. My nipples were erect, causing Jaylin to scroll his tongue across his lips. I turned in slow, tranquilizing circles, then lifted my leg behind my head. Jaylin's eyes traveled straight to my neatly shaved pussy.

"I'm not going to be able to take much more of this," he said in a low voice. "Wrap it up and bring that pussy to me."

I put on my show for at least another fifteen minutes, and once it was over, we indulged ourselves once again. I swear this was almost like a dream, but the good thing about it was, it was a dream come true. I had waited a lifetime to find a man like Jaylin, and who would have thought that I'd find him at a little cozy resort.

We both had exhausted ourselves, and as Jaylin lay peacefully in bed sleeping, I tip-toed around the room, gathering my belongings to go. With my purse tucked underneath my arm, I leaned over him in bed. I placed a soft kiss on my fingertips, then put my fingers on his lips.

"I must go, but I wish like hell that we would have met under different circumstances," I whispered. His eyes were still closed and light snores escaped from within. I touched his thick curly hair, almost hating to leave, but knowing that I had to do it. I made my way to the door, but my steps halted when I heard him call my name.

"Yes," I said, turning around.

"Me too," he said, agreeing with what I'd said. "But it is what it is, and until next time, stay sweet."

He winked, and I left the room with a smile on my face, as well as a very tender coochie. For me, that was the best way to go out!

The End

Book Club Meeting . . .

To me, Kellie couldn't have gone out better, but now, something else for me was confirmed. Jaylin was on some type of James Bond shit, and his mission involved sexy women. I wasn't mad at him and I now knew why he was known as the man women hated to love.

One woman brought up Kellie's and Jaylin's steamy sex session on the elevator and that sparked a chat about bizarre, exotic and fun places to have sex. From the back seat of cars, to the Atlantic Ocean...these women had been there. Kellie named a list of places and some of them made my jaw drop.

"The roof of his house...," Kellie continued. "And in the middle of a cornfield."

"No, no, no," I added. "A cornfield I would not do. I only need one snake in me and I wouldn't even be able to concentrate on sex in a place like that."

Many agreed, some was all for it. I drifted off, still thinking about some interesting places to have sex, then my mind traveled back to Jaylin having similarities to James Bond. I'd been asked a million and one times...what actor would I want to play Jaylin? Now, Denzel Washington was my favorite, but I guess everyone already knew that because of my numerous mentions of him in every book. But a Jaylin Jerome Rogers? No. I threw that question back to the ladies in the room and they made plenty of suggestions.

"Blair Underwood," one woman shouted.

"No," said another. "Terrance Howard!"

"I say Mel Jackson or Morris Chestnut!"

"I got it...Idris Elba, baby, and you can't go wrong with him!"

"Michael Ealy got those eyes, but Boris Kodjoe got that swag...he may be able to pull it off."

"Well I think we should let Jaylin play Jaylin and can't nobody do it better than him. Trust me, I know."

Not only did this woman know, but she was also willing to tell how much she knew. The suggestions about actors came to a halt and she started to tell us why Jaylin referred to her as his one and only Sweetness...

Sweetness
LaLa Estrada

I slammed down the payphone as hard as I could. My cell phone battery had died. I knew Jaylin's ears were sure to be ringing right about now. I could not believe that he would play me for Scorpio's trifling ass. For Nokea, a definite yes, but Scorpio, oh hell no!!! Then again, knowing their history together, yes he most certainly would. Why did he have to mention that bitch's name? I would have been cool with a lie, but we all know Jay Baby doesn't lie. He gives it to you straight and raw, no matter how devastating. Well, that's what I love about him, his honesty, so I couldn't complain.

I walked over to the ticket counter to see if I could cancel my flight to the Republic of Panama, a.k.a. Paradise. I had already secured a fabulous King Suite at the new Nikki Beach Playa Blanca Resort—the sexiest place on earth—according to them, with its luxurious rooms, beautiful white sand beaches and blue waters....so inviting, and so relaxing. It had everything, and the staff catered to your every need. All I could think about for the past five days was having Jay's delicious nine plus long inches all to myself. As soon as the tears started to swell up in my eyes, I put on my Gucci sunglasses so the agent couldn't see how shook I really was. She informed me that my ticket was non-refundable, point blank. What the hell, I guess I would be going to Panama alone, which was all good, because there was plenty to get into. Still, it was kind of hard to think of anyone else when dealing with a man like Jaylin Jerome Rogers. Forreal!

As I walked through the airport heads turned. My legs were on full display in my white miniskirt, and my boobs weren't playing either behind my white jacket...but it was all tasteful, you know. My caramel butter skin was oiled with a mango flavored scent. My curls flowed just right underneath my big white hat, and I had the nerve to have on dark shades. The flight was delayed by an hour and a half—just what I needed, more time to sit and soak about what could of been. Finally, they allowed us to board the plane. I wasn't in the mood for any small talk, and I was glad that the seat next to me was empty. I guess I don't have to explain why it was empty, and thinking about being stood up by Jay just made me sad all over again.

First Class was uneventful. The usual: decent food, plush seats, light turbulence and tons of ass kissing from the flight attendants was it. Of course, one of Brenda Hampton's books, *The Dirty Truth*, was on my agenda to read, so now was as good a time as any to get started. Three and a half hours came and went. We had a smooth landing, thank goodness. It was night time in Panama City, and I had an hour and a half long ride to the resort. I jumped in the car the resort sent for me, and settled into the comfortable seat. I was still distraught about Jaylin not being able to make it, and thank goodness I brought some toys with me to play with.

While riding in the backseat of the car, my hand was pressed against my face. I gazed out of the window at the skyline in Panama. It was so beautiful at night. A lot of tall buildings lined the sky. They had just built a new freeway called the Cinta Costera, which means Coastal Strip. It was absolutely breathtaking. Lights, cameras, action is what played in my mind every time I saw it. We made our way to the Bridge of the Americas, which was lit up in red, white, and blue lights. You could see the Panama Canal from the bridge. This led us to the Pan-American Highway, which would eventually take us to the resort.

I dozed off, and before I knew it, we had arrived. I paid the driver, and grabbed my simple carry-on bag and made my way to the front desk. Panama is a Spanish country, but at most of the hotels, because of tourism, all the employees spoke English, or broken English. The lady at the front desk told me that my room had been upgraded to the Penthouse Suite.

"Are you sure," I asked. "I didn't reserve the Penthouse Suite."

All she did was smile and hand over the room key for entry. "I'm positive you will enjoy your stay."

I shrugged, and without Jaylin, I didn't know if that was possible. "Thank you," I said, admiring all of the fabulousness around me. I got on the elevator, inserted my key and pressed the penthouse button. *Well, I'll be damned,* I thought, as the doors to the elevator opened right into the suite. It was breathtaking and all I could see were candles flickering all over the place. The terrace was open, and the sheer white curtains were blowing inside ever so slightly. The whole penthouse was decorated in white. The living room was monstrous, I mean it was huge. I put down my bag, took off my big white hat, and kicked off my five inch heels. The floor was cold under my feet. White and grey marble was everywhere. With all of the candles burning, and the wind blowing, surely a fire could get started. I walked over to the master bedroom, seeing the most beautiful king sized canopy bed with sheer white material draped all around it. White roses were tossed all over the bed, and my eyes followed the trail of white rose petals that led to the master bathroom. The rose petals stopped at the double French doors that were closed. I slowly walked up to them, taking deep breaths as I could feel my excitement building. My hands turned the knobs and when I pushed the doors open, my body weakened and I nearly fainted. From inside of the dim, candlelit bathroom, those heart piercing grey eyes stared into mine, causing my breathing to stop. I couldn't believe it and my eyes had to be playing tricks on me, so I rubbed them, just to be sure. I blinked several times to clear them, but my vision was correct. It was Jay Baby in the god damn flesh, and I mean that shit literally. He was sprawled out in the gigantic Jacuzzi tub that was centered in the middle of the floor. He held a glass in his hand, and I was sure it was a glass of Remy, no rocks. His gorgeous face and chest glistened in the candlelight. The tub was overflowing with bubbles, and I couldn't wait to sink myself in the tub with him.

"Damn baby," he said with a slick grin on his handsome face. His other hand was in the tub, slow stroking his goods. "What took you so long to get here? The nine has been *up* and waiting for a taste of that sweet pussy."

My eyes were focused in on his rising nine, and I was smiling so hard, I thought my teeth would start to fall out at any moment.

"JAYLIN!" I screamed, loud enough for the whole resort to hear. "You tricked me! And for doing so, you will be punished," I whined, still smiling with a seductive grin.

His head moved from side to side, "Nah baby, you got me confused. I'm the one dishing out the muthafuckin punishments around here." He carefully placed his glass on the side of the Jacuzzi tub, and started touching his sharp lined goatee that suited his chin.

I cocked my eyebrows at him. I wanted to say "Wha cha talkin bout Jaylin" in that Gary Coleman voice, but instead I peeled my white jacket off my shoulders to remove it. Jaylin watched each button pop open, obviously anxious to see what was underneath. His eyes shifted from my eyes, to my chest, and when I dropped the jacket to the floor, my black lace Barely There Victoria Secret Bra was visible. My Full C's stood at attention, looking healthy as ever. I tossed my bra to the side, allowing my titties do a nice bounce for Jay Baby. As he looked on, I squeezed them and stroked my nipples. His tongue moved across his lips, and I could tell he was already hyped. Arousing him more, I turned around and zipped down the zipper of my white matching miniskirt. Granted my voluptuous toned legs were already on display, but I was sure I heard the water splash when I lowered my skirt over my apple booty. Jay saw my black lace thong going to the valley of the sweetest, juiciest, wettest pussy known to him, and I had to bend over to make sure he got the best view in the house. I peeked at Jaylin through my legs and my long hair swung down to give it the most dramatic effect. He smiled, giving me a slow wink. I lifted myself up, and turned around—our eyes connecting once again.

"Am I in trouble?" I asked, seductively sliding my index finger into my mouth to suck it. The water swished again, and I could tell that this was getting good.

"You slammed the phone down in my ear Sweetness (that's what Jay calls me...he never uses my name for whatever reason). My shit is still ringing as we speak. Now, did I deserve all of that? Let me answer that, hell the fuck no! Now bring my sweetness over here so I can tear that shit up. That's the only way to settle this."

I had no problem with settling things Jaylin's way, and when he stepped out of the tub, all the water and soap from the bubbles ran down his nicely cut muscular frame, to the tips of his toes. I wanted to scream from the sight of his body, but as my eyes moved down his front and backside, all I could do was put my fist in my mouth and bite down. Damn, he had it going on!

He walked over to the shower and opened the door. When he turned, all he saw was the look in my hungry-for-him eyes. "That's what you get for teasing me," he said, still holding the shower door open. "Now, shake it off and bring me *my* pussy."

Whatever Jay Baby wants, Jay Baby gets. I wasted no more time and like he'd asked, I brought my pussy to him. The shower, itself, was fabulous. It was big enough for a party of eight, but had just enough room for us to get busy, especially since Jaylin had a thing for showers. I was kind of looking forward to that damn Jacuzzi, but I guess that would have to wait. Besides, I knew I would have to soak my kittykat thoroughly after the beat down it was about to receive, so the Jacuzzi would serve its purpose eventually.

While standing in the shower, the water sprinkled down our naked bodies that were pressed tightly together. I looked up at Jaylin, and could feel his growth down below. I wanted to get a closer look, so I slightly backed up. My eyes dropped beyond his waist, and for the first time, I touched *it*. Lawd have mercy that muthafuckin nine and a half inches was hard as a brick from the Great Wall of China! It was swollen to capacity, and as I eased my hand along the sides of it, I swear I heard the angels go, "Aah Aahhhh all the way from heaven." Jaylin reached for a switch on the wall, and music started playing all throughout the bathroom, including the rest of the penthouse. Glen Jones, "Show Me" was blasting through the speakers. I dropped to my knees in front of Jay, and started licking around the head of the nine with my swift wet tongue. My tongue was a.k.a Lasso, and the tip of it was lethal. I licked Jay's big dick from the tip of the head, all the way down to his loaded balls. I licked my way back up to the top of his now throbbing head, devouring it. I had to admit that Jay tasted delicious. His dick was just beautiful, and in a nutshell, it was definitely all that and then some. Jay knew how to back that shit up and he gave "show and prove" a new meaning, forreal.

His fingers tightened in my hair, and my eyelids fluttered. "Damn baby," he softly moaned. "You see what you do to me? I can't get this feeling any place else or from anybody else but you Sweetness. That's real talk, baby. Gotdamn that shit feels good and you got mad skillz."

I let Jay Baby ramble on, while continuing to show him just how skillful I really was. Besides, I couldn't talk anyway, my mouth was very full. I stroked his big long throbbing dick up and down, while my tongue tasted the tip of his head, and sucked all over the bulging veins that now made their presence known. That shit turned me the fuck on, and I couldn't stop giving Jay's love muscle my special treatment. He started pumping his hardness in my mouth, causing both of our moans to increase. I gagged a little, but being a skillful woman, it was all good. I took him in like a champ, no doubt. I began to deep throat his big swollen chocolate stick, and Jay's grip on my hair had gotten even tighter. I wiggled my tongue across the slit of his dick, over and over again. I swear my mouth was like a damn vacuum sucking Jay's dick the fuck up. I felt his whole body tremble from my immaculate performance and I couldn't wait for him to give a sista a pat on her back. I knew how difficult it was to bring him to this level of pleasure, but there I was doing it. Yeah, that's what I'm talking about....I was actually doing it!

My wet kisses went all the way up Jay's body, passing his ripped abs, until I got to my next treasure...his nipples. I started to lick all over his nipples, flicking my tongue back and forth in a fast motion. That shit had Jay on fire, and so was my kittykat as he fingered it. I massaged his massive chest and thick upper arms as he flexed them for me. I loved it when he flexed his arms and all the veins in his arms were at attention, displaying so much strength. While working his nipples, I stroked his dick and felt it pulsating and throbbing in my hand. It was ready for action, and so was my juicy pussy. Jay was working it like a pro, digging in deep and flicking his fingers inside to make my kittykat tingle. Believe me, it was. He backed me against the wall, and moved my long wet hair away from my face so he could see it. His lips met up with mine and he sexed me over with his tongue. We smacked lips for like forever, all the while he grinded his massive throbbing meat into my wet aching pussy. Needless to say, I love, love, love, the way Jay Baby kissed me and my whole body was on fire from his kisses alone. He nuzzled my neck and licked my ear as he whispered in it, "Sweetness, you smell so damn good. I wanna taste you all over."

Without saying another word, he lowered his head and started sucking my beautiful nipples that were very much at attention. As he squeezed and massaged them, I couldn't speak. My mouth was open, and I was feeling so much pleasure. All I could do was moan and let out a soft, yet relieving whisper of one word— "Jay."

He put his finger to my lips to silence me. "Relax baby. I promise you I got this".

Jaylin picked me up so my legs could straddle his waist. I wrapped my thick thighs around him like my life depended on it. Obviously, he had other plans for me and *his* pussy. He lifted me up some more, and my kittykat was now at his face. It wasn't long before he went to work. His tongue stroked my clit like it was playing a fuckin tune, and my coochie lips were singing, literally. He was working it over like no other. I knew he could taste that mango flavor down there, and all I wanted to do was just scream, so I did. His tongue danced all over my pussy lips and clit. He dipped his magnificent tongue in and out of my now throbbing, slippery tunnel. Alicia Keys, "If I Ain't Got You" came on next over the speakers. Hearing the song changed the rhythm. I removed my trembling legs from Jay's shoulder and my body slithered against the wall.

"Back up a bit," I said, touching his chest. He backed up, and that's when I did a handstand facing him. I opened my legs like a scissor, securing them around his neck.

"Hold me tight," I said, now face-to-face with his dick. I was sure his view of my pussy was even better. I was only 5'2" so my goods landed where I thought it would, right below his chin.

"I got you, baby," he assured. "And you better believe I'm not gon let this shit go."

I grabbed his dick with one hand and started sucking the shit out of it again. Yes, we had a standing sixty-nine going on, and Jay was eating me out like it was his last meal. I was busy working his knob like it was a bomb pop on a hot sweaty day. I felt Jay's long pipe swelling up again like it was ready to explode, so I paused.

"I want to stand up," I said.

He paused, too, but placed a few delicate pecks on my coochie lips. "Damn baby, you trying to turn a brotha out with all that flexible shit. I knew you were flexible, but gotdamn," he laughed. Jay pulled back, and looked at my goods and said, "Beautiful ass pussy...wet and juicy, just how I like it. Umph, umph, umph...I just can't get enough of it." He started licking my insides again, but as I neared an explosion, I begged him to put me down. His feverish tongue was rocking my clit, I mean, I lost it! I held on for dear life, not wanting this feeling to end. My thighs clinched Jay's head, and I knew he couldn't breathe. But when all was said, but not nearly done, Jay Baby let me know how much he appreciated that mango flavor.

"Baby we in muthafuckin' Panama for real with that sweet ass mango flavor you got me tasting," he said.

I smiled, letting my eyes roll to the back of my head and sighing from relief. No doubt, the shit felt THAT damn good.

Jay Baby put me down and turned off the water that was turning cold. "Give it to me," I demanded while touching his dick. "I wanna feel that throbbing hard chocolate stick inside of me now!"

Jay laughed and held his long pipe, "Chocolate Stick, huh?" Jay shook his head and smiled from the compliment that made both his heads swell, the one on his shoulders, and the one below. "Ask once, and you don't have to ask again...you can have all of this good ass chocolate right here, and it will for damn sure be the best chocolate you ever had."

We both laughed as Jay playfully picked me up, and carried me over to the beautiful king size bed. He laid me down on the bed, and spread my legs far apart as he stood between them. He gave me another wink, and began to crack his damn knuckles. We couldn't help but laugh. Seconds later, he took his nine in his hand, and tapped the head of his dick on my melting pussy.

"Is this what you want?" Jay teased.

"Yes, yes, yes! Jay, please quit playing baby and give it to me now!" Somehow, I managed to get that out with an already heaving chest. I guess Jay knew my pussy had marinated long enough, and it was time to put some serious work in, as if we hadn't done enough.

My juicy pocket was heated or *muy caliente* as the Spanish say...very hot. Jay took the nine and placed it right between my legs. He massaged the head around my pussy until a high arch formed in my back. I swear my coochie lips must of grabbed a hold of that thick head, cause the next thing I knew, Jay's big chocolate stick was sucked into the hot and wet tunnel that awaited him. I mean he was deep in there, tearing up my gut. At first, he moved at a rhythmic slow pace you know, winding and grinding my insides and massaging my throbbing clit at the same time. Yes, the brotha had mad skillz, too, that's why I secretly nicknamed him the "Bedroom Bully" because he always tore it up. I watched his big dick glide in and out of me, delivering everything that I knew it would.

"Jay Baby, your big dick feels so good going in and out of me. Take this pussy, it's yours," I moaned in a throaty voice.

Jay's chest was glistening from the sweat that we were creating, and it was a serious workout session. It seemed as if his pipe had gotten even bigger and harder inside of me, and from the look in our eyes, we could tell the other was pleased. "Ahhh baby," he whimpered. "This sweetness is my weakness girl. Do you know how good this shit feels?"

Of course I knew, and I was delighted that he knew it, too. I took the opportunity to flip the script on Jay. I turned him around so quick he didn't know what happened. I stood over the nine, and lowered my sweetness right on top of it. I closed my eyes as that juicy rock hard dick entered me. Jay groaned and so did I. We both felt it. I opened my eyes, and Jay opened his eyes at the same time. Our eyes connected again.

I started out with a slow wind and grind on Jay's manhood. I could tell it was driving him crazy because he squeezed my booty, and then started to massage it with his big strong hands. That shit felt too good. If this shit right here was a crime, we would be locked up for years with no way out! My strokes got faster, and faster as I rode him like I was in a rodeo. By the sounds of it, and all the moaning and groaning we were both doing, we were just savoring every moment, and every second of all this goodness. I felt Jay's love muscle growing inside me again, and I intended to milk all of the juices from it. I could feel it...it was time for the explosion I'd been waiting for and I could tell he was about to erupt.

"Not so fast," he said, grabbing my waist and flipping me over onto my knees. With vengeance, he entered me from behind, ready to show me why this was his favorite position. He took ownership of my pussy, stroking it like it was going out of style. I worked that brick like a master of my craft. Everything Jay gave me, I took. We were sweaty as hell, yet loving every minute of it. I was about to cum, and boy I could feel it all the way down to the tips of my curling toes.

"Jay Baby, give it to me baby, yo quiero leche dulce Papi," I screamed. (That means give me all that sweet milk you got for me Daddy.)

"Oooh, I'm cumin, Jaayyyyy!" I screamed even louder.

His seductive voice jumped right in, causing me to coat him with extra juices, "That's right, baby. Throw that sweet pussy back to me. I'm about to give you some sweet milk too."

His fingers pressed into my ass cheeks and we both came near the same time. While taking deep breaths, we collapsed flat on the bed.

"Wheewww," Jaylin said, moving beside me. "Now, that's what the fuck I'm talkin about! Gotdamn baby, you put it on a brotha— forreal."

I was so spent, I couldn't even talk. I just kissed Jay's handsome face, while he cradled me in his arms. Very comfortable with him, I lay my head on his sweaty chest.

Moments later, I found my voice. "Jay Baby, I love the way you put that nine to work. I love you, and I don't know what I'm gonna do when you leave and go back to your world."

I didn't wait for a response because I knew what I wanted to hear would never be said. Yeah, it was complicated, but we had an understanding. No matter what, we were in this thing together. We had each other's backs. I was his comfort, his sounding board, his home away from home. No one understood our connection, but it would never, ever be broken.

Jay lifted my chin and our eyes connected. Those famous words spilled from his mouth and were no way unexpected. "Baby, you know how I feel."

Enough said. I'll take it!

I luvmesumhim!

All of him.

Jay adored my sweetness. This I was sure of, and that was all that mattered in our Paradise in Panama, even if it was only one night with Jaylin. He will always have a place in my heart, no doubt. All love, all day, every day, no matter what!

The End

Book Club Meeting...

Many of the women were left speechless, simply because, like many of the other ladies, LaLa had brought Jaylin alive. She told it like it really was, and it was obvious that she had a special place in his heart.

"I do love Jay Baby," LaLa said, patting her chest. "He's right here and he's not going anywhere. I understand him more than anyone, with the exception of the author. Even though what he does makes no sense to many, it makes sense to him. Nothing anyone says will make him see otherwise and all of his choices will be left up to him. There is something so sexy about a man who is as confident as Jay is, and I love a man who is in control of his surroundings."

"I'm perfectly fine with that," one woman said. "But Jaylin needs to get his act together. Love should not hurt and the things that he does just make me want to slap the shit out of him. I could just choke him, then I'd screw him similar to the way LaLa just did. That was some mean sex you put on him, girl, and I felt the two of you connect."

I added my two cents. "If it were that simple for us to 'get it together' this world would be a better place. I do my best to show you the struggles some men have with relationships, as well as the women. I know I can make you feel as if you want to pull your hair out sometimes, but Jaylin brings about the good, the bad and the ugly. Everything isn't always peaches and cream in relationships and I like to write about some of the reasons why."

"Well, you do have me acting a fool while reading your books. I mean, I be talking out loudly as if the book can hear me. I must say, that's when you know you have a good...great book in your hand. Great job and we appreciate you more than you know."

The ladies in the room clapped and we all exchanged words of appreciation to each other. Someone touched on LaLa's story again, about what it felt like to be stood up by a man. Even though Jaylin had come through for LaLa, some men were known for not coming through at all.

"That pisses me off," someone said. "And why tell someone you're coming when you're not. There is nothing worse than showering, getting dressed, putting on make-up, doing your hair and waiting for hours and hours for someone to show. I don't know why people aren't just honest when they don't want to be bothered, and if LaLa had said Jaylin didn't show up, I would never read a book about his tail again!"

The lady meant business, so I had to make sure Jaylin never stood up anyone. She continued to voice her opinion about being stood up and then asked LaLa if she thought Shemar Moore could play Jaylin.

"Possibly," LaLa said. "But as I said before, Jaylin can play Jaylin. Just wait, you'll see."

"Frankly, I don't believe Jaylin is real, and if he is," she looked around the room with bugged eyes. "Looks like he has some explaining to do."

Yes, he did. I asked if anyone else had had the pleasure of meeting Jaylin and the last woman jumped to her feet, firing back at what the previous woman had said. Tears were in her eyes and she smacked away a tear that had fallen. "Okay, I'll tell you what's real. Being with Jaylin changed my life! When I get finished, hopefully everyone will know what's up."

Well, well, I thought as I quickly sent Jaylin a text message. How could he bring a woman to tears and what in the hell had he done this time? I had held on to my secret for a very long time, but if this woman knew something that I didn't know, like the rest, I was definitely willing to listen...

What's Real?

Nikki-Michelle

It's ironic how things have a way of happening. Like, it's just funny at times. You never know who you are really talking to over the Internet. You just don't! If anyone would have told me that this "person" that I was conversing with over Facebook was actually the person that was standing in front of me at this very moment, I would have told them they were crazy. Because, see, right now, I think I'm crazy. I think I'm losing it. My eyes shifted around the room to see if anybody was playing a joke on me. Those damn Original Naughty Angels were known for playing jokes.

I locked eyes with the man standing in front of me, and couldn't help but ask, "Is this some kind of joke? Who paid you to do this? This is not funny at all."

His brows furrowed and he didn't break his stare. "Why in hell would you think this is a joke? I told you I was coming, didn't I?"

I turned in my seat, looking around and making sure people could see him like I could see him. At the risk of appearing insane, I asked the white girl next to me, "Do you see him?" I pointed at the man in front of me.

"Oh, hell yeah I see him!" she said, blinking her eyes. She licked her lips and was damn near drooling out of the mouth. So were every other woman and some men in the place.

The man in front of me sighed. "Nicole, why in the hell are you playing? What the hell is wrong with you? You told me to meet you here, so I'm here. Question is...are you going to do me that *favor* or what?"

The problem is I didn't know what *favor* he was talking about. I had told him I would suck his dick and make his eyes roll back like Wal-Mart prices and some other stuff that I don't care to mention right now. Hey! Don't you dare judge me! I am rolling my eyes at all of you right now.....judging me for doing what many of you would do, too.

"Like for real?" I asked, still gazing at him and not believing that he was in my presence. I must have looked like the damn fool right now. "I...I can't believe you're real?"

The second sigh he released implied that I was annoying him. "I told you that your face would crack, if you ever saw me in the flesh. You were one of the main people in My World on Facebook, talking shit about not believing me." He held out his hands. "As you can see, I am *really* standing in front of your ass. Of all people, I thought you would know better, Nicole."

I gave a very visible shiver. My name spilling from his sexy lips turned my boiling insides hot, then cold. Lawd help me! I looked him up and down, then down and up and I couldn't help it, my eyes stopped at his mid section. I swallowed at the well defined lump. I, too, wet my lips with my tongue, and I looked up, only to find him smiling.

"Stop staring at my dick," he said, bluntly. "Come on and go with me. You said you would take me where I needed to go."

His words rang out loudly, and everyone else started to look. I snapped out of my dazed haze and slowly stood. I just had to touch him to make sure he was there, so I did. The Brooks Brothers suit was unmistakable, and I even grabbed his wrist to examine his diamond filled Rolex. After inhaling his panty-dropping cologne, I stood on the tips of my toes, searching into his grey eyes to make sure they were real and not contacts.

He grabbed his crotch and sarcastically asked, "You want to measure my dick too, Nicole?" *I do have a tape measure in the trunk of my car,* I thought. He must have read my thoughts.

"Maybe later," he said. "Right now, I need you to get me to where I need to go. Since you said you would, I would like for you to keep your end of the bargain."

I was reluctant to leave, and kept looking around the room, just to make sure I wasn't in a dream. He pinched my butt hard, slightly turning my skin.

"Ouch," I yelled, rubbing my butt. "That hurt!"

"Hopefully now, you know you're not dreaming, baby. Let's get this show on the road, and where's your car?"

My car? I thought. Oh Lord, here we go. I knew this man was a stickler for image. I hoped my 2009 Nissan Altima was up to his standards. Last thing I would want him to do was call me out on it. Speaking of image, I touched my hair and ran my fingers across my lips. I must have been a sight. I had on House of Dereon ripped hip hugger jeans, some Chanel thong sandals and a no name black wife beater. I glanced at my toes and nails, making sure no cracks or chips were on my French manicure. I wanted to kick myself for being so critical of how I looked. I couldn't believe this fool had me up in here scared to simply be me. I sucked my teeth and rolled my eyes before snatching up my purse. It was apparent that Barnes & Noble on Mt. Zion was not ready for this man. It seemed as if everybody was tripping over themselves looking at him. I passed by a young lady reading *Naughty No More* and watched the way she looked from the book to the man walking behind me. Her mouth was hanging wide open, and the look on her face was priceless.

The man stopped and stood right in front of her. "Good book, huh?"

She couldn't even get a word out before stuttering and spilling hot coffee all over her lap. He chuckled a bit and we walked out into the sun. I hit the alarm on my car. I was so happy I had taken that thing to get a thorough detail earlier this morning. Out of habit, I took his briefcase and opened the passenger side door for him. I used the key to pop the hood to my trunk and placed his briefcase there before going around to the driver side and sliding my ass onto the plush leather seats.

His scent overtook the scent of strawberries and bananas floating around. I watched as he adjusted his seat and leaned back.

"I haven't had much sleep. You don't mind if I just lay back and chill do you?" he asked.

I didn't say a thing as I watched him remove his suit jacket and neatly lay it across the back seat so it wouldn't wrinkle. He then leaned the seat back as far as it would go and propped one arm behind his head, the other hand across his eyes. My eyes traveled from his tanned neck, to his chiseled chest, over to his muscular arms, and down to his perfectly cut abs. As I observed the famous lump between his legs again, I continued on down his thighs, then back up to his lap.

He cleared his throat. "Stop staring at my dick and drive, Nicole."

I smacked my lips together and sucked my teeth. "Nobody's staring at your dick," I lied. I put the car in reverse and pulled out of the parking lot. Once the light turned green at the four-way stop, I asked where I needed to be going. He told me, and I hit 75 North, heading towards Buckhead. I put the address he gave me into my GPS navigation system and glanced at him again. OH MY FUCKING GAWD! I *still* couldn't believe this man was in my car!

"So.....you are really real?" I asked, breaking the silence.

It was a while before he answered. I thought he was asleep. "No. I am only a figment of your imagination."

"Ha! Ha! Ha! Very funny. But no, for real? So you and Ms. Brenda Hampton actually are two different..."

"Yes, Nicole!"

"Ok. Geeze! Was just asking."

I turned the volume to the radio up and let Verse Simmonds ask to buy me a round. Of course I couldn't keep my mouth closed, as I had some shit I needed to say and ask. I turned the volume down.

"So, how are things with you and the wife?" I decided to start off a little slow.

"It is what it is," he answered from behind his arm.

"Are you still addicted to Krispy Kreme a.k.a. Scorpio? I am sure the 'HOT' sign is still always on?"

He removed his arm and lifted his head just a little. "I see you're already ready to start some shit, huh?"

I shrugged, "I'm just asking."

"Why are you asking questions that you either already know the answer to, or don't want to know the answer to?"

"So what does that mean? You're still fucking the cesspool? Impossible that you want your marriage to be fixed," I said, shaking my head.

He didn't respond. Not like I cared.

He finally sat up straight and looked over at me. "Why do women think that a man doesn't love one woman just because he fucks another?"

"Because in doing so, you know it will hurt her. You can't claim to love someone, and then intentionally hurt them."

"Who said I did it intentionally?" Annoyance was laced in his voice.

"How else do you explain sticking your dick in that slut monkey mistress you have and continuing to do so?"

"Why do you refuse to call her by her name? And for the record, she ain't the only woman I have slept with."

"Yeah, but she is the one that's causing you your marriage. But for whatever reason, you don't get that. So, tell me...is it that impossible for you to care about your marriage or your wife for that matter?"

His brows rose. "How in the fuck are you going to tell me how I feel about my wife?"

"Because obviously your ass is confused, or you don't know your damn self."

"Damn it!" he said, looking over at me with seething anger. "I didn't come all the way to Atlanta to do this shit with you! If you want to talk, why don't you talk about giving me some pussy or something?"

I snapped my neck around to look at him. "Pussy is what got you where you are now. I ain't about to give you no pussy. You out of your damn mind? Unlike your side ho, I don't fuck married men."

He quickly calmed himself and laughed a bit. That annoyed me, so I turned up the volume to the radio as loud as it could go. Twenty minutes later, I pulled my car into a subdivision called Castleberry Hills. My mouth hit the floor. The houses in the neighborhood were way over the term mansions. These things were castles. He turned the volume down on the radio and told me to keep driving until I got to 1325 Monte Carlo Drive. I pulled into the long driveway. The house was in a cul-de-sac with a lake view and private backyard.

"Who lives here?" I asked, being nosey.

"Nobody. Yet."

A platinum colored Jaguar pulled in behind us. A blonde haired white woman stepped out of the car. She looked like she could pass for that blonde chick from The View.

"Do you remember when you asked if you could be my personal assistant?" he asked.

I nodded.

"Well, for today, you're hired. I am going to go introduce myself to this ditzy motherfucker. In my briefcase, there are two manila envelopes. I need both, a ball point pen with black ink and my wallet."

Before I could ask where his wallet was, he had stepped out of the car. It took me a minute to register all that was happening. I watched as he smiled on cue with everything she said, or whatever lame ass joke I knew she was telling. I stepped out of the car and immediately her smile faltered. She eyeballed me like I had the black plagued.

"Is uh....is this your wife?" she asked with disdain in her voice.

"No. Nicole is my assistant. She will be helping me with some minor details as we tour the house."

"Oh, okay," the blonde bitch said, quickly ushering him by me. When she walked past me, she moved her shoulders so she wouldn't brush up against me.

Oh no this bitch didn't, I said underneath my breath.

I quickly made my way to the trunk, but when I got to his briefcase it had a number lock. Now, he didn't tell me how to open this sucker. I stood there for a while, fumbling with the combination. I quickly thought back to what I knew about him. He and his son were born on the same day. I put in the month and the day with his year of birth and ta-da! I quickly grabbed the two manila envelopes. Out of all of the damn pens he had, not one was black. I closed the trunk and rushed to grab my purse. Didn't find a black pen in there either. I was on my way up the plethora of stairs when I remembered to get his wallet. It wasn't in his briefcase, so I quickly checked his suit jacket and found it in an inside pocket. I jogged up those steps and into the house. If you thought my mouth dropped just from looking at the outside of the house, then the 12 feet Cathedral ceiling and entrance foyer alone gave me an orgasm.

"Damnnnnnn," I whispered.

I heard him and the blonde chick talking and laughing as they toured the house. I walked into the kitchen and saw that she had laid her legal pad and pen on the bar. I stole her pen. Hey, he said he needed one. He didn't say where and how to get it. I decided to tour the kitchen that was bigger than the whole first level of my townhouse. This was a bad ass spot. I did notice a few things that I thought he would want to see up close, before closing the deal if he was buying this place. Like when I turned on the water, the water pressure wasn't that great and there could have been more quality fixtures in here. Also, there seemed to be water damage on one of the panels near the pantry. I pulled my digital camera from my purse, snapping a few pictures. After they left the front room, I walked behind them. I stood in the middle of the living floor and jumped up and down. Blonde bitch looked at me.

"Excuse me, what are you doing?" she asked. She was clearly annoyed.

I threw my hand back at her. "Oh you never mind me," I said with a plastered smile on my face and the most valley girl voice I could find. He didn't say a word as I jotted down a few notes. Oh yeah, I stole a few sheets from her legal pad, too. Don't judge me!

When I jumped on the floor it flexed, which meant it wasn't solid. I looked up to the roof and it looked neat and properly aligned. There was one wall in the hall that was bowed and not squared. I could tell that I was getting under the blonde bitch's skin, because she kept throwing daggers at me with her eyes over her shoulder, every time she thought he wasn't looking. I was tempted to accidentally push that bitch down the stairs, but didn't want to mess up this deal for him. By the time they were done touring the house, it was almost an hour later. I had used up every inch of those three sheets of paper and snapped more pictures than I knew my camera could hold.

"So, what do you think?" Blondie asked him.

He stroked his perfectly shaped goatee and nodded. "I think I like it. I like it very much. How much did you say it was on the market for again?"

"Seven million, and six hundred thousand dollars," she answered with a smile that said she saw dollar signs.

"How soon can we have this done?"

"Today if you want. It is still early and I've got some friends over at the bank that could take care of everything before lunchtime."

He looked at his Rolex and was about to answer. I interrupted.

"Excuse me sir, but I have a list of things here that you should take a look at before you make any decisions." I handed him the papers. If looks could kill, the blonde bitch would have killed me ten times over. She gave a fake semi chuckle. "I am sure that whatever..."

He instantly cut her off, "When was this house built?"

"Just last year in '09," she answered.

We stood there silent again, as he looked over every single thing I had written down.

He turned to me, "Show me what else you have."

"I actually snapped a few pictures," I answered, moving closer to him. I noticed Blondie had a laptop powered up in the kitchen and started to walk that way.

"You don't mind if we use this do you?" I asked, not giving her time to answer before turning the laptop to face me. I removed my memory card and inserted it into the slot for it. Immediately pictures popped up of the things I had found. I placed a smirk on my face, as he sat on the barstool and looked over the pictures one by one.

I pointed to the picture on the screen. "And also, in the front room, in the very middle of the floor when I jumped up and down, it flexed which means it's either not on solid foundation as it should be, or someone overlooked something."

He slowly nodded, continuing to scroll through the pictures.

"I am sure that whatever problems you find, sir, they can be fixed without difficulty," she said in a sing-song kiss ass voice.

"So you knew about these problems?" he asked, touching the hair on his chin.

Blondie looked a bit nervous now. "Well, sir, we actually just didn't think it took away from the appeal and value of the home..."

"You don't think the floor moving is a problem, or this water damage? What's with the water pressure? I like to keep my ass clean and I would like to know that I could get enough running water to do that. Was it a rush job on the halls, because it is clear that it's not squared as it should be. This is a lot of money I am willing to spend. Not just any money. My money! I don't like to be conned, no matter how big or how small, Ms. Winters."

Oh, the blonde bitch had a name. I smiled at her, showing all thirty-two of my damn clean white teeth.

"Well, I...I am in a position to knock a few numbers off for minor infractions," she nervously spit out.

He folded his arms in front of him and nudged his head to the chair beside him. "Let's talk and have a seat. Since I like this house, I am willing to listen. I did fly all the way from Miami Beach for this, so negotiate."

Another full hour later, the house was down a whole million and five hundred thousand dollars cheaper. If I had a word to describe how that bitch was looking when she handed him those keys, it would have been.... priceless!

"You can either leave the key in the lock box on the door or keep it with you. I will meet you at the bank in the next hour," she said before damn near storming off to her car. I stood at the door, waving at her like I had just bought the house.

I turned to find him staring at me, rather at my ass. "If you take a picture, it would last longer," I told him. I walked past him to the kitchen so I could gather my purse and belongings. I heard him chuckle a bit.

"By the way, good job," he told me.

"Thank you," I said, placing the strap to my purse on my shoulder. "Are you ready to leave?"

His seductive eyes looked me over. "No. Not yet."

Before I could ask why, he had swooped down on my ass like a hawk.

"Well damn," I said, slightly backing away from him. My heartbeat was beating with an unsteady rhythm. "What the hell? Move! You're in my space." Don't know who I was trying to convince to move, him or me.

"That was some sexy shit you did back there. Nothing sexier than a woman who knows how to handle business. You got brains to match your body."

Well I knew I had a fat, round, plump ass, and round hips. My chest held 36D's and my waist was small enough. I was thick in every sense of the word. He had me pressed against the counter and my pussy felt like it was Crip walking in my black lace boy shorts.

"Thank you. Now, will you give me fifty feet?"

I was having difficulties looking into his grey eyes that were so addictive. He was making it hard for me to think with his scent invading my nostrils and my senses.

"Damn you smell good. What is that?" I asked.

He pointed to his chest. "It's called, Me. I give off my own scent. You smell the scent of when my dick gets hard and I want to fuck."

My eyes damn near popped out of my head and throat went desert dry. I tried to swallow, but couldn't.

"I can't.....I don't fuck married men," I quickly said.

He turned me around and pulled my ass directly so I could feel that hardness he was talking about. I dropped my head and moaned out in frustration when I felt him move my hair to the side to expose my neck. When his lips brushed across my neck and shoulders, my pussy juices saturated my boy shorts. So much so that I swear I felt juices running down my legs.

"You know you want to do this. Stop lying to yourself," he said to me as I was shaking my head no.

Wasn't exactly telling him no. I was still trying to convince me, myself, and I. His hands gripped my waist and roughly snatched my ass back into him. His dick was placed right between my ass cheeks, and if clothes weren't separating us, we would have a problem. He reached around and unsnapped the buttons on my jeans, sliding them down just enough to expose my boy shorts and my chocolate ass cheeks. He gave my ass a smack and I felt it jiggle a bit.

"Still don't want to? Don't lie."

I just couldn't bring myself to admit it, so I still shook my head no. He brought his right hand around, slowly sliding it down into the front of my boy shorts.

His wet lips touched my ear. "You're a liar, Nicole. Pussy's wetter than a rain forest in Brazil."

My knees buckled when his fingers stroked my swollen clit and traveled down further. I bit down on my lips to bite back a moan. While using his right hand to stroke me in the front, he took his left hand and pulled my lace boy shorts to the side. He then inserted two fingers inside of me from behind. Both of us could hear what his touch was doing to my insides.

"Still don't want it?" he asked.

I didn't answer. I was trying my damnedest not to give in. I gripped onto the counter, when he squeezed my clit between his fingers and pulled a bit. I wanted to call on Jesus but refused to give in. He removed his fingers and I heard him unzip his pants. What I felt next was my undoing. He placed his head right at my entrance, giving me only a few inches of him. My eyes damn near popped out of my head and I think my mouth was stuck in the permanent form of "Oh". I started breathing like I was having an asthma attack, and I felt a few of my nails break while I was holding onto that damn counter so hard. I even banged my fist against the damn thing. Tears sprang to my eyes, and I bit down so hard on my lip, I broke skin and tasted blood. Oh, I was ready for a lot of things in my life, but good Jesus this wasn't one of them.

"Still don't want it?" he asked again, invading my freaky thoughts.

Oh what the hell? I nodded a very clear yes and he removed his head and his right hand. He then turned me around to face him. He rubbed his wet fingers across my lips, before leaning in to suck my bottom lip into his mouth. When I tried to suck on to his lips, and massage the natural curls in his hair, he backed away. I almost panicked, watching him put his dick back into his pants. He zipped them and smiled with a teasing look in his eyes, "You don't fuck married men, remember?"

Moments later, he turned and walked out. I thought he was playing, until I heard the front door open and close. I put both hands over my mouth and screamed. I wanted to go out there and run his ass over, but it was still daylight and too many witnesses. My damn legs were shaking and I couldn't stop them. Against my will, the orgasm he had brought me to just from fucking with me dropped me to the floor. It took me almost fifteen damn minutes to get myself together and get out to my car where he was standing with one ankle crossed over the other. He was on the phone, but ended the call by the time I got to the car. I put his papers back in his briefcase and slammed the trunk shut—hard.

"Damn," he said, jerking his head back. "What's wrong with you? You mad?"

I didn't answer. I hit the automatic locks and opened his door out of habit. Then, I went over to the driver side and slid into the driver's seat. I turned the radio on and listened to Trey Songz and Luda talk to me about a sex room. He leaned his seat back and hummed to the song. It annoyed me, so I changed the station. Jeremih was singing about birthday sex. He hummed to that song. It annoyed me, so I changed it again. This time to Miley Cyrus' "Partying in the USA". He laughed and pushed his seat all the way back, propped both hands behind his head, and closed his eyes. I smacked my lips and rolled my eyes. While driving, I realized he needed to tell me where we were going next, so I asked him. He told me. Thirty minutes later, I pulled into the parking lot of the biggest Bank of America I had ever seen. I parked and grabbed his suit jacket from the backseat as he got out of the car. I put his wallet back in the pocket and grabbed his briefcase from the trunk. With his briefcase in hand, I held his jacket open and let him slide into it. We walked into the bank. Never seen any shit like this in all of my life. This was the difference in being rich and being wealthy. This bank screamed that it catered to the wealthy and famous. Forget the rich. Blondie ran right up to him and I swear all I saw were dollar signs in her eyes.

She introduced him to the bank manager and then looked at me. "I'm sorry, with this being a business meeting of such magnitude, I am sure you understand that only the three of us can be allowed into the back room," Blondie said as she cast me what she thought was a belittling glance.

"No problem," he said to them. "Give me just a second."

He turned to me and handed me his ID and a black American Express card. "Go across the street to The Ritz and book the Ritz Carlton suite."

"Are they going to let me..."

"Just say you want to book the suite and hand them what I just gave you. They'll know what to do."

I nodded. "And then what?"

"Order me something to eat and you, too, if you're hungry. Then, wait for me."

He took his briefcase and turned to walk with them to the back room. I proceeded to walk out of the front door and waited for traffic to let me across the street. I admit, I was a bit nervous about walking into the hotel with this man's ID and credit card, but I did as I was told. I tried to keep my face in check when I walked into the lobby. This shit screamed money! I was only 26, and if I wanted to be able to live like this, I had to hurry and put my degrees to use. I walked up to the counter, and when the lady asked me how she could help me, I did exactly what he told me to do. Just like he'd said, she knew what to do. A few minutes, and a phone call later, she was handing me the electronic card key to the Ritz Carlton suite. I hopped on the elevator and headed up to the suite. I won't even waste my time telling you how amazing the room was. It looked more like a penthouse than a hotel room. I ran and jumped across the comfortable king bed, just because. Let me stop acting silly and order this man's food. Hell, I didn't know what he wanted, so I ordered us both steak and lobster with a couple of sides and dessert. Got him a bottle of Remy, since it was well known that he liked the stuff. There was already a chilled bottle of complimentary wine, but wasn't sure if he would drink that. I sat in the front room of the suite and watched CNN until room service delivered. Not thirty minutes after that, he was walking into the room.

"It's a done deal," I heard him say to someone, swiping his hands together. He was on the phone. I was being nosey because I heard a male's voice on the other end. I walked over to the dining area and set his food out for him. Old habits die hard. Took down a glass from the cabinets and put four cubes of ice into it before pouring some of the Remy for him. I also got him a bottle of Fuji water.

"Who's who?" he asked the person on the phone. "Oh, I hired a personal assistant for the day and I have instilled a new 'Don't ask me and I won't tell you' policy, so don't ask."

He ended the call and we ate in silence, for a while anyway.

"So who'd you buy the house for? You and the family moving?" I asked, wiping my hand on the crisp white napkin.

He didn't even look up from his food. "Not sure yet. It could become just another investment. Time will tell."

"Well, when and if you move this time, don't bring your side ass with you."

This time he looked up, only to cut his eyes at me. "I only moved her to Miami for my son."

"Boyyyy stop! You lie. You could have your son without sleeping with the whore bag."

He laid his fork down, sighing for the third time today. "Why do you insist on making me talk about this shit? Don't you think I have enough of that every day in my world? And now you want to be directly in my face fucking with me about it too? Can I get a break, damn?!"

My neck moved in circles. "Hey don't be damning me, sir! But I'll leave you alone......for now."

He stood up and stretched. "Good. I'm going to shower. Do me a favor. I have some things I need to fax. Will you do it for me? They have an office downstairs that you can use. Everything you need is in the briefcase."

While he went to shower, I did what he asked. Took me all of thirty minutes. I walked back to the room, and went into the bedroom. He was coming from the shower in nothing but a towel. Lord save me! This man's body was ridiculous. No man's body should be this damn perfect. I mean every damn muscle was in the right place. Wonder if he tasted like butterscotch or caramel? I wanted to run my tongue from his sternum to his abs and past his navel to his dick. I needed to get my ass up out of here and quickly because that towel was doing nothing to hide what was hanging low between his legs.

I shifted my eyes from his dick to his handsome face. "Okay, so I faxed those things off for you and your card, ID, and door key are all on the nightstand right over there by the bed. Do you need me for anything else?"

He inched the towel lower, causing my eyes to gaze at the minimal soft hair above his shaft. "Yeah, I do need you for something else."

My eyes shifted back to his eyes. "Ok. What?"

"You know I want some pussy. So quit fronting."

I frowned at him. "You have such a filthy mouth and I am not giving you any pussy. Told you that already."

He stepped a few inches forward and I watched his dick grow. "That's what your mouth says. Why not let me see that Brazilian wax up close?"

"Because you, sir, are a married man and I have already overstepped my boundaries. So, I will be leaving now."

If I didn't know better, I would think it was dark outside. But it was just the blackout panels in the room that gave it that dark allure.

He picked up the glass of Remy from the table and sipped. "Well, at least have a drink with me before you leave."

I knew I should have turned around and kept walking, but hey, it was only one drink.

"Ok, fine," I said, holding up one finger. "Just one drink, and then I'm leaving."

He grabbed the bottle of Remy, the one in the black bottle, and we walked over to the sitting area of the room where the baby grand piano was. He poured me a shot and I took a sip.

"What the hell are you doing, Nicole? You don't sip that shit. It's a shot. Take it to the head."

I looked at the luminous amber color of the liquid and then took it to the head like he'd suggested. That shit showed me where my heart was. It was burning so badly, I wanted to go pour a whole bucket of ice down my throat. This was precisely why I had a one drink minimum whenever I was out on the town. My ass couldn't handle liquor. So when he poured another shot, I should have said no, but I didn't. Hell, truth be told, I needed a fucking drink. So, I dropped my purse and keys and got comfortable in one of the bright orange chairs.

"Where's your husband?" he asked, sitting across from me.

"What?"

"You're married, right?"

I nodded and looked away from him.

"So where is he? You have been with me for several hours and your phone hasn't rung. You haven't made any phone calls either. I would want to know where my wife was and if she was driving some dude around..."

"He's at work," I lied. Well...yeah, I lied.

I could feel him watching me. He was pushing a subject I really didn't care to talk about. Made me sick to even think about it, let alone talk about it. I got up and walked over to the bay window to look out. It was about to rain. Mood killer. I now hated the fucking rain.

"Why are you watching me," I snapped. I could see his image in the tall glass windows that I looked out of.

He chuckled. "No reason. I just think I get it now."

He struck a nerve. I turned, pointing my finger in his direction "Fuck what you think you know."

"I feel the exact same way. Fuck what you think you know."

I didn't respond, just turned back around.

"Your husband cheating on you, Nicole?"

My chest felt heavy and my breathing labored. I felt like I was drowning.

"No. Why would you ask a thing like that?"

"I guess that's why you are always talking shit, huh? What I do, hit a nerve? Get a bit too personal for you?" He taunted me and I didn't like it.

"No. Told you my husband isn't cheating on me..."

"And, I know you are lying. Is that why you are so quick to judge me and my situation? Because you can't handle your own?"

I quickly turned to him again. I was tempted to throw my drink in his face.

"Why don't you worry about your own shit," I asked, walking up to him with my hand on my hip. "Apparently, your shit is raggedy or you wouldn't be in the fucked up place you are in now. Never understood the secret to your madness anyway. How can you love someone and do something that you know would hurt them?"

"Are you asking me specifically, or do you want to know for your own reasons?"

I stared at him with a hard look but didn't answer his question. I quickly washed my drink down my throat, and as the rain fell hard against the window, I looked back at it. The liquor started to take effect. I moved over to the chair and faced him again. I watched as he stood, making his way back into the bedroom area. My phone vibrated in my purse by my leg and it startled me. I quickly snatched my purse open and grabbed my phone. It was only a text message.

Still in the conference. Call you later, was all it read. It was from my husband. I cringed and frowned at the phone.

"Was that your husband?" he asked, coming from the bedroom.

I jumped and broke out the trance I was in. "No and why?"

"Maybe you should call the man and let him know where you are."

"Maybe I shouldn't and why in hell do you care?"

He shrugged. "I don't."

He was annoying me, or maybe it was the fact that he mentioned my husband and that annoyed me. He had put on the pants from his suit. I watched the way they fit perfectly around his waist. The man even had pretty feet. My leg had started to shake. Always did that when I was upset or annoyed. He handed me another drink.

"Want to talk about it," he asked.

The rain had my attention. It was taking me back to a night I would rather forget.

"Talk about what?" I said, starting to nibble on my nails.

"Your problem. Hey, it's fair game. You know all of my business and you definitely know me to be a Naughty man."

He stood there with his arms folded across his chest. There was something akin to a smirk on his face. I couldn't really tell.

"I know what you tell me and most of that is probably a lie. I mean, if you can't be honest with your wife then who the hell am I?"

He wasn't amused and his facial expression showed as much.

"I take it you are having a moment of misguided anger. You seem to have a lot of those. I get it now, it's because you are mad at your husband and you are too chicken shit to say anything to him, so you come at me all the time like you have lost your gotdamn mind."

I squinted with a touch of fury. "There is this intersection that is known for the amount of pedestrians that have been killed crossing the street. How about I drop you off there and see if you can become another statistic?"

He only gave a curt smile.

"My husband isn't cheating on me," I continued. "Just because you have a tricky dick doesn't mean all men do."

"No. Just me and your husband," he replied with a smirk.

"Fuck you!"

"I offered, you refused." He shrugged. "Your loss," he said before walking over to pour himself another drink. "You probably should take me up on that offer though. Judging by how tight your pussy is, your husband hasn't been in it for a while. Your choice or his?"

He put the bottle of Remy down, and then picked up his filled glass. While folding his right arm under the left, he crossed one leg over the other, looking as if he was actually waiting for me to answer that shit. Right then, thunder shook the earth and lightening lit up the sky.

"Whatever the choice, it's the same one your wife made."

When his eyes darkened and his jaw flinched, I smiled. Like a game of chess...check! He slowly walked over and took the seat in front of me—again. The rain was bothering me. My phone vibrated beside me—again.

Going to have to stay until tomorrow. Call you later.

I wanted to take my phone and stomp it to hell, but I simply placed it on my thigh and took a swig of my drink. My leg started to shake again. That sick feeling that you get in the pit of your stomach when you know something is wrong and can't do anything about it settled in. Pissed me off.

"I take it that was your husband. Damn, he could have the common courtesy to at least call."

I was so mad and breathing so hard that my shoulders moved up and down. I could hear myself inhale and exhale.

"I really meant that from the bottom of my heart," he continued, irritating the hell out of me.

I decided to get him where it hurt. "Did your wife leave you yet? She should. No woman should subject herself to total bullshit and disrespect. I hope she never comes back."

He fired back. "Your husband probably started cheating because you talk too damn much. Sometimes, a man just wants peace. Maybe he wasn't getting it at home and decided to get it somewhere else. That's what happens when you annoy a man. They tend to go out and look for what they can't get at home."

I bit back my anger. "Well, you're proof of that being a tall ass lie. Like I said, just because your tricky dick likes to come up with lame ass excuses as to why you like jumping from pussy to pussy, doesn't mean my husband does."

"Seems like your husband is jumping from everybody's pussy but yours. Still wondering if that's his decision or yours?"

Before I could stop myself, I stood and threw my drink in his face. Before the drink even got to his face, he returned the favor and threw his drink in my face. I was so stunned that all I could do was stand there and let out a startled scream. I couldn't see a thing. I screamed again.

"This shit burns!!!!" I yelled out. I tried to open my eyes as best I could, just so I could find my way to the bathroom. Once I found my way there, I turned on the cold water to wash my face, but as soon as I did, I heard him come into the bathroom. He used his hip to boot me out of the way. I couldn't see, so I ended up stumbling over something and hit the floor hard. If I would have been able to see, I would have tried to kick his ass. I heard him washing his face, and I opened my eyes just enough to see I was near the shower. I quickly felt for the knobs to turn the water on. I crawled in with all my clothes on and washed my face. By now, the whole area around my eyes was burning. I let the cold water from the shower wash over my face, all the while trying to keep from drowning myself. A feeling of defeat washed over me just as the water did and I gave in to my tears. He couldn't see them because they blended in with the water from the shower. But that only lasted a second. He turned to look at me before leaving. I was sitting under the water with my knees pulled up to my chest. This would not get the best of me. I stood and pulled my clothes off, choosing to stay in the shower a while. No doubt, I needed to get myself together. I stayed in the shower for about ten minutes, just letting the water drown out the sound of the pouring rain. Although I couldn't hear it from the outside, the sound inside of my head held me hostage. I turned the water off and grabbed the white robe from the back of the door with the Ritz emblem on the left side. I walked out the bathroom and he was lying in bed watching the 47 inch flat screen LCD TV mounted on the wall.

"Asshole," I called him as I sat at the foot of the bed. The bed was big enough for about four adults to sleep in comfortably.

"Shut up. I'm trying to listen to the weather report," he snapped.

"That was rude. Don't tell me to shut up you jerk!"

He used his foot to push me off of the bed. I turned the TV off, and on the way out of the door, I picked up a pillow and threw it at him. I rushed from the room, pulling the doors closed behind me so he couldn't retaliate. I picked up the Remy bottle and the glasses, taking them to the kitchen area. I grabbed a few paper towels and cleaned up the mess I had made. My phone vibrated under the chair. Must have fallen when I threw the drink. I got down on my knees and picked it up.

Where are you? Why you ain't at home? He had some damn nerve, I thought. Another text came through. *Why haven't you answered my texts?*

I walked over to the mini bar and drank a full mini bottle of Crown Royal. They were such small bottles that I didn't feel as if one would do the trick, so I drank another. I slipped the phone into the pocket of the robe and went back inside of the bedroom. I heard him moving around in the restroom. I needed to get in there, so I could get my clothes out to dry. My phone vibrated again. Two messages back to back. The first one stopped my heart. The next one killed me. I groaned out in a flash of rage and the phone flew from my hand, aiming for the closed bathroom door. Instead, he opened the bathroom door and the phone hit him. He looked at me like I had lost my mind. I was up and over the bed so quick, it looked like something out of a ninja movie. Moving so fast, I hurt my damn ankle when my feet hit the floor. The alcohol had my head spinning, but I was steady.

I quickly explained, laughing a little inside. "That was not meant to happen. It was a mistake."

Didn't think he would hit me, but he was known for choking people and I was not taking an ass whooping of any kind.

"Need to get a better fucking aim," he snapped.

"Shut up! I said it was a mistake." Those text messages had rattled me. Had my nerves on end. Could be the alcohol too.

I watched as he picked up my phone and placed it on the dresser. He then turned to me. He raised his eyebrows and smirked.

"What are you smiling at?" I asked, folding my arms.

"You have big chocolate titties." He chuckled. I didn't even realize the robe had come open. I quickly closed it tightly around me.

"Perv. You could have told me my robe was open."

He shrugged. "Why in hell would I do that? Let me touch your titties."

"I will not."

"You let me touch your pussy, but I can't touch a titty? That's kind of backwards, isn't it? You know you want to let me touch'em anyway. Fronting ass."

"I am not letting you anywhere near my pussy or my titties."

"You mean again, right? I have already been near and damn near in your pussy. Damn, that text from your husband must have messed up your way of thinking. What? Did he come out and tell you he was fucking somebody else in a text message?"

I glared at him from across the room. "If he did, at least he would have told me. You on the other hand..."

"You have no idea what the fuck you are about to speak on. So silence yourself!" Yes! I was getting underneath his skin.

"Well at least you are an honest lying cheating tricky dick bastard."

"Something you wish your husband was, huh?"

I needed to move from this window. The rain was bothering me. I stared at him as I moved from around the bed and headed to the bathroom. I tried bumping my way past him, but that didn't work. He grabbed my waist and sat me on the dresser. He used his legs to give my legs a nudge apart. Loosening the tie on my robe, it fell from my shoulders. With both of his hands, he grabbed a handful of my breasts and gave a firm squeeze to both. My nipples were so hard they ached. He flicked both his thumbs across them and made me shiver. My phone vibrated beside us and my husband's number and name flashed across the screen. The phone was flashing and vibrating like warning bells. I eased my hand over and pushed it until it fell on the floor. I was caught off guard when his damp velvety tongue closed around my right nipple. My back arched against my will and a moan escaped from within me.

He shrugged. "Just wanted to see if you tasted like chocolate." He still had a handful of my breasts....massaging them.....squeezing them. He wrapped one arm around my waist and pulled me closer to the edge of the dresser. My phone was dancing on the floor. I was vibrating and moving around like a fish out of water. My husband must have known. He must be feeling what I felt that night when I saw death flash across my eyes. I was almost a murderer. A killer, I could have been. I was so close to the edge. Don't know what made me follow my husband that night. Wish I would have stayed at home. It is true. What you don't know will never hurt you. What I found out killed me.

The man in front of me brought my attention back to him, when I realized he was naked in front of me. He had pulled me even closer to the edge of the dresser, pushing my legs further apart. With my pretty round mounds of almond joys still cupped in his hands, he ran his lips from my shoulder all the way over and up my neck to my ear. Thunder shook the earth—again. My phone danced on the floor—again. My pussy vibrated and ached. My back arched and my legs came up and secured his waist. *Nicole, you can't fuck a married man,* that little voice inside of my head screamed at me. *You can't do this,* it pleaded. *You're married yourself. There is no coming back from this. Just because your husband is a whore doesn't mean you have to be.* Where were you when my husband was...when he was...

My mind went blank, as soon as I felt his fingers creeping around my Brazilian wax. I let out a breath of release when his fingers found their way back inside of me. He brought them out and wiped his wet fingers across my lips. He then leaned in to suck my bottom lip into his mouth and then the top. I believe I could have stopped if he wouldn't have let me taste his tongue. I probably could have stopped, but a kiss always changes everything. A simple kiss betrayed Jesus. This kiss made my body betray me. One hand fondled my breast. The other cupped my neck and brought my face closer to his. I don't know why or how my hand was holding on to the hand that held me hostage to his lips. Don't know if you had ever tasted honeysuckle, but his kiss tasted like honeysuckle. Like what they tasted like first thing in the morning, when the dew was still on them. My hands moved to his shoulders, then chest, then down to his abs. I explored his body like I was an explorer. Touched everywhere. Touched everything. My hands had become voyeuristic for my eyes. I gripped his ass before coming back around and grabbing a hold of his dick. His dick was heavy. Heavy and thick and hard. Heavy and thick and hard and long. Better than anything I had ever held in my hand. At this moment, I felt as if I was holding an Oscar. His dick felt like the greatest reward for a role I had never played. This was somebody else's Oscar I was about to steal for the night. He closed the gap between us and moved my hand. His hand replaced mine and he guided his dick to my abyss. I swear my pussy was leaping. Jumping up and down for joy. She was about to get something she hadn't received in months. Almost a year. I braced myself, feeling his head break skin. My body tensed and I bit down on my bottom lip. I let out "fuck" before I even knew it.

"If you relax this would be much easier. Your pussy shouldn't be this tight. What have you been doing? Obviously, not fucking."

I tried to relax, but good gotdamn!!!! This shit was lethal. This man's dick needs a license to be carried around. This was a weapon. My walls were stretching from here to yonder. My heart beat was slow and hard. I needed to remember to breathe. My head fell back and I yelled out as my back arched and took in all of him. I was tripping like a motherfucker. I was about to OD on the biggest dick in the state of Georgia, Mississippi, Missouri...hell, all fifty states! Imagine putting a Cadillac where a ten speed bike was supposed to go. I had never been in so much pleasurable pain before in all of my life. He didn't move for a while. I felt his muscles moving inside of me and my inner walls responded. His dick. My pussy. They were getting to know each other. After a while, he pulled back until he was almost out of me and slid all the way back in. My nails dug into his arms, until I realized that he was not my prized thoroughbred. You couldn't send someone else's steed back with bruises and scratches. I removed my nails and gripped onto the dresser. When he found his rhythm, I was a moaning fool. I couldn't even think straight as he pushed in and out of me with a steady beat and precise motion. My body didn't know whether to convulse or suction. I slowly moved my hips back and forward to match him stroke for stroke, thrust for thrust. It was hard trying to keep in sync with him, especially when he mastered the art of multiple orgasms. I wiped the drool from my mouth and looked down to see my come all over his dick. I watched as he moved in and out and a fresh batch would coat his dick. It was thick, creamy and white. Almost like whipped frosting. He picked me up and moved me to the bed.

"Face down, ass up," he ordered. I served.

With no questions asked, I did what he'd said. I put my best arch forward and gripped the covers because I already knew I wasn't ready for this. Before I could even prepare myself mentally, he gave a hard thrust and I yelled out. Don't know if it was from pain or pleasure, or both. He gave a whole new meaning to the words rock your body. My hair cascaded around my face and flowed with the waves he was causing. With his hands around my waist, keeping me planted in the arch and the angle he wanted, he literally beat the pussy up. My thighs were weak and burning like I had been running a marathon. I don't know why, but in my head he was fucking me to the tune of Jazmine Sullivan's "Holding you down (Going in circles)". Or that could have been playing on the TV in the background. Either way, I moved my hips back to the same rhythm until his breathing changed. His grip tightened around my waist and he went deeper and harder.

"*I keep going in circles, circles. Round and round. The way you doing me so wrong and I just keep holding you down. I feel so stupid. Foolish. Loving you this way but what can I say? I wanna go, but I keep coming back.*"

The chorus of that song had me throwing my ass back like we were dancing on the dance floor.

He halted the motion. "Oh you fancy, huh? Throwing the pussy back to the tune of the song?"

I didn't respond. At least not with words. The harder he pounded, the harder I threw it back. I fucked him back like it was revenge. I gave it to him like it shouldn't have been given to any man that wasn't my husband. I arched lower and felt him fall deeper into it. I moved my ass like I was hypnotized and fucked him like I didn't have a husband. Flashes of the night I followed my husband lit across my mind like lightening lit the sky. The man behind me grabbed a handful of my hair and pulled me up. He had my hair like it was reigns and pulled me hard back into him again and again and again, until I felt him swell and release. He slowly released my hair and I fell face first into the mattress. He fell next to me. My breathing was intense and I needed a minute. After a while, I got up and made my way to the bathroom. My legs were like cooked spaghetti. I almost fell three damn times. I pulled myself together and turned the shower on. I didn't even realize I was sweating until I looked in the mirror. I quit looking at the woman in front of me and stepped into the shower. The hot water felt good against my sore muscles. Felt like I had been worked over and under. I saw the bathroom door open and he stepped into the shower with me. Dick was still semi hard. My pussy was still jumping jumping like a Destiny Child's song. I took a towel and lathered it with soap. Old habits die hard. I turned around and washed him from head to toe. All he had to do was stand there.

"You do this for your husband too, Nicole?"

I shrugged and kept washing him. I kneeled down so I could wash his thighs, legs, and feet. I even took the time to rinse the soap on his dick off and placed a couple of kisses here and there. Ok, so I sucked his dick. What? Don't judge me! I guess you want to know if I swallowed, too, huh? Sorry, I haven't received a swallow-ship yet. I let his seeds spill onto my chest and legs. I re-washed him and moved the shower head so I could rinse the soap away. He stepped out of the shower and I followed a little bit after. After tidying up the bathroom, I walked out. He was on the phone. I minded my business and picked up my phone. Ten missed calls from my husband and fifteen text messages. The last one read that he would be coming home tonight after all. Claimed he was worried because I wasn't answering his calls.

"Does he know she is sending you pictures of them together?"

"What?" I asked. He caught me off guard with that question.

"Does he know she is doing that trifling shit?"

I swallowed away the feeling in the pit of my stomach. "I don't know what you're talking about."

"I saw the picture when I picked your phone up off the floor."

It took me a while, but I shrugged.

"A man knows, Nicole. Not talking about the pictures either. Your husband knows something is up. That's why your phone is ringing off the hook."

I shrugged again. I had cotton mouth. Tongue felt thick.

"Remember there is always a difference between the woman a man will fuck and the one he will marry," he added. "He may be fucking her, but he's married to you."

That annoyed me, and finally I said his name, and said it out loud. "That shit doesn't make sense Jaylin! That makes no fucking sense!"

"Yes it does. You just don't want it to."

"That's the shit men come up with to try and pacify…"

"Not trying to pacify anyone. It's the truth. If I wanted to pacify you, I would stick my dick back in your mouth."

Before I could respond, my phone vibrated. *My flight will be in at six in the morning. Say something to let me know you got this message. I'm catching the first plane out tonight.*

He was in L.A. Thousands of miles away with somebody else. I stood there and stared at the phone for the longest time. The robe I had on was wide open and Jaylin had a towel wrapped around his waist. In a sense we were strangers, but not so much. I was comfortable enough to let him see my body in the open. Took me months after my daughter was born to get this body back.

"Yes, Jaylin," I said, plopping back on the bed. "My husband is cheating on me."

He sat next to me, holding my hand with his. "Well, I knew that. You needed to admit it to yourself first."

I shook my head. "I followed him."

"What?"

"I followed him. About a month ago."

"Damn, baby. If you had to do all of that then you already knew."

I shook my head again and chewed on my bottom lip. "I had to be sure. I had to see for myself."

The rain outside started to fall harder and the lights went off in the hotel as thunder and lightning danced together in the sky. The hotel phone rang and gave him a courtesy call, telling him that the backup generators would kick in soon. I inched back on the bed, closing my robe and laying on my back. He lay on the other side of the bed with both arms propped behind his head. I opened my mouth and let my demons escape. Told him about the night I followed my husband. My husband had been too anxious to leave the house. It was midnight and he said he needed to smoke. My husband was a smoker. Said he needed some more Newports. Disgusting shit to be a smoker. I finally gave in and told him he could go. We always argued about his habit. As soon as I saw the car leave, I put on my Nike Shox and pulled on my Polo raincoat. I ran out of the house and through the wooded area that was like a pathway to the gas station my husband was going to. I ran like my life depended on it. I made it just in time to see him pay for the cigarettes and hop back into the car. Instead of coming home, he turned the corner and went down the back street where a shopping mall was. I was like a hunter as I ran. I took the rest of the pathway and ran like I had been running track since high school. Of course the car was faster than me, but I kept running anyway. I was hoping he was just going to the Burger King to get a late night snack, so I kept running. I stopped when I saw two cars parked at the back of the darkest part of the shopping mall. There was my Nissan Altima and a black Lincoln sedan. My heart fell out of my chest. I don't know why, but I inched closer to the cars. Rain was coming down hard and my vision was blurry, but I just had to see for myself if this was my husband. I walked up to the front of the car. I didn't hide. I saw him. I saw him with her skirt pushed around her waist and my husband's face was buried in between her legs. He was eating like he hadn't eaten in years. My heart fell to the ground and I threw up. I guess the rain or the music playing in her car drowned me out. When I got myself together and stood back up, her eyes were on me. She was looking right at me like she knew I would be there. She didn't move. She seemed to get off on the fact that I was standing there. My hand went into my coat pocket and the gun that I carried came into my grasp. I pulled the gun out, slowly aiming it at her. She tensed and her breath caught, but the bitch didn't scream or move. She never even tapped him on his shoulder to tell him they both were about to die. Her eyes stayed on me. He came up and immediately went inside of her. They were in the back seat of her car. Her back was against the driver side door. I could have blown his brains out right where I stood. She still kept her eyes on me, as he thrust in and out of her. She even kissed him with her eyes on me. I removed the safety from the gun and cocked back. A sound erupted the night. A baby crying in the distance brought me back to reality. I had left my kids at home with my little brother.

"Somebody's baby, my kids, stopped me from committing a double murder that night."

Jaylin was looking at me with a frown on his face. "No man or woman is worth taking you from your kids. You need to think about that shit before you jump stupid next time. No man is going to leave his wife for a woman who lets him fuck her in the backseat of a car in a parking lot."

"That's not the point. I just don't understand. I do everything for this man. I cook. I clean. I wash. I keep those kids attached to my hip all day so he can relax..."

"Men don't think about all of that shit. Were you fucking him every day? Men want pussy. Give a man some good pussy and he's happy. You have an abundance of good pussy. Were you giving him any?"

"He never went without sex. Even when I didn't feel like it, he got it. Some of you motherfuckers are just selfish. Guess my pussy just wasn't good enough."

He moved his head from side to side. "Not about it being good enough."

"Well, what the fuck is it about?" I asked, pounding my fist on my leg. "Please help me understand!"

We didn't say anything for a while, and I guess Jaylin really didn't have an answer.

"He's with her now," I said. "They're in L.A. together."

"Does she work with him?"

"No."

I wiped the tear away that fell down my face. He turned sideways to look at me. "Are you crying?"

"No, my eyes are leaking. What reason would I have to cry? It is what it is right? Men will be men."

Each of our minds must have drifted off somewhere because neither one of us said anything after that. The room was dark, except for the floodlights lining the floor. My phone vibrated in the pocket of the robe I had on. It was my mother.

"Yes," I answered.

She told me my husband kept calling wanting to know if I was okay and alive. Told her I was. She asked what was going on between me and my husband. I lied, telling her everything was fine. She told me the kids were fine and were eating. She asked me where I was and I told her. She didn't say anything after that and hung up on me. To my family, my husband could do no wrong. I placed the phone back in the pocket of the robe, and before I knew it, I had fallen asleep. Fell asleep with leaky eyes and a heavy heart.

The phone vibrating in my pocket jerked me awake. It took me a minute to realize I wasn't home in my bed. I sat straight up and then fell back against the pillows. It was three o'clock in the morning. I shook Jaylin to wake him. After the third try, he woke up.

"What time does your flight leave?" I asked.

"Seven-thirty," he groaned, still sounding sleepy.

"You want me to drop you off?"

He nodded and closed his eyes. I got up and went to the bathroom. After I was done there, I was going to climb over him and back into the bed. Didn't quite work that way. I tried to climb over him and he grabbed a handful of my titties. I laughed out loud.

"Thought you were sleeping."

"I was until you put your titties in my face. You have big, round fucking titties. Surprised they sit up like that. These tits real?"

"Hell, yeah, they are real!"

He continued to examine them with his hands. "Why are they all fluffy?"

"Fluffy?"

"Yeah. Got milk?"

I laughed again. He pushed the robe off of my shoulders and gripped my waist.

"What size are these?" he asked.

"Thirty-six double D, sometimes."

"Sometimes?"

"Yeah, depending on the time of the month."

He pulled me down and wrapped his mouth around the right one, then the left one. He had a way of making my nipples hard enough to hurt. I felt his dick move under my ass and remembered my pussy was sore. That didn't stop me though. I slid down and removed the towel from his waist. Took his dick that I had named Oscar into my grasp and then inserted it into my mouth. Moved my tongue from the end of his shaft, back up to his head and closed my mouth around his whole head, taking him to the back of my throat. Made my throat and my mouth as wet as possible.

Moved both my hands up and down in swivel motions, turning my head at different angles. Did that until I felt his head swell and his hands gripped both sides of my hair. He pulled me up and on top of him. I moved up and let him push his way inside of me. I don't know what he hit, but it made me stop taking him all in. He held me in place and pushed me all the way down on it. He told me to take that, take that like his name was Diddy. My eyes rolled to the back of my head.

"Oh.....wowwww," was all I could say. I may have thought I knew how to ride a dick before now, but I was sadly mistaken. What worked for the average dick, didn't work for this one. This big dick bandit was a killer. Took me a minute, but I got it. I rode that dick like a motorbike. I was used to automatics. His dick was a stick shift. I had to switch gears to keep up. I was catching the worst cramp in both my legs but I couldn't stop even if I wanted to. I grinded and winded on his dick like my ass had springs attached to it.

"I guess this makes you a slut, huh?" he asked.

I knew his reason for asking. So I just smiled and kept moving.

"No. Wait. I think you call it a whore bag slut monkey," he said, correcting himself and smiling.

"Yeah, and it makes you a man whore."

Quicker than quick, he had me on my back. He pushed my left knee all the way behind my head and fucked me hard. His hips pounded against me as he moved in and out of me with primitive force. He then moved my right knee to match the left one. I wasn't prepared for that shit and tried backing away a bit. Didn't work. He had my ass on lock and I could feel him in my stomach. My back was arched, and my head and back, lifted from the mattress. The short strokes were killing me, but the long, hard strokes were bringing me back. When he pulled out and moved his mouth down to replace his dick, I quit. I tried tapping out over and over and over and over. His whole mouth covered my pussy as his tongue sucked on my clit. I screamed and tried to move his head. You would have thought I was having an asthma attack with the way I was carrying on. He moved back up and back inside of me. The orgasms that I had, caused me to hyperventilate.

"I quit," I said to him.

"Bullshit!"

He pulled me closer to him and used his hands to lift my ass and spread my ass cheeks so he could get deeper.

"OH MY FUCKING GOD!! I QUIT!"

I don't know what spot he had found, but that shit was driving me mad. I grabbed a pillow and put it over my face. He snatched it away and drove deeper into me. By the time he let me go, I didn't even know my own damn name. I was delusional and incoherent. I was down for the count.

He woke me up two hours later.

"Come on. Get up. I like to get to the airport early."

It was 5:00 a.m. I got dressed quickly. I didn't put my underwear back on. Stuffed them into my purse with my phone. I helped him to make sure he didn't forget anything, grabbed my keys and we left. On the way to the airport, Jaylin fired me as his personal assistant. I laughed. He actually handed me a pink slip and a white envelope. I had no idea what was in the envelope. I stuffed them in my purse. Thirty minutes later, we sat at the airport. I was nervous. My husband would be landing soon. Jaylin waited with me, as I waited for his flight to arrive.

He came to sit beside me. I sat quietly while he talked on the phone. He moved to the other side of the room, when his conversation got heated. Almost forty-five minutes later, my temperature went hot when I saw my husband. She was walking a few paces behind him. She was a halfa. She was half black and half Puerto Rican. A halfa. Her short shorts caused men to eye fuck her as she walked. Her body was that of a video vixen. I saw her eyeball Jaylin and he turned to look at me as if to ask if it was her. I nodded. He didn't look impressed. She almost ran into my husband she was staring at Jaylin so hard. She followed his eyes to me. She looked from me to him and from him to me. She wrapped her arms around my husband from behind and tried to kiss his ear. My hand went to my purse and I panicked. I went to grab my gun, but it was gone. I looked over at Jaylin and he was shaking his head. He must have taken my gun. I stood when she tapped my husband and pointed to me. He then pretended as if he didn't know her and came directly for me. When he got to me, I wrapped my arms around his neck, tiptoed and gave him the best public display of affection ever invented. I gave him the sloppiest kiss I could. Stuck my tongue all the way down his throat. When I was done, I looked around my husband and Jaylin looked disgusted. Not because I had kissed my husband in front of him, but because during those forty-five minutes that I waited for my husband's plane to arrive, I followed Jaylin into the men's restroom. I dropped down on my knees in one of the stalls and gave him some of the best head in the game, and this time, I received my swallow-ship. I let him release his seed into mouth, and out of spite, I used my tongue and washed his seed around my mouth and swallowed it. I didn't wash my mouth off or rinse it out. I turned to pick up my purse and waved bye to Jaylin. I smiled at my husband and we walked out to my car. I helped him out of his suit jacket, took his briefcase, and opened his door for him. I popped the trunk and slid his briefcase in. I walked around to the driver side and slid my ass onto the plush leather seat. Now...you can judge me...

The End

Book Club Meeting. . .

The ladies clapped and laughed out loudly. Even if you wanted to judge Nicole, you couldn't. Her husband had it coming and seems like she had gotten the revenge that she needed. Been there, done that. Revenge became the subject at hand, and for a while we talked about how so many women were frustrated with Jaylin because they saw him as their own significant others. They wanted him to be Mr. Right, but he just wasn't there yet.

"I kind of got this love/hate thing for Jaylin," Nicole said. "More so love, because he's willing to tell you the truth, even though it may hurt. He knew that I was having some issues with my husband, and I had much anger pent up inside of me. Lord knows I was so happy to release it, and from the moment that I saw Jaylin, I knew he would help me release all that I was feeling inside."

"What about you and your husband, Nicole? Where do things stand with the two of you right now?" someone asked.

"All I'm going to say is it's a work in progress. I don't know what the future holds, but we're working on our marriage."

"That's all you can do," another woman said. "But, I have a question for you and some of the other women that were intimate with Jaylin. If his dick is as painful as you all make it out to be, then why continue? I think Tonja was the only one willing to call a time-out, but Nicole you really seem like you got battered and bruised. Breasts and all."

So many laughed, even Nicole. "I don't know how I can say this without sounding so nasty, but when the 'D' is that good, you will yourself to muster the pain. I don't know about the others, but I wasn't willing to pack it up anytime soon."

All of the ladies who had told their stories agreed, adding that you never let that kind of goodness go to waste.

After their comments, one woman gave her input, "What I want to see is growth in Jaylin. He's still doing some of the same things that he's done since forever. At some point, a person has to grow the hell up and act like they got some sense. He's not a young adult anymore and my only hope is that when *Jaylin's World: Dare to live in It!* hits the stores, we don't read about a man who is still selfish and only thinks of himself. Don't get me wrong, I love me some Jaylin Rogers, but I'm pulling for him to show me that he's capable of getting his life together. I think Nicole said it best when she said it's time to leave the cesspool, Miss Scorpio Valentino, alone."

There wasn't a person in the room who wasn't hoping for Jaylin to make some major changes in his life, but many debated if he should remain with his wife Nokea, Scorpio or with no one. I knew the answer, but in the room the verdict wasn't in yet. I spoke up, "I can't say right now, but we all have to wait and see. My struggles with writing this story was accepting the fact that, sometimes, people don't progress as we may want them to. Making changes in your life is easier said than done, and was there ever a designated age where people just wake up and say...okay, today is the day that I grow up and know better? No, there isn't, simply because people show progression on their own time, not when others want them to. Yes, the older we get, the wiser, but that doesn't apply to all. I know people in their 40's, 50's, 60's...still clowning. Still cheating, still playing games and still not ready to settle down. I refuse to knock those people, because part of that is reality. With Jaylin, again, you'll just have to wait and see."

The conversation continued, and by now, it was getting pretty deep. The room was so loud and no one could hear what anyone else was saying. I was doing my best to calm the noise, but to no avail. Then, the moment of truth came and my ongoing worries about this moment hit me like a ton of bricks. The double doors to the entrance flew open, and in came a settle breeze that quickly cooled things down. Not only that, but Jaylin's presence had silenced the entire room. No one was moving, no one said one word. Not me, not him, not one single lady. All eyes were on him and I didn't have to tell anyone what kind of suit, shoes or watch he wore, as you already knew. I didn't have to say how his hair was styled or the way he sported his goatee...it was on display. The mention of his nine plus inches was embedded into many brains, so there was no need to stare at the bulge in his pants. His cologne was already filling the room, so no need to ask what kind it was. Yes, there he was, standing in the flesh, leaving us all frozen in time and still...speechless.

Somebody...anybody, say something, please, I thought. Maybe it should be me, but as soon as I got ready to open my mouth, several women stood and there was a rush towards the double doors. I couldn't even see Jaylin anymore, and as the entire room cleared out, the doors shut behind the last lady who had left a shoe behind.

I sighed, even though I expected something like this to happen. "Thanks for coming," I said, hearing my echo. "Had a lot of fun and can't wait to meet again next year."

Yeah, I was talking to myself, but oh well, it wouldn't be the first time. I gathered my things to go and left plenty of books, t-shirts and other goodies on the tables, just in case some of the women returned. As I was folding some of the t-shirts, the door came open. Jaylin came inside with part of his torn shirt pulled from his pants, lipstick on his cheeks, and for the first time, his hair out of whack.

"Gotta love your readers," he said, walking down the middle aisle.

"Yes, I do, but I don't know what to say about you Jaylin. I heard some stories today that just blew me away. I hope and pray that you've stopped being Naughty, because people are getting into my shit about your actions."

He smiled, obviously loving every bit of it. "But they still love me, though. No matter what, we're all going out together and most will appreciate my *changes.*"

I shrugged, always skeptical about believing him. "I hope so. And what's with this James Bond thing you got going on? It's like you're on some kind of mission and why are you having sex with so many women? That dick of yours has to be worn out and I'm surprised you didn't hurt yourself after all of that sex."

Jaylin softly snickered and touched his goatee. "I still have plenty of juice left in me, and you know better than anyone how much I love pussy. Each woman that I was with brought something different to the party and I don't regret being with any of them."

I couldn't help but ask. "Well, what about Nokea? Scorpio...the kids?"

"Kids are good, but pertaining to the women in my life...I have some work to do."

"You got that right. So please get back on that plane and go home to Nokea to make things right. You got us hanging in limbo, and even I'm confused about where to turn."

"Ay, you're the writer, so I go wherever you want me to go."

"No, I go where you take me."

"Then, I'm taking you with me. A hotel, across the street...just the way it used to be, all right? While the other women told their stories, you did tell your story, too, didn't you?"

I snatched up *Naughty One* and flipped through the pages. "Excuse me, but I've been telling the story for years. The women know who I am, so no need to reiterate it."

His brows rose. "You sure about that?"

"Positive. Now, goodbye and hold it down on being Naughty. Just a little, but if you can't do it, I understand why."

Jaylin laughed and reached into his pocket. He dropped a condom on the table and looked into my eyes. "I may not be able to stop being Naughty, but remember...you're the only one who can stop me. Now, meet me across the street in fifteen minutes. If you don't show, I'm out."

He turned, slowly making his way towards the doors. Even I had to admit how much love I had for this man, but my situation with him was very complicated. Once the doors opened, Jaylin disappeared. I picked up the condom, thinking of what we'd shared, as well as debating if I would continue to be a part of the Naughtiness too. I said I'd be *Naughty No More*, and after *Jaylin World* is released, I wasn't sure if any of us would dare to live in his world again!!

If Only For One Night

The Naughty Series

Naughty 1 (Two's Enough Three's A Crowd)

Naughty 2 (My Way or No Way)

Naughty 3 (Change Don't Always Come)

Naughty by Nature

Too Naughty

Naughty No More

Jaylin's World: Dare to live in it! (Coming Soon)

Other Brenda Hampton novels include:

Full Figured 1: Who Ya Wit

Full Figured 3: Who Ya Wit 2, also featuring Nikki-Michelle's *Tell Me About It!* (Coming 2011)

Don't Even Go There (Coming Jan. 2011)

Two Wrongs Don't Make a Right

The Dirty Truth

SLICK

Girls from Da Hood 5: Trick Don't Treat

How Can I Be Down?

No Justice No Peace

Who or What is in that Closet?

www.brendamhampton.com